Fishing for Māui

Fishing for Māui

ISA PEARL RITCHIE

First published in 2018

ISBN 978-0-473-43754-1

A catalogue record for this book is available from the National Library of New Zealand

Typeset by Paul Stewart
Cover design by Katrina Berry
Author photo by Sabrina Grabow

Te Rā Aroha Press

For Mum, Jane and Grandad

PART ONE

Calm
Spring 2011

Elena

I love the early mornings. I don't think I've naturally woken up this early since I was a small child, but the hormones, combined with that sinking instability – low blood sugar from the long stretch of night with no food – leave me wide awake before first light. I lie in the stillness and listen for the first bird calls, bringing in the dawn chorus of another chilly spring morning.

Staying still feels almost unbearable. I push back the duvet, tuck it around the sleeping, snoring Malcolm, and I'm out of bed. I don't mind the cold; my body is running on overdrive trying to sustain this new life growing inside me. It doesn't feel real, but at this time of day nothing is.

The world is grey. I look out the kitchen window at the cluster of north-facing trees that obscure the sunlight and protect us from the world. Today something is different. I notice one of the old plum trees is leaning on a strange angle. It's probably been dead for some time. You can't tell in the winter because all deciduous trees look dead, but now that spring has sprung and peridot peppers their grey, licheny branches, it's obvious which ones have been left behind for good.

When a tree falls in a dense forest the noise it makes is minimal. There might be a cracking sound as the trunk breaks away from its roots, or they might have softened to a point not much stronger than bread. It doesn't really fall; it just leans on those around it and slowly decays. Every particle returns to the ecosystem. That's what happens in the suburban forest around our cottage. I didn't hear it in the night; it just leaned forward, like a sigh, surrendering its burden.

I make my cup of peppermint tea and sit by the window, nibbling at yesterday's scones. It is a sick paradox. I am nauseous because I need to eat, and I don't want to eat because I'm nauseous. But here, looking out at the garden, I always feel at peace. The morning sickness is fading now that my first trimester has ended and I can enjoy this personal time.

The garden next door is lush with plant life. I love the way these two properties sit, small houses with sprawling jungles, compared to the tight compartments of suburbia all around us. From where I sit it creates the illusion of more space, as if both sections combine into a wilderness and the fence is irrelevant. For me it is the illusion of freedom. I don't know if I've ever been truly free. It would be terrifying to have no attachments, no restrictions – but the illusion is liberating.

I reheat some gelled porridge, presoaked and cooked yesterday. When I blog about porridge I call it oatmeal, at least in brackets, so my American readers know what I'm talking about. I have a whole blog post dedicated to explaining why people traditionally soaked their grains. Blogging is about all I have the energy for lately. Even the slight exertion of making my breakfast is taxing to the point of exhaustion.

I go back to the window and sit with my legs propped up. I sip my cooled tea. At least herbal tea is still pleasant when it's no longer hot. I look out at the garden, in full swing now that the sun has risen. The bees dart about, busy gathering nectar, contributing to their role in the life cycle of other living things. It makes me feel lazy.

We moved here when I was almost three months pregnant, the bulge of my belly just starting to peep over my jeans, just starting to 'show'. I thought it would be impossible to find a better home than the one I was leaving, the 1960s state house with the kitsch linoleum and my best friends in the world, Henry and Tanya. My chosen family. I resented Malcolm and his excitement; he couldn't wait for it to be 'just us'. I told him it would be hard to find a place I'd be happy with. I actually thought it would be impossible, but it only took a week.

The first time I saw this little cottage with its sprawling overgrown garden, so close to the university – the section so big compared to the house it could easily be in the country – I knew it was perfect.

It had belonged to an old woman, obviously. The Romanesque statuettes in the garden, the seven dwarves on the back porch and the old-fashioned ornamental plants were a testament to her.

'She passed away – not in the house,' the real estate agent assured us. She fidgeted nervously with her hot-pink manicured nails. I'm not ageist but she did look too old for that shade of pink. They were so long they looked dangerous as she raked them through her bleached blonde hair.

'She was in a rest home. The family have decided not to develop the property.' Her tone was disapproving. I could tell she thought such a large garden was a waste of space. She quickly righted herself and continued in the pseudo-positive tone that made half of me cringe, while the other half struggled not to laugh.

'The garden is lovely. It's fenced off so will be safe for the little ones.' She glanced at my protruding abdomen, making me feel self-conscious. 'As you can see, there's lots of room to play out here.' She gestured around as she walked us through the quarter-acre, its winter branches bare and still. Early daffodils peeked up at me and I knew it was right.

I love it here, as I knew I would. I watch the wax-eyes darting from branch to branch, knowing that this perfect morning will be over soon and I will have to face the day. The grey slowly turns to green. I hear Malcolm stir, confirming my thoughts. As soon as he is up my peace will be interrupted and once he leaves for work I will suddenly be rendered lonely, aimless, with just my blog to keep me company.

My shoulders sink into the faded pumpkin-coloured cushions of the couch, my mind comfortably blank. I've never in my life been able to sit still for as long as I have the last few weeks. I can spend an hour or more in the bath, not minding the cold. I can sit here and not realise the whole day has slipped by. It's as if my body, in its all-consuming effort to produce this baby, forgets to give me time, or perhaps the baby, as it grows, is consuming more than just my energy – perhaps it is eating time. My conscious mind is deprioritised, but at least I'm never bored.

My blog is the only thing that keeps my brain ticking over; it helps me feel as if I'm still connected to the world outside this garden, this cottage, this pregnancy, outside the insular nest that Malcolm and I have created. The food that I make just disappears, but the photos last. The recipes that I type up are shared with my followers and anyone who stumbles across my blog looking for a healthier version of apple crumble (cobbler to the Americans) or instructions on how to make your own jerky. The comments I receive give me a boost. I feel like this network – this community – of other food bloggers, are my friends. Even though we've never met we support each other, we commiserate and joke, debate and philosophise, marvel and praise. The blog posts sit there, in cyberspace, proof that I've been doing something these past few months, seemingly permanent in a world where nothing seems to last.

It's already 9am before I remember it's Sunday. Market day. I feel a rush of excitement and then wonder briefly what my life has become with a trip to the farmers' market being the highlight of my week. Malcolm still hasn't stirred from his Sunday slumber so, rather than risk missing out on fresh, local produce for the week, I go it alone.

The tree-lined car park bustles with activity. A chill still clings to the morning air as I climb out of the car, guiding my slightly bulging belly through the small space allowed by my terrible parking. The man sitting in the new-looking navy blue sedan next to me glares as my door brushes his car. I smile cheerfully at him anyway.

I do my usual circuit, scoping out all the stalls before I settle on purchases. I'm excited by the first strawberries of the year and by the luscious looking asparagus. I also pick up some sourdough bread (since mine won't be ready for another day or two), more venison salami and a jar of raw honey.

I stop by the herb stall and buy a pot of lemon thyme before heading back home to the cottage surrounded by trees, back to Malcolm and my cat and my blog.

Michael

Cold water saturates my wetsuit, the only barrier between me and the ocean. It chills a changing thermometer line up my spine. I float with my board, scratching designs in the wax while I wait for the perfect wave. Now and then I look out at the land on the other side of the harbour mouth. Sometimes I wish I could erase everything along the horizon – so there's nothing else in sight – just me and this perfect line.

Today the sea is calm – a tarp of water with creases that peak as they reach me. My wetsuit chafes around my crotch, but nothing can distract me from the surf. The waves are paced so that in between each worthy one there is a rest. Sometimes I paddle out or in more, judging the best vantage point, but more often than not I just sit, half submerged, bobbing in the water like a fishing buoy. This could be my whole life right here, right now: the calm, the anticipation, the thrill of the ride and then the come down that drops back into waiting.

You can only push yourself so far – reach your peak – before you start to decline. It's the curved graph we studied in sports psychology last trimester. I always push myself too far, too fast. The challenge is to hold back, just that little bit. Don't paddle out too far, let go of the wave before it mashes you into the rocks, stop while you still have the energy to get back up the hill or you won't be keen to get out of bed tomorrow. Even though I know this I still always push myself too far.

It's time to call it a day when every muscle in my body aches and the sun is well on its way to setting. In the summer on a full moon I could stay out here all night, but spring is freezing and it will be dark in ten minutes.

I unzip the back of my wetsuit, feel the release as I pull it off my arms, chuck on a hoodie and make my way over the rocks toward the bush path that leads me home. With the canopy overhead it's dark already, and as I reach the old karaka tree I know I'm in for a special show tonight. There they are, thousands of them, bright lights in the dark of the clay bank, randomly placed like stars. I sit on my favourite rock, roll a joint and watch them for a while.

Out of the corner of your eye glow-worms twinkle like stars too. I guess that light is supposed to bring in their dinner – what a life, eh? The sun shines out your bum and attracts tasty food. Fuck, that would be awesome. I crack up at myself. Then the laughter stops and I feel peace. Maybe it was the calm water and the workout from the surf, maybe just the weed or the glow-worms making me a light show without even trying, but this is the most relaxed I've ever felt – well maybe not ever – but definitely in the last month or so. Uni must have been getting to me. Sometimes I wonder why I even bother studying when my real life is here, in Whaingaroa – or Raglan if you want to use its Pākehā name – surfing and chillaxing.

Maybe if I was dropped into the middle of nowhere by chopper, I could look around and breathe it all in before Tangaroa takes me. I imagine him down below, the Māori Poseidon, with a taiaha instead of a pitchfork, ready to stab me in the backside if I step out of line. Maybe you don't know what a taiaha is. I probably wouldn't either if I didn't try so hard to find my culture. But these days you can just look it up on Wikipedia and find out it's a traditional Māori weapon, a carved wooden spear. Tangaroa is the main god of the sea and has been since the separation of the earth from the sky. He's the boss of this whole damn ocean.

These are the buzzy thoughts that go through my mind as I walk the track up to Nan's house. As soon as I roll through the sliding door she's making me a Milo. Grandmas are the best.

'How are you, boy?' she asks, stirring the mean mug of hot chocolatey goodness.

I almost reply automatically, the way you normally do, 'good' or 'fine' or 'sweet', but the walk up from the surf is still with me.

'Like I feel nothing,' I say, trying to put my mood into words. 'But it's peaceful.'

Nan nods. She understands. She walks out of the kitchen, towards the deck. I can hear her wavering voice drifting back as she sings. The words wash over me: '*Te kore, Te tīmatanga*'. The nothingness, the beginning. It seems to all make perfect sense but I have to ask her.

'What are you singing about?' I call out.

Nan turns to face me. Her eyes wrinkle so much when she smiles you can barely see them. Her voice is slow and warm. 'Come out here, boy. The kitchen isn't the place for these things.'

I follow her out. This must be important. Sacred. Tapu. Not something that mixes with the kitchen.

'It's a song my māmā used to sing about the beginning of the world.'

I know she's not talking about Genesis. Nan has never been religious.

'You mean like Rangi and Papa?'

'Yes, they came after, but in the beginning was Te Kore.'

'Like a void.'

Nan nods again. 'The beginning of everything, that is.'

'Then what?' I've never heard this version before, just the creation myths in kids' storybooks.

'Te hauora.' Her voice reverberates around the room.

'The breath of life?' I ask.

'Good boy.' Her arm reaches up to pat my back. I only learnt Māori at school so it's not the best – nothing like the fluent language Nan can speak.

She starts singing again, '*Te atamai, te āhua.*'

'Ah … āhua – the way things are?'

'Shape and form, you might say, but there aren't proper words in English. English words are all in the head – not here.' She pats her chest above the heart. Manawa. 'They're all about what should be but nothing about what really is.' She shakes her head. That's the problem. Nan is nothing like Mum. I don't understand how Mum is even her daughter. Mum is all in the head – always right, always busy. She doesn't understand any of this.

'*Te wā, te ātea.*'

'Time and … ātea?'

'Space, boy, space.'

'It sounds just like philosophy,' I laugh. She pretends to smack me in the head and laughs too.

'You've been reading too many Pākehā books, eh?'

'Nah – not enough if you ask my uni tutors.' I sigh and rest my hands behind my head, leaning back on the deck chair. 'So we have time and space. When do the gods come in?'

'That's where the song ends.' She lights a cigarette and inhales deeply. She never smokes in front of Mum – doctors hate smoking. I help myself to one from her pack and spark up. I want her to tell me more, I know the stories from kids' books but I don't know how they all fit together. I need to know how this beginning fits in with Rangi and Papa, the sky father and earth mother, and the gods that are their children. I need to know how these gods relate to the demi-god Māui. Every story Nan tells is different, every time. I want to ask but I know I have to wait for the right time.

It's funny. My story starts with nothing, just like the creation myth. That was what I had as a child. No culture, no heritage. I was just white-bread normal. But that was the problem. I knew there was more to it. I knew my grandmother was Māori, even if Mum lives as if there's no such thing. I always felt ripped off because Mum had the chance to know about her culture and to teach me, but she never even tried. At primary school I loved the books of Māori myths and legends, the gods, the stories of Māui and all the adventures. I wasn't interested in reading anything else. I find it a bit sad now – that I had to learn my own culture from storybooks. I had to learn my own language at school. It wasn't until I started to learn that I discovered Nan knew so much more, she just never said anything before.

'I didn't think you'd be interested, boy,' she said.

And I know she only thought that because of Mum. Mum

never cared, but I do. I need to. I guess you might not understand if you've never been through it. Some people don't seem to need a cultural identity. Or maybe you already know all you want about where you come from. You're lucky. I don't even look Māori, but I am, I need to be. I've only just skimmed the surface of my culture. I don't know if I will ever make up for what Mum lost. There are so many places and names, so many stories. It's a whole different world, Te āo Māori, so different from Te āo Pākehā, the Western view, where everything is black and white. I can't even begin to explain it. I wish I could. Nan tells me stories about her ancestors, their names and what they mean and I still feel like an outsider, or maybe like a traveller, lost at sea, who's finally coming home.

Nothing is what I was taught to believe in as a child. That was what happened after death. Nothing. I don't think I understood it at the time, it was just another meaningless adult mystery, but everything comes back to that. Mum didn't really get into religion until Dad left; by that time it was too late for me. So I grew up knowing that at the end of all the trials I faced in life there was nothing waiting for me.

After a rough night sleeping in the hut at Nan's I wake up knowing I'm twenty years old today. It's my birthday and that means family obligations. Nan is already in her best dress when I get into the kitchen.

'I'm just waiting for my chauffeur,' she says in a posh voice.

'You're a cheeky one. What's for breakfast?'

'Excuse me, Master Michael. Who's being cheeky now? It's eleven o'clock already and you can make your own breakfast.'

'On my birthday?' I pretend to be offended. Not that it matters. Nan pulls a plate out of the oven loaded with fried potatoes and sausages.

'Happy birthday, my darling boy.'

I give her a kiss on the cheek and stuff myself full with the delicious salty goodness.

On the way into town we swing by Dave's to pick him up. He's one of the boyz and probably my best mate. He's always keen for a free feed and Mum will be cranking my favourite lamb roast. She's a good cook even if she won't touch the gravy herself. I guess she had to be a good cook with Nan for a mother.

It's 12:15 when I pull into Dave's driveway and toot the horn. I'd be running late if Nan wasn't on my case. She's been sitting like a queen in the passenger seat the whole way in from Raglan.

'How's it, Gov?' Dave asks as he dives into the back seat with his longboard.

'Pretty sweet, eh.'

'Good afternoon, Nan,' Dave's a sweet talker. I bet he checked the car clock to make sure it was actually afternoon.

As soon as we open the door at Mum's all I can smell is delicious roasted lamb. Evie won't be impressed.

Mum comes out of the kitchen. She's actually wearing an apron. It looks strange. She hugs me. Evie smiles at me from the couch where she's watching TV with Malcolm. He's Elena's partner and a bit of a twat, but he's alright compared to all the other weird boyfriends she's had.

Elena comes out from the kitchen all smiles and gives me a hug and a kiss on the cheek. I guess that's okay now that we're adults but a few years ago it would have been weird. Elena is older than me by a few years and she's pregnant. I put my hand on her belly and say hi to the baby. Elena hands me an envelope.

'Happy birthday,' she says. It's a subscription to a surfing mag.

'Thanks.' That was pretty nice of her but I guess she wouldn't know what else to get me. We've always been pretty different.

'Michael!' Rosa rips down the stairs and jumps on me. My kid sister is awesome.

'Hey, smelly. How are ya?' I pat her head.

'I just had a bath,' she argues. 'I'm not smelly – you are!' I let her chase me around the lounge for a bit while Malcolm looks annoyed. I bet he's gonna be a crap dad.

I grab a couple of beers from the fridge, pass one to Dave and sit down in an armchair. The TV shows fields of corn and some old guy talking. It's probably about peak oil or something. I grab the remote and change the channel to the Sunday fishing show. Malcolm doesn't say anything.

Malcolm is blond and Elena has dark hair, the way Nan does in the photos of when she was younger. I wonder who the baby will look more like.

John comes down the stairs looking like he just woke up.

'I didn't know you were here, little bro.'

He grunts the way teenagers do, sits down and watches the fishing. Mum comes in and glances at the TV.

'You didn't invite your father, did you?' I'm about to reply when she sees John has joined the party.

'About time you got up,' she says. 'Give us a hand and set the table.' John doesn't move so Evie sets the table.

We could be a perfect normal family. That's if you don't look too hard. If you do you'll see Evie glaring at the roast and Elena glaring at Evie. I don't really know why they don't get on. They both care too much about food.

'Have you had the tests yet?' Mum asks Elena casually.

'What?' Elena almost chokes on her lamb.

'For Down syndrome.' She says something else but it's probably some kind of technical medical thing.

'I'm not going to,' Elena says. That's the voice she always used to use before she had a big tantrum.

The next thing I know the phone rings, and Mum has to leave on a call-out. Elena has left the table and gone to the computer room anyway. John goes back to the TV, Dave's bailed out the door with his board and Nan is taking Rosa to the park.

So it's just me and Evie with her plate of asparagus without butter. No cake. No celebration. Some birthday.

Evie smiles at me and I stop feeling sorry for myself. I'd rather be here with her than the rest of them put together.

Evie

Nothing will benefit human health and increase the chances for survival of life on earth as much as the evolution to a vegetarian diet. ALBERT EINSTEIN

Pythagoras was vegetarian, so was Saint Francis of Assisi. So many enlightened individuals have come to the obvious realisation that harming living, breathing creatures is morally wrong – and yet we live in a world that sends 150 million animals, cows, chicken, sheep and pigs to slaughter every day. This is what I ponder as I sit outside and watch the stars.

Sound travels differently at night. Intermittent cars can sound like the ocean. I take a drag of my cigarette and breathe smoke at the stars. I like it out here, on Tara's porch. It makes Hamilton seem further away. The garden around me is overgrown with flax bushes and bamboo, the neighbours' houses are barely visible in the daylight. I could be anywhere. I hear a train in the distance, the cars on every side – but far away. The sound swallows me up and I feel like I could drown in it. I'd like to. I'd like to lose myself.

Silence follows me into the house like a shadow. It creeps up the door frame, over the threshold, into the kitchen, engulfing me. My footsteps lead the way; behind me is nothing.

People like to think that farm animals have nice, happy lives until they're packed off to the slaughterhouse. I grew up on a farm, so I know what it's really like. My dad and brothers used to kill animals. Not in the humane way that people talk about (how the hell can killing be humane?). They would shoot cows in the head and then we would be served them for dinner. The same cows that we saw every day, that we fed handfuls of grass to and patted. That wasn't the worst of it. When there was a drought and there were too many sheep with not enough food they would be culled. It might sound like a nicer option than letting them starve to death, but if you'd seen my dad and brothers out there with spades and baseball bats, whacking them in the legs, cracking their brittle bones, smashing their heads in, having fun doing it, you probably wouldn't think it was for their own good.

I left home when I was fifteen. I left school even though I was supposed to stay another year. There was nothing they could do to stop me.

I hitched all the way to Wellington. I didn't even care who gave me a ride. One disgusting old man tried to grope my thigh. I made him stop the car in the middle of nowhere and let me out. I only accepted rides from certain people after that. Women are usually okay, but some of them are uncomfortable to talk to. I won't get into the car alone with old men anymore, especially if they're wearing collared shirts. The straighter they look, the more they have to hide. I'm good at judging them now. I haven't had any close encounters since that first time.

I hitch all around the country and feel safe. Free. I love the feeling of freedom, of only having my knapsack and the clothes I'm wearing. I store my possessions with friends I can trust and take off into the world, like a bird into the air, free from the burdens of society.

I never stay in one place too long and I always come back.

I come back to see Tara and Amy, and of course I come back to see Michael. Him and Valerie are the closest things I have to family. He is like my rock, weathering me from the storms of my mind, and his mother is so welcoming – so gentle and kind and open-minded. So unlike my own family. Elena is nice too, but we always argue.

I sit on Tara's couch and take out my pipe. A friend I met in Southland carved it for me and it makes the most beautiful sound. I carry it back out into the night and play myself into oblivion.

Valerie

For the longest time I thought I remembered nothing of my childhood. My early childhood, before my school years. It's funny how you can always recognise the things you love. I saw him in a home décor magazine that was flipped open and abandoned on the coffee table in the waiting room, and suddenly I remembered. It was a collection of vintage toys; nestled in the middle lay the little brown teddy bear that I slept with as a child. The memory was a blur of soft lighting and warmth: my father tucking me in and telling me a bedtime story. Not from a book, I think he must have made them up, different every night. The memory was beautiful, but I instantly wanted to reject it; it went against all the other memories I have of Dad. I suppose no one's all bad.

For a moment I thought of tracking down the owner of the little bear in the magazine. Maybe I could find an antiques dealer who could source the exact kind of teddy I had as a child, but it was just a momentary lapse into fantasy. I'm a sensible woman, a doctor. What would I possibly do with a teddy bear?

My waking thoughts drift, vague and aimless, as I muster the strength to face the cold post-duvet air for the few seconds between my bed and the welcoming hot shower. A to B, that's how my life seems to work. I don't have the luxury of meandering the way young people do – especially these days – adolescence stretching so far into adulthood that it never actually ends.

As I step out of the shower, steam billows out around me. My feet hit the heated tiles gratefully. I've spent so many years of my life living in houses with sub-standard heating that I don't take the warmth for granted, even after fifteen years of living in this house, which I still think of as new although it's starting to show its flaws. I wipe the mirror clear with the corner of my towel.

I don't know how this got to be part of my morning ritual; I never like what I see. My limp, greying hair hangs loose around my shoulders. My body shows the telltale signs of ageing – spots are beginning to show on my skin as it thins. I remind myself that it's not noticeable from a distance, but I know I can never hide from myself. The circles under my eyes are darker. I suppose it's lack of sleep, perhaps iron deficiency.

Maybe one day I'll learn to avoid my reflection entirely. Cellulite textures my thighs, flesh hangs over my waist – I'm obviously overweight. But doctors are often terrible examples of good health.

My skin in the mirror bears its wrinkles like scrunched paper, the colour of muddy water. I may look Māori but I don't really consider myself to be. Other people assume I am, that it's part of my identity, even though I don't feel that it is. Strangers smile at me at supermarkets, service stations, as I walk down the street, taking our matching skin tones for granted, kissing me on the cheek like family.

When I was growing up it was shameful to be Māori. We never learnt the language. Mum was told not to speak it to us, that it would hold us back. Like the last survivors of an apocalypse, her generation was forced to adapt, surrendering their dying culture, never even fathoming the revival which was to come, just decades later in a monsoon of red, white and black spirals. I missed it completely. I still feel the shame even though I know it's wrong.

When Michael started learning Māori at school I was proud – of course I was – but at the same time I couldn't escape that feeling. The look my mother gave me, like she was holding all that pain in. Now she smiles at Michael and they speak together in thick, solid syllables, dulcet, rolling, that I can't understand. I feel the unfairness, the jealousy, even if it's irrational. I worked so hard to make it in a white world – to be successful. Now I can't go back.

There are only so many hours in a day, most of them dominated by work, my volunteer rounds at the nursing home and the regrettable fact that I need to sleep. There are also other important things like family time, the evening news, church and catching up with friends. Meals are often rushed; when I have time to cook I usually lack the energy to do anything fancy. I'll slap together a tuna salad or pasta, the healthiest, quickest things I can find, but while I eat I worry about the possible mercury poisoning from the fish, the high calorie count from the carbs, the dressing I use that is loaded with fat. I should buy the lite one next time.

I stare at my body fat in the mirror that is becoming cloudy again with steam. I could stand to lose a few kilos. My body mass index is through the roof. If I was my patient I would check for cholesterol, blood pressure, iron deficiency. I'd probably recommend a whole host of prescription medicine. But there's really no time to think about myself, let alone wallow in self-criticism.

I apply my moisturiser that promises to take ten years off my face and fight the seven signs of ageing. I'm not sure what they are or who came up with them but anything is worth a shot. I cover my face, my patchy skin and wrinkles with foundation.

When I'm dry I go back to the bedroom and dress for work. My blouses were once white but they now look cream, almost threadbare, getting old – just like me. They need replacing. Yet another thing on my agenda: clothes shopping. I'll see if Elena will come with me on Saturday; maybe I'll bribe her with the promise of a maternity belt to hide the tummy bulge that tops never seem to stretch over. Something I wish had been invented in my day. She's showing already, at four months. No one could tell I was pregnant with her until I was almost six months into gestation. I kept working until the day my water broke and, fortunately, I didn't have far to go. I was already at the hospital, working as an intern.

My pants feel tight, another thing I should replace. I'll probably have to unfasten the top button after lunch so I put on a long cardigan just in case. It's green, but not a shade that could be attributed to anything. Not apple, forest or mint. It was expensive but now I don't know why I bought something in such a lifeless colour. Elena would call it frumpy.

In the kitchen I make instant coffee with skim milk. I've always drunk instant coffee because it's quicker to make, but now I can afford the fancy kind that comes in little glass jars and is advertised on TV by perfect Italian women.

I take a women's multi and my Paxilla, Paroxetine, from the same family as Prozac: selective serotonin re-uptake inhibitors – SSRIs. Don't get the wrong idea, I'm not depressed. It's technically an anti-depressant but it's also supposed to help women deal with the day-to-day stresses associated with being female: hormones, work, children, men, having people judge you on your appearance, having to maintain composure. I think it's brilliant that a little pill can help to solve all of those previously uncontrollable problems. It does relieve the stress, a little, but I probably need a higher dosage.

Elena doesn't know I take Paxilla. She'd probably go nuts if I told her. She hates medication, which ironically is involved in 90% of my profession. It's a strange thing to find out one day that the child who developed inside you, that you nursed and raised is suddenly a completely different person, diametrically opposed to your views on life. Drugs have side effects, I'll give her that much, but they also save lives. I see it every day. Being so young and healthy makes her easily prejudiced. It's easy to see the world as black and white, pharmaceuticals as bad and 'natural medicine' as good, even if it's unproven.

Elena hasn't called me since I reprimanded her about not getting the baby tested for Down syndrome. She's so sensitive; I don't think she would cope with all that extra work, with a child who is likely to be more dependent, for longer. It would be easier, in the long run to terminate the pregnancy, regardless of what God thinks. I may be Christian but I still put my children first. If God has any compassion for us he would understand.

Rosa is already up, watching TV downstairs. I walk past her

on my way to the kitchen. 'I've made my lunch!' she calls.

It's probably just an excuse for me not to turn the TV off. I inspect her lunch box: three packets of Tweezels and two berry fruit ropes, a pot of yoghurt and three chocolate chip cookies, wrapped loosely in cling wrap. I sigh. Is it really worth a battle?

I knock on John's door and make sure he doesn't sleep through his alarm again. I make him a sandwich for lunch while I'm making one to add to Rosa's lunch box. I put one of the Tweezels and a cookie back in their rightful places in the pantry, calling out, 'Three packets is too many.'

'Cindy has three! Mum! It's not fair!' But soon enough she's absorbed in whatever violent-sounding cartoon is playing at this hour of the morning.

Michael technically lives here too, but in reality he spends more of his time sleeping on friends' couches or staying at my mother's – not because he wants to spend all his time with his grandmother, but because she lives just above a good surf break. I suppose that's just the age – twenty-year-olds aren't known for their strong family values. He spends so much time with his mates that they've almost developed their own language, the way twins sometimes do. I can barely understand a thing he says when I overhear a phone call; it's always 'cobba' this and 'lordish' that. Always one to judge, Elena calls it a 'patriarchal subculture'.

When Michael's not with 'the boyz', as he calls them, he's with Evie, who's so different from any of his previous girlfriends. She's like a bird with a broken wing – the kind of vulnerable, beautiful creature my children would always bring me. She heals and flies away again and comes back broken every time. I wonder if Michael realises. At first I wanted to protect him from the inevitable loss, but more and more it's her I worry about.

For breakfast I eat a piece of wholemeal toast with margarine and sugar-free jam on my way out the door, careful not to leave crumbs on my clothing. Doctors are judged more than normal people on the way they appear. Strangely enough, we're not expected to be healthy; we are expected to be professional, tidy and preferably old. We are expected to be experts, use technical language and speak in calm, even tones. We are expected to listen to our patients and know exactly what they need, to give advice and write prescriptions. We are expected to solve everyone's problems, satisfactorily, in ten minutes flat. That's all it takes to be a GP. We're trained to be superheroes, or at least to appear as if we are. I'm old enough and wise enough to see the flaws in the system but I also know that it works. We treat infections with antibiotics, lower temperatures, and relieve pain by recommending paracetamol or prescribing combinations of half a dozen other pharmaceuticals. We refer patients to specialists if they need it; occasionally we send them straight to the hospital emergency ward. We perform pap smears, prostate checks and STD tests. We save lives, or at least stop them from getting worse.

As I drop Rosa off at school she gives me the sternest look, it's quite strange on her baby face.

'Mum,' she says. 'I don't think you should eat that margarine. Elena says it's a cancer food.' I'm stunned.

Of course she believes her beautiful, charming older sister over her boring, old mother. I once overheard a nurse at work commenting that her children were the harshest judges of her character. I've never heard a truer word spoken. Michael isn't too bad. In fact, I think he's a little too laid-back about everything. John is too wrapped up in his own teenage bubble. Occasionally he hurls abuse at me when he loses his temper but it's blunt and reactive, hardly calculated, like Elena's critiques. She is the first to call me on any mistake. Even when she was younger she always seemed to be hovering around when I dropped a plate on my foot and swore or ran a red light or enacted countless other small trespasses.

Rosa seems to take after Elena. I suppose my girls have been sent here to keep me on my toes, to make me more aware of myself, but it gets tiring. Everything I do is really for them, my children. They are my world. I just wish I could protect them from their father.

Rosa

The sky is grey. I think it might rain soon. The air smells damp like mushrooms. I look down at my feet. My new pink and white sneakers are already dirty. Mum might tell me off, if she notices. She won't be home 'til six o'clock. I used to go to after-school care when I was seven but I hated it. It was boring, so Mum said that John could watch me after school. John said that he would stop flushing me in the toilet if I didn't tell Mum that he's never home after school. So now I just walk home and watch TV 'til someone makes dinner.

John is my brother but not a nice one, and Michael is my other brother but he's cool and likes to swing me around and stuff. Elena is my sister, but she's really a grown-up. She's having a baby and I'm going to be an aunty even through I'm only eight years old. Chardon says that means I'm poor because only poor kids with big families are aunties when they are eight but my mum is a doctor and Chardon's mum is only a nurse, and everyone knows that doctors are better and get more money. Chardon is mean and I wish she would die or move to a different school so I don't have to see her every day.

The ground under my feet is heavy. My bag is heavy too. It makes my shoulders hurt. The footpath is covered in little stones that are stuck into it but stick out and scrape against my shoes. I don't like the noise but I keep scraping my shoes anyway. My legs are tired. I kick a stone and it makes my toes feel funny on one foot so I kick my other foot into the ground to make it even. I look at the fences and the houses that I walk past. This one is pretty and white. I like the blue deck chairs. They look relaxed, like the kind that a mum and a girl would sit in them with sunglasses and sun hats on a hot afternoon and drink lemonade – like on TV. The garden looks like it has someone spending time with it a lot to make it tidy. I reach out and grab a leaf off a bush. It's red and green. It feels like paper. I crush it into tiny bits and sprinkle them on the ground. Then I pick a flower. It's pretty. Bluey-purple and shaped like a bell, a bit like the ones that fairies have on their heads as a hat. It smells gross, like glue and puke. Probably to stop people from stealing the fairy hats. Mum says fairies aren't real, only God is, but we can't see him either, and I've seen lots more pictures of fairies then I have of God. And why would people write books about them if they aren't real?

I stop and sit down under a big friendly tree. The grass around me has little hard things, like cones but with velvet underneath the outside skin. I rub it with my thumb. Mrs Mills says there could be lots of things that people don't know yet. I want to be the first to find the door to a different world. I know that it might not be real, but maybe it is. Maybe there are some magic words or some kind of code. I think I've spent my whole life waiting. I'm always waiting.

I watch the cars go past and think maybe Mum is in one of them. Maybe she's finished work early and is looking for me. Mum used to pick me up from after-school care but she was always late. I was usually the last one to leave and I felt bad, 'cause the carers had to go home and cook dinner and I was making them late. When I was seven, or maybe when I was six, Mum tried to finish work early so she could pick me up when school finished. I would wait outside, on the fence. It was okay for a while. There were usually kids I knew from my class who I could play with, but then everyone else left. I watched the other mums pick up the other kids and sat by myself. I waited and looked for silver cars like our car to come, and sometimes I would wish that maybe she had borrowed a different car because ours was in the garage being fixed, or maybe, when I knew the car coming down the road wasn't Mum, I wished that it would turn into her car. Sometimes it would rain and I would feel sad, and I would think that the sky was crying so I would cry too, because I was lonely and Dad had got a divorce and that's supposed to make you sad.

Sometimes there was another kid I knew, Hannah. Her mum had six kids to pick up first and so she was late too. Sometimes, if I asked Mum, I could go to Hannah's house. It was new and smelled like sawdust. Then her mum would drop me back home at six when her brother's piano lessons finished. One time we made truffles.

It's starting to rain now. I get up and pick up my bag. It's so heavy because of the books for homework and because I put some special stones in it. I hope they're really special because I want everything to change. I want to get out of this world. It sucks, like John says. I never asked to be born here. I want to be somewhere fun where people like me.

Elena

How I got into this stuff

For a long time I felt like I was searching for something. It turned out it wasn't a culture or religion, but it was something to believe in. Now, for the first time in my life I feel like I have it.

I've always wanted to be healthy. My mother is a doctor and I used to believe everything she told me about good foods and bad foods. I used to read health food magazines until I noticed they were riddled with contradictions. One week coffee is good for you, the next it's evil. If I were to believe everything I read I'd be living off blueberries and tofu – I even tried that once and made myself sick. My health got into such a state from eating 'healthy' – trying to follow all these different recommendations. I had terrible eczema, digestion cramps, my skin and hair looked terrible and I felt anxious and depressed. I gave up and switched to junk food and made myself feel even worse. Then my best friend, Henry, introduced me to Nourishing Traditions.

A whole world opened up to me and it's so simple and delicious. It all started in the 1920s and 30s with a man named Weston A Price. He was a dentist who noticed his child patients had worse teeth than their grandparents. He guessed that this was caused by modern food, and set off with his wife to research the teeth of people eating indigenous diets around the world, from the Swiss Alps to Africa to New Zealand. He compared them to those eating new foods such as white flour, sugar and processed vegetable oil, and in every case the traditional diets trumped the modern ones. But it wasn't just teeth that were affected. Price found that within one generation of eating modern foods, babies were born with much higher rates of club feet and crowded jaws, were more susceptible to tuberculosis and suffered from worse health overall.

It makes sense when you think about it. For the last ten thousand years our bodies have evolved to eat these raw and traditionally processed foods and only in the last hundred or so our diets have changed so dramatically that your great-grandma wouldn't recognise most of the popular food in the supermarket.

This blog follows my journey into traditional nutrition. Now that I'm eating for two, I'm doubly interested in making sure my body is getting food that it knows how to deal with.

I proof the post for errors then hit the 'Submit' button,

committing my words to the cyber world. The people who read my blog generally appreciate it. I've never had a troll causing trouble or even someone – a vegan, most likely – who genuinely disagrees, voicing their opinion through the comments. I suppose people who are already on the same buzz are just more likely to come across it. We congregate online, a strange collection of very right and very left-wing people: conservatives who want us to go back to food the way God intended and hippies rebelling against the dominant corporate food system. If I keep my (non-food related) politics out of it and just focus on the food, we don't have any disagreements.

I never get too personal, either. In some ways it's an escape from the personal. The facade I present to my readers is free of my daily struggles, family dramas and relationship tensions. Most of the other blogs I read are the same: informative, casual, occasionally funny. Sometimes they're almost too perfect, these 'happy woman' bloggers with perfect children and perfect meals. I remind myself that no one actually lives like that – even Martha Stewart got done for the fraudster she really was.

I don't feel like I'm being fake. On the contrary, I really believe what I put out there. But I have to admit, I sometimes embellish. Sometimes I pretend to be happier than I am, I leave out the gory details of my slothful housekeeping, I pretend Malcolm is as involved in eating as well as I am, I don't ever mention that we're not married in case I offend the sensibilities of my more conservative readers. It's just a small fragment of the bigger picture of my life, after all – the part that's focused on traditional food that our bodies can actually digest.

Of course my mother, the doctor, thinks I'm crazy. They only get one lecture on nutrition in Med school – one lecture on nutrition and six years of studying illness. But I suppose that's appropriate in an inherently ill society.

I'm still not talking to Mum. I know it sounds childish. It probably is, but she really upset me and I have this irrational urge to punish her for it.

I want this baby no matter who he or she is. I don't want to be faced with horrible choices. I don't want to focus on everything that could go wrong. I'm young so it's not a high-risk situation, but even the ultrasound tests they could have done earlier in the pregnancy are inconclusive and further testing, amniocentesis, carries the possibility of miscarriage. Strangely, this is another issue where I would find common ground with right-wing fundamentalists. It just proves that Mum doesn't really believe in her own religion. It's a crutch and it makes life easier for her. It's a religion of convenience.

I don't want to constantly worry about illness, disability or disease – I don't even want those things to cross my mind. Having a baby growing inside me is miracle enough – I don't want my power taken away by biomedical interference. I want my pregnancy to be a *healthy* thing, but Mum doesn't understand health – just sickness.

Evie

There is no fundamental difference between man and the higher animals in their mental faculties ... The lower animals, like man, manifestly feel pleasure and pain, happiness, and misery.
CHARLES DARWIN

The night air almost crackles with anticipation, and fear prickles my spine as I jump out of Jason's van and walk quickly, with the others, towards the death factory. The whole place gives me the creeps. Most people would ignore it, they would say that a chicken's life doesn't matter as much as a human's. Who are they to judge?

Homo sapiens is the most vile, most evil and destructive species on this earth. I am unfortunate enough to fit into this category, but at least I have the power to do something to stop some of the hideous suffering inflicted by my species, and at least I do it.

I climb through the chicken wire that Jason cut the night before, giving us easier access. I'm careful not to snag my jeans. I can see Tara, with her purple dreads, and Jason in his black hoodie at the door already, trying to get through the lock. Tara tries to pick the deadbolt and when that doesn't work Jason gets out his mallet. It's noisy as hell but no one lives within a kilometre of this place. Who would want to?

Tara has cut the wires of the security system. It will send a signal to the rent-a-cops who patrol this place, but at least it won't blast open our eardrums. We have ten minutes.

I try not to cry as we walk through the door. My eyes and lungs are burning from the ammonia, a by-product of the faeces piling up on the floor. The ammonia levels are worse for the birds raised for meat. This can mean chronic respiratory disease for the chickens, as well as sores on their feet and breast blisters. It sometimes makes them go blind. The next time you buy a packet of chicken breast or a dozen 'barn-raised' eggs I hope you remember this. The smell is overwhelming, putrid. It's a chicken concentration camp. They are stuck in cages, one foot square, stacked on top of each other in rows, worked to the death for their eggs. Most of their feathers have been plucked out, by themselves or their neighbours, revealing mottled pink skin. Their beaks are clipped so they can't peck each other to death, some of them can barely stand. I bet if they could have chosen their own evolution they would have been less useful to humans. Even extinction would be better than this.

The wretched creatures turn towards us, thousands of beady eyes that we will not be able to save. We only have time for a few cages. We get to work.

It used to scare me, reaching into a cage towards a chicken, but I don't care if they peck me now. Through my gloves, it isn't painful and I am saving them lives of pain.

We only get about twenty when we hear Jason's cell phone ring – a warning from Mark, our designated getaway driver. I walk as quickly as I can with the two travel cages Tara has borrowed from her work, the SPCA, trying not to bump them against my legs too much. These poor birds have had a hard enough life as it is.

Mark revs the van as we carefully stash the refugees in the back.

'Well done, my brothas and sistas,' Mark says, grasping to pull us into the van.

We make our getaway. My heart pounds in my chest as the van lurches into motion, accelerating at a speed you would think was impossible for a clunky old vehicle. We swoop around the corner, catching sight of the security car in the distance, too far away to get our plates. I'm grateful it's not the cops. They have the right to chase us, pull us over, arrest us and even get us put in jail for some inane reason. All we are doing is rescuing the oppressed. We might have to do a bit of damage to get in there, but we wouldn't do it at all if we didn't believe that what is being done to these living creatures is wrong.

Our rescued chickens cluck away as if they know they are on their way to a better life. They probably do. They are intelligent creatures. It's an hour's drive to the farm sanctuary where they'll be allowed to wander around in the grass, in the sunshine for the rest of their short lives.

It's the middle of the night but we are expected. Derek invites us in for cocoa while Jeanie gets the chickens settled into their new home. They are both wonderful, kind people who have turned their family farm into a paradise for rescued animals. Most of them are legal. They ask to take the sick and dying animals that factory farms don't budget for.

Jeanie is a retired vet and she does what she can to save them. I'm sure they know these are illegal refugees but they don't ask questions. The less they know the better it is for them. They sit

on the fence between morality and legality, knowing as well as
we do that the two concepts can be worlds apart.

45

Michael

Something about cold mornings makes me want to sleep in, even though I could get a surf in before uni. As soon as the thought crosses my mind I'm there already, riding the crest of the wave. I can almost feel the adrenalin. I get out onto the deck and try to spy the waves through the bush. If I had an early class I would probably skip it today. I can hear the surf crashing below and I know it's gonna be mint.

I pull on my wetsuit and I'm halfway out the door when I see Evie. She's looking pretty rough. Her hair is limp and there are dark circles under her eyes. She's always in this kind of state when she gets back from her travels, but she's smiling that cute pixie smile.

'You're up early,' she grins at me.

'Be back in half an hour.' She knows it will be more like a whole hour, but she stands aside and I peck her on the cheek as I pass. She smells like stale cigarettes, disgusting, but it's all part of her charm.

Evie is different, different from anyone I've ever met. Not in the same way that Elena is, although they're both a bit strange. There's always been this tension between us. I think that's what makes it exciting.

I remember it clearly, the first time we met. It was pouring with rain, and me, Dave and Nico were hitching back from Gizzy. We walked to the outskirts of town with our hoodies over our heads, getting absolutely soaked. That was when I saw her.

She was so small, wearing those strange clothes of hers. Her jeans were covered in colourful patches, and over them she was wearing what looked like three or four layers of silk nightgowns, dyed black, and her skin was so pale, almost white. I remember thinking how strange she looked.

Three people is not a good number to hitch with. Most cars only have room for two extra people, and it's threatening for drivers who are travelling alone, so we'd already decided we would split up. Dave and Nico were going to hitch together because I volunteered to go it alone, but when I saw her in the rain I thought we both could do with some company.

I don't usually introduce myself to strangers and she looked like she might be a bit scared of me at first, but after a while she got used to me standing there making a dick of myself by telling a complete stranger all about the embarrassing time I'd had the night before. She even smiled when I told her about how I'd accidentally pissed on some guy's tent because it was green so I thought, in my drunken state, that it was a really smooth type of bush. Then she told me I was an idiot and laughed.

We got picked up after ten minutes by this Rasta guy with a big beard and dark glasses – jumped into the back of his van before we saw that there were no seats, just bags of old clothes and boxes of books. It was a bumpy ride because his driving was insane. We had to hang onto the back of the front seats so that we weren't thrown around the van. I honestly feared for my life, but she – Evie – seemed to like it, as if it was normal for her to be in this kind of situation. That's when I realised she had actually been helping me out when she agreed to hitch with me, and not the other way around.

It was much more entertaining and less terrifying, being flung from side to side in the back of the van with her there, laughing at me. That was when I noticed she was beautiful. Not in a typical blonde beach babe kind of way, which is probably the kind of chick I'd usually go for, but in a wild, untamed way. With her dark hair and piercings, her torn clothes and patches, her pale skin and green eyes. I think she caught me off-guard – and kept me there this whole time. She's not trying to be anyone else but herself. She's independent and fiery and slightly terrifying, and she doesn't pose for anyone.

It was one of the first things she ever asked me. 'Do you eat animals?' she asked, in her tough little voice, and I knew from the words she used and from her tone that she didn't, and that she thought it was wrong.

I tried to sidestep the question. 'Not living ones,' I joked, but she didn't laugh. There was clearly no way of getting around it so I put my head on the line. 'Yeah,' I said, looking her in the eye, trying to be casual. 'You don't?'

'No!' she said it in a fierce way, as if I was accusing her of murder. I guess, to her, it sounded like I was.

'I do everything in my power to stop cruelty to animals,' she explained a few minutes later. 'I'm vegan.'

'Does that mean you don't drink milk too?' I asked. I didn't really know much about it. She nodded at me. It was a bit patronising, actually, like I was a little kid.

'I don't eat any animal products. I don't wear them either.' She looked down at her scuffed black leather boots. 'Unless they're second-hand.'

'Whoa, really?' I thought it was pretty strange. 'Aren't your dresses silk?' I admit I was trying to catch her out.

'No. They're satin, they're synthetic – and second-hand. I don't buy silk, I don't support the murder of insects.' I couldn't fault her on that.

'Do you eat honey?'

'No.'

'That's intense … So my shoes are out – what about this beanie?' I say, pointing at my forehead.

'It's wool – from sheep farming.'

'So you're not even gonna let them shear a sheep?'

'Haven't you ever thought it might be wrong to raise animals just for our own use? I won't wear wool unless it's from an op-shop, I don't want to support an industry that is cruel to animals.' She said it as though she was really proud.

'So … umm … what do you eat?'

'It may surprise you,' that condescending tone again, 'But there are millions of products out there that don't hurt animals.'

'Like …?'

'Bread, beans, potatoes, nuts … ever heard of vegetables?' She was starting to get irritating.

'Is that all?'

'Soy milk … and there are other soy products. I can even get sausages and burgers made of vegetable protein, and vegan cheese and yoghurt, and fake bacon.'

'What's the point?' I laughed. 'If you want to eat meat so

badly that you're eating a fake version … It sounds like you're depriving yourself.'

'Meat is disgusting!' She folded her arms and it seemed as though she was closing in on herself, obviously unhappy with me. I didn't care.

'It tastes pretty good, actually.'

'Maybe to *you*. I suppose you don't mind making yourself into an animal graveyard?'

'That's a bit extreme.'

'Well it's true. You are what you eat. All the cells in your body are made up of bits and pieces from other cells and some of those cells are coming from dead animals …'

'So you mean atoms and shit?'

'And bigger things.'

'In that case I think you're breathing in dead animals right now. It all gets recycled, you know?' I'd read about it in Bill Bryson's *A Short History of Nearly Everything*. Atoms are always passing between everything on earth, so tiny and prolific that if a person has been dead long enough, like Da Vinci or someone, it's likely that every person's body contains at least a few thousand atoms that were once part of him. That kind of shit makes my head spin.

She made a kind of 'hrmph' noise, surprised that I could out-smart her.

'Well at least I don't contribute to the pain and suffering of more than fifty-five billion animals around the world that are kept in horrible conditions just so that people like you can have something tasty to eat.' Her arms were still crossed in front of her, leaving her unprotected; the erratic driver chose that moment to suddenly pull off the road. She was flung into me as the van juddered to a halt. She pulled away as soon as she found some stability.

'You crazy kids …' The driver was smiling back at us, making me feel slightly uncomfortable. 'You smoke da ganja?'

He pulled a little tin out of his glove box, which was packed with sticky green buds, the smell of them made my mouth water – the sweetest perfume. We watched as he broke up the herb and began to roll a long spliff, mixing the pieces of green with a pinch of tobacco.

It was just what I needed. I took a toke and relaxed, forgetting completely about Evie and her weird ideas. After a few more I passed it to her. I was actually surprised that she took it. No coughing. Like a pro.

The water is ice cold, even through my wetsuit. I grit my teeth as I step over the boulders. When I'm up to my waist I launch onto the board and start to paddle. The air's so cold in my throat it's hard to swallow. Real refreshing. There are a couple of other guys out but I don't know them. I'll just stay out of their way. I wait my turn, unlike some locals around here who will cut in as if the break is their bloody property. I get out to where the surf is breaking, too late for a primo wave but there will be more to come. I duck under it and the freezing water is in my ears and dripping down my spine.

I see my first wave coming. I inhale and feel my heartbeat

pumping through my whole body. I get a zingy feeling when I can see the ridge aligning with where I need to be when it breaks. I paddle out just a bit, the wave shadowing me. I jump on my board and feel the exhilaration as the wave lurches me forward and, just for a few seconds, I'm flying.

When I'm too tired and hungry to focus I paddle back to the rocks and find my footing on solid land. Glad to be back. It's a good kind of exhaustion, but I better get some food before I faint like a girl. I bet Evie will make me marmite on toast – it's all she ever eats – but I'd rather cook up some bacon and eggs, which will make her angsty, but there's no point denying the truth: food is food.

It used to seem like every time I saw Evie she would try to convince me to become vegan. It got pretty heavy sometimes, every time I ate a pie she would look like she wanted to slap me. We used to argue about it a lot. At first it was a challenge, a fun debate and something to talk about, but it got old pretty quick. I felt like she was trying to convert me to her religion.

'If I want to be preached at I'll go to church,' I yelled one day after that she stopped pushing.

Now, when I get the bacon out of the fridge, all she does is roll her eyes. *You can't change me.* I don't even need to say it. She knows.

She pulls a half full bag of cheap bread out of her backpack and a jar of Marmite. She always brings her own food even though Nan would love to fatten her up.

She doesn't say anything 'til we're sitting out on the deck in the sun with our plates. Then she's full of stories of her travels.

'You wouldn't believe this guy, Michael. He didn't wear pants the whole festival, just a rainbow jumper that looked like it was falling apart, and he kept trying to hug everyone.'

'Damn hippies.' I say this every time.

'Oh, that wasn't the worst part. He would go up to people and wave his arms around their heads and clear away the bad karma. That was pretty hilarious, but then he kept telling everyone what to do. He told me I should smoke dried mānuka leaves instead of tobacco, that I should let my hair grow long and that I was wearing too many clothes.'

'I hope you told him to shove it. The guy sounds like a creep.'

'Yeah, but that just made him want to have a peace circle and hold hands.'

Evie complains about this kind of thing, but she must love it, otherwise she wouldn't keep going to hippie festivals. Sometimes she comes back from something and raves about how trumps everything was and I wonder if I would have enjoyed it. And sometimes after she leaves, I lie in bed wishing I was that free; that I could just fly away and hitch all over the place and not give a damn. But most of the time there's nowhere I'd rather be than here.

I do know why she does it though. The thing she always talks about the most when she comes back glowing is the feeling of belonging, of being part of something. That's something I wish I could have, but I doubt I'd find it in the forest with a bunch of half-naked hippies. I don't know where I'd find it. Maybe Nan can tell me.

Valerie

It must be Sunday. My brain is still foggy from sleep, or lack thereof, but I can negotiate a few facts from the shipwreck of my mind. Yesterday I did the laundry, my socks and underwear are probably still wet and if Saturday is laundry day, today is Sunday. I haven't needed an alarm in years. My body clock knows that seven is wake up time, but today when I look over at the digital numbers by my bed I'm perplexed: it's 8.49. I'm going to miss the morning prayer meeting. It's a shame. I have four young adults to pray for.

I stand up but I feel light-headed so I sit back on the bed and wait for the room to come into focus.

I can't count the number of times I've been asked, by friends and family, how I can keep my faith in such a science-based career. Don't I believe in evolution? Don't I have to favour the power of science rather than God's will? I suppose they are thinking about those cases on the news – the religious family who won't seek treatment for their child's monstrous tumour, the sects that won't allow for blood transplants or organ donations.

Maybe some Christians have a deep distrust of science, but I don't. I don't see it as a conflict of interests at all. Evolution certainly doesn't explain everything, regardless of what John, with all the certainty of a sixteen-year-old, tells me. Why couldn't God have created evolution? Who am I to claim to know the mysteries of creation? All my life I've known I'm here to help people. My job gives me the means to do it and my faith keeps me going. If God didn't want me to interfere I'm sure he'd stop me, or find some way to let me know. If John's right and it's all a delusion – then at least it's a practical one. It helps me get through the day. I have gone through hard times, times when I considered giving up, but when I feel spirit moving through me I understand that I'm exactly where I need to be. It's a relief to know that I'm following a greater plan, that it's not just a pointless struggle.

When I arrive at the church car park all the spaces are taken. I find a spot on the next street over and tolerate the uncomfortable feeling of my damp underpants. Maybe I should have taken the day off. Would Jesus mind? I can just picture him shaking his head with that compassionate look on his face. *I died for you and you're thinking about neglecting me?* I pull myself together as I get to the door. Brian, a man I've only spoken to a handful of times in the ten years I've been coming here, hands me a newsletter at the door and smiles. Usually he seems kind but today I notice just a pinch of self-satisfaction. Maybe he noticed my absence this morning; maybe I'm imagining things.

I find a seat next to Audrey, my best friend, possibly my only friend apart from Cynthia, who wouldn't be caught dead in a church. She smiles at me and I find myself suddenly relieved. She has her baby godson, Tyler, on her knee and her eight-year-old son, Josh, clinging to her arm.

'I want a muffin,' he says.

'In the break,' Audrey hisses.

The church band take their places and the morning worship

begins. The music always makes me feel safe and secure, as we sing 'In His Arms' I feel beautiful, calming energy circling the building – his presence, the Lord's grace, all around me, inside me. I would never tell anyone at work this kind of thing. They'd think I was nuts. But everyone here understands and so it's okay for me to raise my palms and receive this love, this blessing, to close my eyes and lean my head back slightly, to pray for Elena, for Michael, for John, for Rosa, for Evie, for Malcolm, for Mum, for myself. I pray for Alice, the nurse at work who's having complications in her pregnancy, for her husband and her unborn child. I pray for the murderer on the news last night who couldn't show any signs of human emotion. I pray for my patients: for the woman with the autistic son, for the man who's an alcoholic and won't accept it and for his wife who has almost given up. I pray for the teenage girl whom I gave a prescription for the pill; I pray that she's careful and that she finds God in her own way. I pray for the old man with the heart condition who has severe side effects from his cholesterol-lowering medication.

And as I pray I begin to understand a small part of something greater, as if the Lord is showing me something, a vision. I see that this man could be one of hundreds of others I have treated, that all these patients I'm praying for could be the exact same patients I prayed for last year and the year before that. I see the same desperation, pain, exhaustion, confusion and fear every day. This is the human condition.

'Is this your work?' I ask Jesus in my head.

'This is our work,' He replies.

'Are you responsible?' I ask.

'We are all responsible.'

The singing seems to go on forever and when I hear the prayer begin it seems like no time at all has passed.

'Thank you, father,' the singer is saying into the microphone. 'We fall on our knees, father, we worship you, our Lord. We pray for all of the sinners that they find your grace, Lord, that they find your love. In Jesus' name, amen.'

I'm still feeling God's love as I sit down, as if his arms are wrapped around me, rocking me. I hear the smooth, familiar voice of the pastor, Bill, say it's break time and Josh is already rummaging in Audrey's purse for a gold coin to pay for his muffin.

The sermon today is about life. The projectors on both sides of the room display pictures of a precious newborn baby, wrapped in a silky blanket.

'God's greatest blessing to you is this life.' Pastor Bill begins to speak and the humming of voices dies down. His voice is friendly, confident. Charismatic, I suppose.

'He has made us all, since Adam, from the clay. He has crafted us as his children; each of us has a path, a destiny under God. How did Adam repay him?' There is a murmur of laughter around the room. It strikes me that the words Bill is speaking aren't exactly funny. It's his tone, as if he is giving us an insight into the folly of mankind.

'He didn't say, "Yes, sir"…' Bill raises his hand in salute, '… and obey the one simple request of God. Oh no! He listened to the temptation of the serpent, Satan. He ate from the tree of knowledge and was cast out of the Garden of Eden. You'd think we would have learnt from his mistake.' His voice is still comical, amused.

'God gave us free will and this means we all have the power to sin, to do evil, to think evil thoughts. But God loves us so much that he gave his only son. Jesus died so that we could be free from sin, so that we can, today, repent and be forgiven.' He speaks passionately, the volume of his voice rising, and for the first time in a long time I notice the way the sound echoes in here. There must be speakers all around the walls, surround sound, in this strange shaped building which used to be a supermarket before it was converted into a church.

'We have been blessed. Truly blessed.' Now he sounds sincere.

'And how do we repay him?'

I'm not sure quite what he's getting at here.

'We all have times when we disrespect life – the lives of others or our own lives. We think hateful angry thoughts; we have all done things that disrespect the gift God gave us.'

'A woman came to see me a few years ago. She had been blessed with a child; she was three months pregnant and she was shaking with fear. She told me there was a genetic disorder in her family, that her baby could be born severely disabled and she didn't know what to do. The doctors had been talking to her and had asked her to take some tests to find out if her baby would be in this difficult condition.' Pastor Bill's sermon continues. 'I asked her, "Do you have faith in the Lord?" She nodded but I could see that she was still plagued with fear. I said, 'These doctors are doing their job, but that is not the job of faith.' I said, 'If the Lord has decided to bless you with a child who has special needs would you turn away from him? Would you step off the path he has set out for you?' Tears began streaming down her cheeks. 'No,' she said. She was shaking and I asked if I could pray for her and the second I laid my hand upon her shoulder I could feel her whole body relax. I could feel her faith return.'

I look down into my newsletter, thinking of Elena. I feel guilty that I advised her to have those tests but I feel even more contradictory guilt that I would do it again, regardless of whether she would listen to me. I look across at Audrey and she has a puzzled expression on her face and suddenly I realise she knows what I am thinking and her expression changes into one I don't recognise. I feel her stiffen next to me. Maybe she's not thinking about Elena, maybe she's thinking about the abortions that I sign off in my day job. I don't talk about that at church. That is work. At work my duty is to help people in the only way I can. Pushing my faith on them wouldn't help. If I was a pregnant teenager I sure wouldn't want a doctor to tell me it was God's will that I drop out of school and give up my life to a child I don't have the resources to raise. Bill the preacher would disagree with me, but maybe abortions are part of God's plan too. I don't want to get into it here, with Audrey. Thank God she's too polite to bring it up.

I take my mind off the whole situation the only way I know how: by being busy. I go to the supermarket to make sure I've got everything I need for dinner then call in on a couple of elderly patients on the way home. It's lonely when all your friends have died and your family is too busy to care and Sunday is the worst day of the week to be lonely.

As soon as I'm home I start cooking. Sunday dinner is probably the only meal I spend more than twenty minutes on all week. I make a roast, beef, chicken or lamb. I bake the vegetables separately in olive oil. I started doing that when Evie started coming to our family dinners. I also make a salad without cheese or eggs or honey dressing so that she has something other than roast vegetables to eat.

Elena comes early to prepare the gravy. She refuses to eat the packet mixes I used to make because of the MSG and any ingredients with unrecognisable numbers and letter combinations. She always tries to convince me to put something non-vegan in the salad.

'What about home-made aioli?' she asks, only half serious. I briefly wonder if it's a coping mechanism she developed as a child so that if she got into trouble she could claim she was joking.

'You already know what my answer to that is.'

'We could tell Evie it's made with tahini or something, and anyway, it would be good for her to get some more B vitamins.'

'How would you like it if I served you some battery-farmed eggs with canola oil and MSG seasoning? Anyway, *you're* not supposed to eat raw eggs.' She sighs.

'I wouldn't poison her, Mum. It would be good for her, and I'm sick of eating iceberg lettuce with refrigerated out of season tomatoes and cucumber as a side dish. My body can handle a few raw free-range eggs.'

I'm saved from any more of her subversive arguments by the doorbell. Michael has lost his keys again.

'I'm sure you've left enough sets of house keys around that everyone in town must have some by now.'

'Yeah, yeah,' He says, giving me a brief hug and a peck on the cheek. Evie is behind him, still as quiet and shy as the first time she came. I'm not sure if it's just because she disapproves of my life so much she has nothing nice to say, but she smiles at me and I take it as a compliment. They join Malcolm in the lounge to watch the six o'clock news that Elena refuses to watch in case it pollutes her mind. I am suddenly in a mental gap. A few years ago these were my babies, dependent on me. Now here they are with their partners, all grown-up. Except for John, who is up-stairs on his PlayStation no doubt. He'll be down when food is offered. And my baby, Rosa, who is wise beyond her eight years.

Elena is in the kitchen violently tearing lettuce. She's still not happy with me but I got her to come today out of sheer guilt and family responsibility.

'What did it do to you?' I tease.

'I thought maybe it would be less bland if I abused it.' It's unlike her to be so snarky. 'Don't tell Evie. She might be offended that I'm disrespecting the life of the plant and then we won't get her to eat anything.'

Now it's my turn to sigh.

'She comes here and eats some potatoes and lettuce. For all we know, it's her only decent meal all week and she's not even getting protein. No wonder she's so emaciated. Veganism is a moralistic version of an eating disorder!'

'If you think she should be eating protein I'll get her some tofu.'

'Mum!' Elena is yelling now, I wonder if the hormones are affecting her. 'Do you ever listen to a thing I say? About how unhealthy soy is or how soy crops are destroying the rainforest?' She begins to calms down.

'So what should I do?'

'Oh I don't know, cook her some lentils and rice or something. Buy some organic tempeh; at least it's fermented and doesn't stop the absorption of minerals like tofu does.'

I know Elena and Evie sit on different sides of the fence but I still find it strange to witness. Elena normally ignores the things that bother her, something she has a natural talent for but I am still learning how to do. There's just something about Michael's quiet vegan girlfriend that makes Elena breathe smoke. They're probably more alike than they'd like to think. They even look similar somehow, maybe it's the passion of youth. Elena glares at me if I say anything positive about veganism. She won't believe me even if I read it in a medical journal, even if I'm a trained doctor, even if I'm her mother and twice her age. She's still the expert.

'What are you going to do after high school?' Elena asks John.

'Dunno,' he says, eyes downcast.

'He wanted to be an author a few years ago.'

'No, Mum. I wanted to be an Auror – when I was ten years old. I never wanted to be a stupid author.'

'Auror?' Michael asks.

Malcolm suppresses a giggle.

'From Harry Potter? The dark wizard hunters?' Elena is talking about this as if it's an everyday thing, not something straight from a child's fantasy.

'Well, that sounds to me like something in the police force, a detective maybe?' I'm trying to be helpful but Michael gives me a stern look. John almost chokes on his food.

'Fuck the police!' His voice is loud, angry.

'Don't you use that kind of language at the dinner table, John Martin Joyce!'

'Don't you use my fucking middle name, you bitch!'

'Don't fucking swear in front of Mum!' Michael contradicts.

'John!' I'm appalled. I try to think of something to say to make it better, or to punish him. I can't decide which is more important. Too late, he's already left the table and his half-eaten meal and gone back upstairs. The slam of his bedroom door echoes over us, guiding our eyes down to our plates and away from each other.

Rosa

Aroha is my best friend. She's in my class but she sits at a different table with the tall girls who have pretty hair: Christen, Melissa and Chardon. Aroha says doesn't really like them, but she swaps lunch with them sometimes. They hate me. Chardon pulls my hair when she stands behind me in the line outside the classroom after lunch. She's a bitch. Aroha is different in school when she's around them. They say they have a secret club and I'm not allowed in, but I don't want to be in their bitch club anyway.

At lunchtime and playtime me and Aroha go and sit behind the pool on the little wooden seat that no one else ever sits on. One time we saw some teachers there smoking, but we ran away. This morning it's cold, and when the playtime bell rings we go to our seat.

'Christen says I'm black,' Aroha tells me.

'She's pretty stupid if she doesn't even know what the colour black looks like,' I say. 'Maybe you should ask Mrs Mills if you can move and sit by me.' That would be so much cooler.

'Nah. I think we should just kill her.'

I laugh. That would be impossible, but it's funny to think about. 'How would you kill her?'

'We could garrotte her with wire.'

'What's that?' I ask. Aroha knows lots of different words.

'It's like strangling, but you get really strong wire and pull it around someone's neck and it kills them.'

'How do you even know about that?'

'Charlie told me. He saw it on this movie once,' Aroha says.

'Charlie isn't real.' Aroha talks about him all the time but he's a 'maginary friend, which means he doesn't really exist.

'He's real. He's just invisible. How else would he see movies?'

'But your mum said you had to stop pretending because she was worried about you being mental.'

'I'm not mental. She just can't see him, that's why she thinks he's not real.'

'Like God?'

'God's not real,' Aroha says. She's an atheist because her mum doesn't believe in God.

'My mum thinks God's real.'

'Well, I think Charlie is real, so I'm just as crazy as your mum.'

'She's pretty crazy.' We both laugh.

'Maybe you're not real and you're my 'maginary friend,' I say. Aroha looks cross.

'But everyone else can see me. I have to be real.'

We sit on our seat and dangle our legs. Aroha gives me some of her muesli bar and I give her some chips.

'You don't really want to kill Christen, do you?'

'Nah, but it's fun to pretend.'

I'm a bit disappointed because it was exciting to think about. But it's good that we won't go to jail or anything and it's good that Aroha doesn't like Christen.

'We could decapitate her,' I suggest, but I'm not sure what that means.

'Then we could gouge out her eyes with teaspoons,' Aroha says.

'Eww, gross!' I say, and we both crack up laughing.

Elena

The supermarket car park is not as full as usual, so I'm surprised to find the produce section a hive of activity. They always put the produce section first because it's one of the few types of food in here that will naturally decay. Like Michael Pollan says, shop the perimeter of the supermarket. Everything around the outside of the isles gets the highest foot traffic because it's actually food; if you don't eat it soon it will go off.

Fortunately I never need anything from produce. My organic fruit and vegetables are delivered to my door on Fridays and if I ever need anything else I go to the local greengrocer. The artificial lighting is bright white. It makes everything slightly surreal. I weave the trolley around other shoppers while trying to remember the list in my head. Rice. Toilet paper. Coconut cream. As I pass the sourdough bread stand I pause briefly before reassuring myself that I have some starter rising at home. It was only a few months ago that I noticed real bread in the supermarket, absent of the additives: preservatives, hydrogenated protein, flavour enhancer or raising agents, all with different number codes. This bread has an ingredients list like: flour, water, yeast, salt. Full stop.

A woman walks past me wearing a pretty black-and-white print dress with vivid scarlet poppies. I stare for a moment too long.

I pass the drinks section and then remember the coconut

cream. Check. Toilet paper. Brown sugar. Tomato paste. What else? I should have written a list. Peanut butter? A short-haired woman in a tie-dyed T-shirt is examining all the jars.

'They're all made in China!' she exclaims in exasperation.

She's my kind of shopper. I pick a few of them up and scan the labels.

'Oh. This one's Australian-made,' she reports.

'Here you go.' I pass her the organic one, made in New Zealand, and pick up a jar for myself.

I browse the chocolate section, checking to see if my favourite fair trade organic kind is on special. The young man in front of me is either taking his candy very seriously or he's standing there awkwardly, waiting for me to leave.

Tomato paste: check. Ingredients: Tomatoes, salt. I would get the organic one but it's twice the price, and on a limited income I have to compromise sometimes.

I pass countless food imitations in bright colourful packets with ticks for low-fat and added folate. Rubbish. Most of the time low-fat equals high sugar or, worse, artificial sweeteners. Human beings have become bizarrely good at deceiving themselves. The food we've created tastes like the things we naturally crave: sweet, salty, fatty, sour. In nature these tastes mean nutrition, in our new world they mean crap.

The guy stocking the shelves with pasta checks me out then notices my baby bump. I smile to see his slight embarrassment. I'm sure I've forgotten something. Maybe the baby is eating all my brain fuel. Toilet paper: check (the more environmentally friendly option). Feta: you can never have too much. I remind myself to learn to make it. Meat and dairy are always around the outside of the supermarket because they, like produce, have been known to go off, a sure sign of real food; if the microorganisms don't want to eat it then neither should we. I don't need meat because we get it in bulk from the farm. Cleaning products? No. I don't think so. Raw cat food: check. Dr Pottenger found that cats fed only cooked food would become sick and infertile after a generation or two. It would be hypocritical of me to feed Serah the cat the equivalent of McDonald's.

Sometimes I examine the ingredients lists on random products, but by now I know what to buy and what to avoid; anything with more than five ingredients (usually), everything with unrecognisable ingredients (definitely). I've memorised the most evil ones, known to cause seizures, chest pains, headache, nausea, burning sensations and face rashes. MSG E621. E627, E635 and E631, sulphites E220-E228, nitrites and nitrates, E249-E252 … the list goes on. Basically, you're safer avoiding anything with a code number.

The woman in front of me in the queue has brown politician hair. I watch as she loads her shopping: a telegraph cucumber, a red capsicum, an avocado. If she looked at my trolley she might think I was anti-fresh fruit and vegetables, or the worst kind of vegetarian. I only come here for the things that I haven't found better sources for yet. I make a mental note to look into finding a local organic co-op. I swipe my Fly Buys card – Henry assures me it's some kind of market research conspiracy but I just want to get enough points for fancy French cookware – then pay for my food ($25.99) and guide my trolley back out into the real world. I can't wait to get home to the bunches of asparagus I picked up at the farmers' market.

Spring asparagus soup and seasonal strawberries

When you shop at your local farmers' market, you always know what's in season. This morning we encountered the first strawberries of spring and bright, healthy looking asparagus spears in green and purple. I know that these are fresh and bursting full of nutrients; the asparagus is so sweet I couldn't help but nibble it raw!

It's quite odd that supermarkets stock all manner of produce all-year round – it has created a generation of people (myself included) raised clueless of the seasons and their respective bounties. It wasn't until recently that I became acquainted with the close relationships fruits have with their seasons. I wasn't totally clueless before, Feijoas – a Kiwi favourite, have always meant autumn; mandarins are so much cheaper in winter, strawberries are what summer's all about – but supermarkets are always stocked with sweet, bland grapes, chalky pears, and mangoes that don't even grow in this climate.

Not only is the food at my local market fresh and mostly free from toxic pesticides, it's also local, which means it doesn't need to be shipped across the country, wasting fossil fuels. In the US, produce is often transported thousands of miles across country, subsidised by the government, which means that cheap Californian tomatoes can out-compete small local growers around the country. New Zealand is a small country but all of our produce is still wastefully transported to central depots before going to outlets, so even if you buy a supermarket cabbage grown on a farm down the road it's probably travelled a few hundred kilometres.

These strawberries are so delicious I can't bear to do anything to them except slice them up and serve them with a drizzle of cream and a splash of vanilla essence.

Asparagus has long been one of my favourites. I can't stand to boil or steam this tasty green. My absolute favourite way to cook it is to gently fry the whole spears in butter and/or olive oil for five to ten minutes. When it's almost done I sprinkle on some salt and squeeze some fresh lemon juice over them. The lemon juice compliments the unique flavour of the asparagus while highlighting its sweetness. These always disappear quickly at family dinners.

Spring asparagus soup

This simple soup is perfect for warming up when there's

still a chill in the air, while still being full of freshness and vitality. I love the way the tendrils of asparagus are almost pasta like, without being heavy. If you prefer a creamed soup, simply blend it before you serve it.

Ingredients:

2 onions

2 Tbsp. butter

1 tsp mustard seeds

2 bunches fresh asparagus

1 litre good quality chicken stock

Juice and zest of one lemon

1 tsp thyme, roughly chopped

Good quality sea salt and black pepper (to taste)

Sour cream (to serve)

Dice onions and brown in butter with the mustard seeds. Add stock and bring to boil. Slice asparagus lengthwise and add to stock. Cook for approximately 5 minutes (careful that it is still vividly green). Remove from heat and add thyme, lemon and zest. Season with salt and pepper.

Serve with a heaped spoonful of sour cream, or substitute with fresh cream or yoghurt (bearing in mind that the sourness of the yoghurt will add to the sourness of the soup).

Michael

I can't move. Hungover as fuck. It was a big night with the boyz and I should get up and see if Nan will cook me a feed but every time I lift my head the pain throws me right back down again. Instead my thoughts drift to Evie, I'm worried that something is up with her, and my fucked up family, and I hope that Elena's baby is alright, and then I hear Nan calling out and I know I have to face the world.

The sweet smell of coffee hits me as I walk into the kitchen. Nan hands me a mug.

'This is the business,' I tell her.

She's still in her dressing gown, smiling at me as I squint out at the sunlight. 'The Panadol is in the drawer, boy.' She smiles, but doesn't give me any shit for being hungover this time.

I grab my sunnies and follow her out onto the deck. Something is missing and it's time to ask about it.

'Nan, the other day you were telling me about Ātea, about time and space.'

She nods.

'How did we get from there into the gods – you know – like Tangaroa, and Tāne?'

'Let me see …' she begins again. 'Then there was Io.'

'God?'

'The godhead,' Nan nods, 'who created Ranginui and Papatūānuku.'

'The sky father and the earth mother.'

'Not yet. Don't rush, boy. There was no sky or earth yet, just the mother and father. They had seventy children.'

'Jeez, that's a lot of kids!' I joke. Her hoarse laughter ripples the air around us. It never made sense to me, this story. But I suppose myths don't have to make sense – gods that became the world, why not? It's about as likely as one very strict God who created everything in six days and then had a nap.

'You don't know the half of it, boy – all those kids, squashed tightly between their parents! You'd bet they wanted nothing more than light and a bit of space.'

'That's right. So they got together to sort that shit out.'

'Watch your mouth,' she snaps, but she's smiling.

'I can tell you the rest of the story.' I'm showing off now. I put on my storyteller voice: *'The kids had a hui to get down to business.* I see Nan's eyes twinkle in the dark as she smiles. *'Tūmatauenga was aggro as – he wanted to kill his parents but his brother Tāne Mahuta said, "Hold your horses! Let's just push them apart and get some more room down here!"'*

Nan and I both crack up. 'Nah, but seriously,' I say, finally. She's still laughing at me. 'Seriously …' I get back to the story.

'Everyone took Tāne's side except Tāwhirimātea who didn't want anything to change. The kids all took turns to show what they were made of. Tūmatauenga, Tangaroa, and the others all failed to get their parents to move. Then Tāne – the ultimate – placed his shoulders against his mother and his feet against his father and strained and heaved until they finally began to separate. Then, for the first time, the children saw the light of day.'

'Te Ao Mārama,' Nan says and gets up. 'I'll make us a feed.'

'I'm not finished,' I call to Nan, already in the kitchen getting out pots and pans.

'Carry on then, boy.'

I carry on speaking as Nan gets the bacon out of the fridge and cracks eggs into a frying pan. I look out at the ocean and raise my voice. The story stops being casual and takes on a life of its own.

'The sky and the earth had been created. The children looked out across the rolling plains of Papatūānuku, the earth mother; they looked up at the wide open space and saw Ranginui, now the sky father. They felt the rumble of their unborn brother, Rūaumoko. He became the god of earthquakes as he turns inside her womb. Tāne Mahuta became the god of all creatures and plants upon the land; his brother Tangaroa became the guardian of the sea and sea creatures. Fierce Tūmatauenga became the god of war. Tāwhirimātea took to the sky, angry at what his brother had done. He became the god of winds and storms. To this day he continues to punish his brothers with violent gusts and cyclones.'

A sudden gust of wind hits me as I finish speaking I feel a surge of power, then it's gone.

'Tēnā koe, e tama,' Nan calls out from behind me, honouring me. I've been trying for so long, but now I'm finally connecting with my heritage.

I used to wake up in the night when I was a toddler and climb into Mum and Dad's bed. Dad didn't want me there because I'd inevitably stretch out horizontally between them, pushing and kicking them apart the way that Tāne separated his parents.

It wasn't until I read the legend at primary school that I made this connection and that was when the guilt hit me. Did Tāne ever regret what he did? Maybe on some level I was responsible, in some small way, for the divorce. Pushing them apart as a metaphor, straining their relationship, making them argue over me, making them lose sleep, making them grumpy. I know it wasn't my fault, but I still feel that guilt, because maybe there was something I could have done to stop my family from falling apart.

Malcolm

The students look down at me. The shape of the lecture theatre amplifies my voice, but I'm not sure if they're really listening. Some of them are, or at least they put on a good show of paying attention. Some are almost bursting with questions and contributions, waiting for a pause in my monologue where their words can fit. But most have that typical first year glazed-over-waiting-for-the-class-to-end look. A few are eating or chewing gum, and one or two are texting or listening to MP3 players. It's their choice if they want to miss the whole lecture; they're paying to be here. I don't mind as long as they don't disturb other people.

Today I'm giving them more thought experiments, ridiculously crafted situations in which morality is not black and white: the fat tour guide stuck in the cave, trapping a group of people who will drown as the tide comes up and happen to have a stick of dynamite.

'Kill him,' Kim, an alternative-looking girl with dark hair and sharp features in the second row, says. 'If it will save the rest.'

'That is a typical utilitarian response,' I say, trying to drill the word into their minds for the upcoming test. 'The greatest good for the greatest number.'

'It's his fault,' a tanned boy in a singlet declares. 'If he worked out more he'd never have got stuck. What is he doing – being a tour guide – anyway?'

'So, because it's his fault he deserves to die?' I raise my eyebrows. 'Okay, say it's not his fault, say it's a genetic condition. Say the group of people specifically asked him to be their tour guide, does that make it their fault? Of course there is no right or wrong answer here. Morality is never that simple.'

'He's probably going to die of heart disease anyway. His life is expendable,' a guy with spiked hair and a black band T-shirt adds.

'He's actually very healthy, despite his size. But that is an interesting point. Did you know that when they give organ donations to people who need them, they decide based on how long the person is expected to survive afterwards, not just how long they've been waiting in the queue? So if you and I both need a new kidney, and I've been waiting ten years and you've been waiting five, but you have a life expectancy of two years after the operation and I only have a life expectancy of one, then you'll get the kidney if it's a match.'

Kim furrows her brow. 'Is that fair? If you'd gotten the kidney sooner you might have had a longer life expectancy.'

'That's true, but in a system with limited availability they have to make a judgement somehow. Fair? I'm not sure – that depends on your perspective. Back to the fat man: what would you do if you were in his place? You are the fat man. Do you say, "Blow me up, please, save yourselves"?'

'I'd probably not want to die,' Kim admits and looks down.

On the next slide is an example of a man who robs a petrol station and accidentally shoots and kills a cop. He gets away but the next day is paralysed in a car accident.

'He deserves it,' the spike-haired boy says. 'He killed a guy.'

'Okay, so he deserves it … Does that mean he's already been punished and the court should let him off the charges?'

'No.'

'Why not?'

'He deserves worse,' he says. 'He should be executed.'

'For manslaughter?' I've taught this class for three years and I still find myself shocked by the opinions of my students.

'Well, maybe he shouldn't be put to death, but the law is supposed to treat everyone equally, regardless of what's happened to them through other incidents,' says a blonde girl in the third row. *Law student.* I make a mental note.

'Alright. And is the law the same as morality?'

'Yes,' she says. 'Isn't that the point of law – to enforce what's right?'

'Well, I'm no expert on logic, but I do recall a logical fallacy – a flawed argument called "conflating morality with legality". Law is defined in print, created by the government, enforced by the court and the police. It's designed to maintain social order. Morality differs from person to person. It depends on your background and your experiences. Some people believe morality is absolute, that there are some things that are always wrong, like killing, lying or stealing. Who here agrees?' Half a dozen people raise their hands.

'Who thinks morality is subjective – that it depends on people's perspectives?' About the same number of hands go up, this time cautiously. I poll the class again and add a third option. 'Who doesn't know?' This time it's divided into roughly thirds with a few more voting for absolute morality and a few still not bothering to raise their hands.

'Immanuel Kant believed in absolute morality. He spent years of his life arguing for it, but every time he wrote something convincing some other thinker would challenge it. He said it's always wrong to lie. Who here believes that?'

About twenty hands go up.

'But what if Jews were hiding in your basement during World War II and Nazis came to the door asking if they were there? Is lying to save someone's life moral? Most people would agree that it is.'

'So back to the example on the slide,' Kim pulls the conversation back on topic. 'If there was more to his story – if he was robbing the store to feed his family or if he was mentally deranged,' (I love the language) 'or something, maybe he was abused as a child – does that mean he shouldn't be punished?'

'That's a good question.' It is. 'The law sometimes takes those factors into account. Insanity can – very occasionally – mean that people are not convicted of murder. Most of the time it doesn't work. It's seen as an easy way out. The person is treated as a patient rather than a prisoner. Sometimes a judge or jury will feel sorry for someone who's had a hard life, but not usually sorry enough to let them off. The whole legal process is based on a concept called 'free will' which means it's your choice and your responsibility, regardless of circumstances.' I see some glazed eyes.

'Okay, here's another question: is it worse to commit an armed robbery and steal a hundred dollars or embezzle a million dollars through white-collar crime?'

'Armed robbery might kill someone,' Kim points out.

'Well, it could. It's an interesting issue – in the USA a few years back some states introduced laws that guaranteed long prison sentences for armed robbery, even if the weapon isn't real – say a toy gun. Who do you think this would affect the most?'

'Black people,' Leon, a Samoan boy who always sits at the back, calls out. Some of the students look around uncomfortably.

'Well, I hate to say it, but it's true. This kind of law targets poor people, many of whom are from ethnic minorities, especially in the US. Who's likely to risk their lives in prison for a couple hundred bucks? So an executive could steal a million dollars from his employees and get a six-month suspended sentence, a fine and a black mark next to his name – it's usually a man – or some desperate guy goes to jail for ten years over a handful of money. Is this fair?' No one answers this time.

'Morality is never a simple thing, especially when you look at the big picture.' And my lecture finishes in perfect time; the classroom clock is at exactly 4pm. The students who have been watching it are already out the door before I've closed my PowerPoint. The students who were nodding off have regained consciousness. There are always a few who are bursting with questions about the next essay or want to debate with me – typically philosophy majors.

By the time I get out of the doors I'm tired. I'm ready to go home, but when I think of home all I think about is Elena and her blog. Elena and her ceaseless obsession with food and health, Elena always having to be right about everything. There's no room for me in that little house. When I'm at work my mind is free to challenge and question, at home I might as well be wearing a panda suit; I might as well be an inflatable man.

Don't get me wrong. I love Elena, she's gorgeous and intelligent and a really good cook. She's the clichéd best-thing-that's-ever-happened-to-me. Ask me about her any other day this week and I would have smiled, but today I'm just not in the mood.

I head back up the three flights of stairs to my office, avoiding the gaze of anyone I pass in case they want to chat. I'm not in the mood for small talk either. I felt great in the lecture, I realise. It was probably because I was the centre of attention for a change. Now I'm staring at a computer screen, just like everybody else. Sometimes it seems like the world we human beings have created is too comfortable. Nothing is real. We socialise through Facebook, rather than have real conversations. Elena would rather blog about her life – a fantasy life – than live her real one.

Elena

You may have noticed by now that I have a different idea of what's healthy compared to most people. It's true I eat liberal amounts of unrefined sea salt and animal fat. I love butter and cream. I avoid 'low-fat' food at all cost. I actually avoid anything with a long ingredients list. I'd rather make my own food.

I didn't know much about nutrition four years ago, when I first moved in with Henry and Tanya, but they seemed to. They were always going on about protein and zinc and things I'd never even heard of like amino acids and lipids. Our typical 1960s style flat had that outdated yellow/brown floral carpet and those tiny high kitchen cupboards, painted mint green, the kind used for storing jars of preserves when people still made them. Everyone was always in the kitchen, talking over the breakfast bar, cutting up vegetables and cooking strange-smelling things.

At first I thought I wouldn't fit in with my eccentric flatmates. Henry is bisexual, the type of person who seems to have a slightly sexual relationship with everything in the room. I'd never call him sleazy. It's not that. It's more an undercurrent running through him. He's electrically charged. I think it scares some people. Tanya is goth-looking and has the kind of presence that fills an entire room, but under her don't-fuck-with-me façade she's really a sweetheart.

It was just the three of us, most of the time. We'd go to the farmers' market on Sunday, as a flat. It was always like an adventure. We never knew when we would see the first strawberries or rare fruits like cherimoya, or when the smoked salmon people would be there. Even supermarket shopping was fun. Henry would scoot down the aisles dropping strange sauces and preserves into the trolley, while Tanya and I would read the labels of everything and then put anything with strange sounding additives or numbers back on the shelf. We managed to save a lot of money. We skirted the perimeter of the store, buying mostly fresh things, yoghurt, fish, butter, free-range eggs when we couldn't get them at the farmers' market. Only a few inner aisles held anything remotely healthy. Canned tomatoes, rice, cold-pressed olive oil, dark chocolate with 80% cocoa solids. Sometimes we read the labels on the margarine and laughed at the preposterousness of anyone mistaking it for real food. We got our red meat from Henry's uncle, with his organic dairy farm. We only ate free-range chicken.

It was bliss to live with people who cared about the same things that I care about. Malcolm understands the philosophy, on an intellectual level he gets it, but he doesn't really care. For someone who teaches ethics he is surprisingly lacking in them.

'It's all just different discourses, Elena.' We are in the kitchen doing the dishes. He's drying.

'Don't you pull that postmodern shit with me,' I smile. It's not a real argument, just a surface level tease of something that's actually a problem under the surface – like the iceberg that sunk the *Titanic*.

'I know they're all discourses – but mine is better.' He tries to whip me with the tea towel and fails.

'Well yours is getting popular with the privileged and middle class … just like most food ethics discourses.' He's really pushing my buttons, but I refuse to show it.

'And you're on the soapbox for the underdog today?' I jab him in the ribs.

'Hey, everyone wants to be right.' He wraps his arms around me and I relax, letting my soapy, wet hands soak into his white shirtsleeves, exposing the tone of his forearms beneath. Everything's fine, I assure myself and our baby. This is not my parents' relationship. I am not my mother.

Mostly, everything is fine. Mostly, we get along really well. But perhaps this difference between us – that I care and that he doesn't – is so deep that it will never be resolved.

'I care about you,' he assures me when I challenge him on his apathy.

I believe him. But I suppose I want to. What else do I have?

Evie

If slaughterhouses had glass walls, everyone would be a vegetarian.
PAUL MCCARTNEY

Traditional societies did a lot of unethical things. I don't see Elena advocating genital mutilation or infanticide. But I guess she is selective about her truths, like everyone else.

I actually met Elena before I knew Michael. It was a cold, stormy night when I knocked on her door and asked her to join Greenpeace. It was my job at the time. The light on her doorstep was dim and for a minute I thought she was about twelve years old.

'Are your parents home?' I asked. Big mistake.

'They don't live here,' she laughed at me.

'But you're over eighteen?' I had to be sure, for even as my eyes adjusted her soft features still looked young.

She skirted the issues for a while, said she didn't agree with everything we stood for. She said she believed in sustainability, organic farming and positive initiatives but she thought activism was a waste of energy. Of course it irritated me.

'Don't you care that there are people out there murdering whales, people who are quite content to keep killing until there are none left?'

'It's terrible,' she admitted, 'but putting my energy into stopping them isn't going to help.'

I liked her, even though she was naïve and stubborn and a

little self-righteous. She even invited me in, unusual for someone who doesn't actually want to sign up. We kept talking for over an hour, and I kept thinking that maybe she would change her mind, that I was inches away from winning her over.

'What difference does it make if I give you five dollars a month?' she asked.

'Five dollars and your support is the same as one hundred signatures in the current system. We take your money and your support to Parliament; it's the same as what the industries do in the United States.'

'I don't like that system,' she said. 'You can't use the master's tools to disassemble the master's house. You can't dissolve the system by becoming part of it.'

She was one of the few people I met while door knocking who offered me a cup of tea. Most people think Greenpeace are crazy violent activists or pot-smoking hippies. Elena said she didn't care about that. Personally, I think Greenpeace is too PC. That's one reason I don't work for them anymore: they get too caught up in bureaucracy, they don't have enough action, they worry about bad publicity.

'Do you have any green tea?' I asked in the light of her retro yellow-brown kitchen, complete with pale green cupboards. She wrinkled her nose a little, in that cute way she has of expressing distastefulness, and suggested liquorice instead.

At first I trod carefully, introducing issues slowly, but the more we talked the more I was surprised at how much she knew. Our conversation ranged from sustainable power generating technologies to critiques of the monetary system, and she agreed with me, right up until the point where it came to money.

'It's not about the money,' she insisted. 'Not really. I used to be a member of Greenpeace but every time I got their letters and emails it all seemed to draining and depressing.' I could almost hear the underlying thoughts in the tone of her voice: *as much as I believe in justice, I can't fight all the world's battles.*

'All you have to do is show your support … We have victories,' I assured her. 'We stopped Panasonic from using lead and mercury in their products, we got KFC to insist their supplier, Tegel, uses non-GE corn to feed their chickens.'

'Those are great,' she said, her eyes so soft, almost pleading. 'But so much energy is wasted on resistance. You may win some battles, but it's a bit like having an argument with your partner. Even if you come out on top, no one really wins. So much energy has been put into resistance when it could have been put into a positive initiative instead.'

'What kind of positive initiatives are you talking about?' Did she seriously think about these things?

'Well, instead of putting all that energy into stopping GE you could support farmers to go organic. You'd set up funds and produce material that would help people to do the things you want them to do, rather than trying to stop people from doing things they have already made up their minds to do. Encourage people to grow their own food and create so much free abundance that the monetary system is unnecessary and collapses.'

I liked the way her eyes lit up when she hinted at the kind of world she wanted to live in. A true idealist, one who isn't weighed down by the world's problems, is a rare thing. This must have been the way she protected herself.

'But GE is a *real* problem,' I said, frustrated. 'The pollen from genetically engineered corn with scorpion DNA can drift to other farms and infect them.'

'I just think it's a waste of energy to worry about the things you don't like. If someone has a set way of thinking and you challenge them, they're just going to resist you more and more. If your organisation only supported productive campaigns I'd be happy to give you money. I'm just not comfortable with wasting my energy on resistance. It only keeps the problems there.'

That's what it came down to.

'I only want to support things that I *do* want, not waste energy on things that I don't want. I would support an organisation that just did positive things.'

'You won't find one,' I said, although I knew that Greenpeace wasn't the be-all and end-all of political activism. I was angry that even though she could see these causes were worth fighting for, she wouldn't fight. At the time I thought it made her weak, but since then I've often wondered whether she was right, usually in my darker moments when I'm just about to give up, on activism and even sometimes on life itself.

This is something Michael's family doesn't know about me: I'm usually attracted to women, at least I have been for most of my adult life. Most of my relationships have been with women, probably because most men disgust me.

When me and Michael started going out it surprised me. I suppose gender is just one factor that most people happen to pay a lot of attention to, not the only defining feature of a person. I can't help who I'm attracted to and I admit I was drawn to Elena that night when I first met her, with her soft voice and dark eyes, intrigued by someone so far from me who I didn't immediately hate. She wasn't like most people; she had values and ethics that could have been related to mine and she wasn't exactly apathetic. She deliberately cared about the things that she thought were the best use of her energy. She was infuriating because she made me question things I never question: the things that mean the most to me. That's what makes me edgy around her.

Valerie

Tonight it's Elena's turn to choose the DVD. It's Sunday and we've just finished dinner with minimal arguments.

It's Michael Moore's *Sicko*. I was worried at first because a political documentary could cause even more family conflict – more so than one of John's zone-out Hollywood action flicks, anyway. But Elena won't stay to watch something she considers to be 'filth', so this time I let her choose.

'Blackmailed by my own daughter!' I joke.

The surprising thing is that I really enjoy it. We all do. Well except Rosa who gets bored after five minutes and demands Elena put her to bed.

America's health system is a shambles compared to ours.

'It actually makes New Zealand look good!' Elena is incredulous.

Malcolm just sits there nodding like one of those plastic dogs you see in the back of cars. As if he already knows it all.

Evie seems to be enjoying it too. She's always ready for a good critique of a corrupt system. Even Michael's enthralled. For once I feel as if we're a real family.

John swears every time he sees something he can tell is obviously wrong, but just to be controversial he becomes the devil's advocate.

'So what do I care if those people die? People suck.'

Evie smiles at him and he hides his blush by turning away, not used to his adverse opinions being welcomed. We pass around a bowl of salted popcorn Evie made. Elena doesn't complain that it's not buttered.

I'm appalled at how bad it is. I feel sorry for the older couple who have to move into their daughter's spare bedroom because, despite having health insurance, their health problems meant they had to sell their house, and the 79-year-old cleaner who can't retire because he and his wife need medication.

'If there are golden years, I can't find them,' he says.

I'm disgusted at the exploitation. I even feel sorry for the employees of insurance companies who are paid to ruin people's lives.

Health isn't a business. It shouldn't be. It's a necessity. It's a right. It shouldn't be about profit.

My heart went out to the young woman and her son who lost a husband and father because the insurance company wouldn't fund an 'experimental' bone marrow transplant that would have saved his life. They just leave people to die.

The real losers are the poor who have no power.

I'm a little bit jealous of the UK's public health system. I know it's not perfect but it seems to be better for the people. New Zealand doctors have always resisted being on state salaries. We can make more by running private practices subsidised by the government. In my practice clients usually pay $60 per visit and the state tops the rest up. It's what they call a General Medical Subsidy.

We all laughed when Michael Moore asked the British pharmacist where all the bread and detergent and candy was.

The film ends and Elena looks conflicted.

'I'm not sure what's worse,' she says in a quiet voice. 'Providing healthcare that is terribly flawed to everyone or making it unattainable.'

I can't answer that without getting into an argument. She probably wants to send all the patients off to a chiropractor or a homeopath but some of these cases are severe. They need surgery.

As if in answer to my thoughts she adds, 'I suppose there are some things mainstream Western medicine is good for: blood transfusions, bone marrow transplants, that sort of thing.' She looks me in the eye and for a moment I think she might be giving me some credit for a change.

'But for everything else …'

Rosa

I work into the school. Its old. I go into the elavayta and press up. The doors close and it shaiks. I go to the top flor and then I put the secaret coad on the key pad. And the elevata chainges from silva to being maid of wood and it keeps going up past the top flor to the secaret ofis. The doors open and maik a buzzing sound and then misst comes in and its purpil

Mrs Mills looks at my story and tells me to look up the words I don't know how to spell in the dictionary. I take the dictionary off the bookshelf and take it back to my desk. I don't know which words I can't spell so I look words up that are funny instead, like 'bitch' and 'penis'. Then I get bored. I look up Mum's job.

doctor

• *noun*: person who is qualified to practise medicine. 2. (Doctor) person who has the highest university degree.
• *verb*: to change in order to deceive; falsify. 2. to adulterate (a food or drink) with a harmful or potent ingredient.

Does that mean Mum is all of those things? I don't know what some of the words mean so I look up 'adultery'.

adultery

• *noun*: voluntary sexual intercourse between a married person and a person who is not their spouse.

Mum says sex is only for adults and I don't need to know anything about it 'til I'm a grown-up but it's how people make babies and if anyone tries to do sex with me or shows me their penis or touches me under my clothes it's wrong and I have to run away and tell her and they can go to jail because I'm a kid. Sex is the same as fucking and I'm not allowed to say that and John said that's what Dad did and that's why he doesn't live with us anymore. I asked Mum why he wanted to make more babies because he already has four kids. Mum said that he doesn't want babies, he was just having fun. Mum says that he just wanted to live in a different house and so he moved to up north so he could have more room for his motorbikes. Elena says that Mum and Dad should have broken up a long time ago because they were unhappy.

Michael says Dad is a coward because he always runs away, but Michael is always away at the moment, and acting weird like he doesn't care anymore. Elena doesn't talk about Dad. John says that Dad is a fucking retard who can't keep his dick in his pants and that it was just an excuse for him to leave us and he doesn't blame him because Mum is ugly and a bitch. I don't think Mum is ugly. I like her hair when she goes to the hairdresser and gets the different colours like yellow and white and gold in it. Mum is nice when she's not mad and she smells like roses and she tucks me in every night. Dad was nice sometimes, but he smelled bad and he slept on the couch and watched sport all the time and wouldn't let me watch cartoons.

When I stay with Dad in the holidays we get fish 'n' chips and he takes me on his four wheeler on the beach and we go fishing, but it's boring and smells bad, and he tells me I can come and live with him. But I miss Mum so I go home after a few days.

Michael

Up close, the skin flake is covered in ridges, a pattern like tree bark that I don't normally notice on my chest. I'm holding this thin, transparent membrane, made up of millions or maybe billions of my former skin cells. For a second I wonder if the short lifespan of a skin cell would seem just as long as my life, with no bigger stretch of time for comparison. If that cell was conscious would it feel just as satisfied in its existence as I am now after a good surf, carrying with me the feeling that if I were to die right now I would just let death take me? I release my thumb and forefinger, letting the skin flake fly in the breeze. Those cells have jumped ship after an assault by the sun, surrendering themselves to the skin underneath the way I was surrendering to the waves when I got burnt a couple of days ago. I like that word 'surrender'. It's like in that moment when you're up on the board and the wave is propelling you have this limited control with your feet and your arms directing you where to go. You can stay in your mind, calculate every lean, every curve of the board – or you can let go and let your body take over, blending like alchemy with the wave, with the ocean. That's where the real rush is.

I should have been wearing my wetsuit but I couldn't find it. Must have left it at Mum's, and the surf was calling me. My arms were already brown from wearing singlets but my chest was as white as fuckin' virgin snow after a winter in the dark – some fuckin' Māori! I'm looking pretty half-caste about now, and the sunburn is red like my redneck heritage on Dad's side. I wish I could peel it all away. I never say this shit to most people. They don't know half of what goes on inside my head.

The boat rocks and I realise my mind has been drifting with it. It was Dad's idea, this fishing trip; quality time with the boys, maybe, or just another excuse to go fishing. Although he's never needed one of those, according to Mum. She takes everything too personally; anything Dad did was about her. If he wanted to go fishing, it was as if the fishing was more important than her. None of us have caught anything yet. John looks bored.

'I bet I can catch a bigger snapper than either of you,' Dad says. 'I've got the skills and the experience.' He slaps his thigh.

'I reckon I need a spear gun.' John's voice is deeper than it should be. It's always an act with him, trying to be tough. 'Fishing rods are for pussies.'

Dad grabs John around the neck and pretends to wrestle him. The boat rocks from side to side and Dad stills himself.

'Wanna bet?' Dad's always been a gambler.

'Whatever,' John replies, straightening his T-shirt.

'I bet I'll catch the first fish.' Dad never gives up.

'Bet's on!' John's smiling like he's been waiting for the opportunity. 'If you lose you're buying me a speargun for Christmas.'

I look out at the horizon, scanning the hills on the other side of the harbour inlet. Māui, the demi-god, fished up this island, or so the legend goes. He snuck into a fishing trip he wasn't invited to. His brothers were pretty pissed, probably more so when he hauled up the world's biggest catch using his grandma's sacred jawbone as a hook and his own blood for bait. It's no wonder his bros started carving up the country leaving these gaping wounds, jagged mountains, hills, ravines, while Māui was trying to make peace with the gods for the ruckus he'd caused. Pretty ridiculous I suppose, but wait a thousand years and see what people think of our modern mythology? Will $E=mc^2$ squared be a joke? Will what we now call physics seem mystical and archaic? Who the fuck knows? It amazes me that Māori myths with their larger-than-life characters, sentient mountains and sacred jawbones were plausible explanations, but people mostly believe what they're told, don't they? None of us can see molecules or atoms or germs with our naked eye, but we're heard about them – they seem to explain things – so it must be true.

'Oh yes!' John grunts, pulling up a medium-sized snapper; our first catch of the day.

'It's just a little sprat.' Dad downplays it.

Māori tradition would have us throw the fish back: give away your first, your best, your only. If I had caught it, I would have returned it to Tangaroa. John smashes it in the head with the butt of his fishing knife. I'm glad Evie isn't here. A conversation I had with her a few weeks ago drifts through my mind.

'We're at the top of the food chain,' I said.

'We're not at the fucking top of the food chain. We have no right to be. Our ancestors worked hard to get to the top of the food chain – we're just the lazy descendants living off the trust fund.'

I crack up and Dad gives me a funny look. He must have

thought it was aimed at his butt crack – exposed as he bends over to bait a hook.

Evie seemed to leave in a hurry this time and for some reason I wanted her to stay. It's almost summer which is festival season and I don't expect either of us to stick around, I was surprised at my own reaction but held it back, smiled and waved. See ya.

Evie

What else is it that should trace the insuperable line? … the question is not, Can they reason? nor, Can they talk? but, Can they suffer?
JEREMY BENTHAM

This time I didn't leave for the reasons I said. I packed my bags this morning, told Michael I was going down south for a festival. Nothing unusual. Most of my friends are camping out in parks around the country, joining in the Occupy movement, protesting against the corrupt power systems that exploit the world. I would join them but I can't.

Yesterday I got a letter. My mail gets delivered to Tara's. It has been like that for years. So when I popped in to have a cup of tea and a chat yesterday I wasn't surprised to find an envelope waiting for me. I just wasn't prepared for the contents.

Valerie is my doctor. I go to her because I like her and I trust her more than any stranger, and because she doesn't charge me. Before I met her I hadn't been to a doctor in years. I felt uncomfortable. I need to go more than most people because I need B12 injections sometimes. It's hard to get enough without murdering animals. If I don't get them I start to feel dizzy and weird, then I get tingles in my arms and legs and they start to lose feeling. I know that if I don't listen to the warning signs I could end up in temporary paralysis. That's why I'm so relieved to have a doctor I can trust. I just hope she can keep my secrets.

The letter says: *Abnormal CIN 3.*

Last time I saw Valerie I let her take a smear. It is pretty weird having your boyfriend's mother down there, but she is very professional. I'm glad that it was over quickly. But now I know it's not over, not really.

The letter tells me I need to go into the hospital for a colposcopy. It sounds awful. Tara's been through this before and I'm grateful for her support. I'm going to sleep on her couch for a while and sort myself out. Tara isn't into Occupy because her ex is a real creep and is involved with organising it here, and she can't stand the sight of him. I'm grateful that she's around to be supportive and also give me space when I need it.

'It's not something you need to stress about,' Tara says, but that doesn't stop the build-up of tension in my body. I know there is something seriously wrong. She's sitting on the porch next to me. We're wrapped up in a king-size duvet; protection against the cold night. She's smoking my cigarettes but I owe her more than that.

'You should probably stop smoking these,' she says. A hypocrite. Tara has natural looking dreads. She wears raggy clothes like me. We often fire-dance together.

'I did, when I got my abnormal smear,' she adds. I look down at the burning roll of tobacco between my fingers, wondering if its light could spell out a word in the dark like sparklers on Guy Fawkes. I would spell out some kind of silent prayer: *hope* and *help* and *why?*

'I ate lots of vegetables and no bread or anything for about a month, and my results went back to normal.'

She has told me that thirty per cent of cases spontaneously

regress. I wonder how 'spontaneous' it really is.

All I know is that the cells of my cervix have something against me. They're mutating out of control and if I don't do something about it I could get *cancer*. I'm only twenty-three and I already have to think about this sort of shit. I can't believe it. It's mind-blowing.

Valerie must know but she can't contact me professionally, except by letter. She can't tell Michael either. It would breach patient confidentiality.

I get a letter three days after the first; it tells me my colposcopy is booked for two weeks' time. I'll need to go to the woman's outpatient clinic in the Elizabeth Rothwell building. Even though I've been expecting this, it makes me shiver.

Malcolm

I'm supposed to be writing a lecture but my mind drifts into vague fantasies. The secretary fantasy is one I've had since I was a child. I still do. Sometimes, when I'm working, I fantasise about Elena coming into my office in a short skirt and bending herself over the desk. Sometimes, when it's quiet I lock my door and jerk off over it. In my fantasy she's not pregnant, of course. And that's not the real fantasy, just a role play. The real fantasy is about power. The boss has the power, the secretary wants it and she seduces him. In that act she has power. I'm not sure why it turns me on, in particular.

My somewhat inappropriate thoughts are interrupted by a knock on my office door before it's pushed open. Kim pokes her head in.

'Busy?' she asks. Very casual.

'I was,' I reply automatically. I tug at my shirt collar but I doubt she notices. She's not her normal hard-line self. Her eyes are puffy, mascara smudged, cheeks red. She's holding some crumpled paper. I guess I shouldn't have given her a C.

'I worked so hard on this,' she says, collapsing in the chair opposite mine. 'It's my worst mark ever – EVER!'

I take the essay and reread it. Ambiguous use of terms – or maybe just misunderstanding the question.

'Kim. It was a simple assignment. You made it too complicated.'

'A utilitarian is a person too,' she argues. 'It's not just a construct that academics can wank over.'

I look at the ground.

'The whole point is a utilitarian would work in the weapons factory, because if he didn't get the job, someone else would and there would be no net loss; there would be no more destruction whether it was him or not,' I explain.

'Can't he have a conscience?'

'Well, his conscience would say it wasn't a problem.'

'Well, then, what about my argument that he'd take the job and use it to throw a spanner in the works? If making weapons that contribute to warfare is, overall, a bad thing – not the greatest good for the greatest number,' Kim insists.

'That's not the thought experiment.'

'I hate thought experiments!' Her passion reminds me of Elena and for a moment I'm entranced.

'Look, I appreciate that you tried a different approach,' I coax. 'The point of the assignment was for you to demonstrate that you understand utilitarianism, and I know you do – you just want it to be more flexible.' She almost smiles. 'The main flaw with utilitarianism, in my opinion, is that it isn't flexible enough. These situations can occur, in lame-ass thought experiments or in real life,' she actually smiles that time, 'and the right thing to do by utilitarian standards is not – really – the right thing.'

'Will you change my mark?' she asks.

'You deserve better,' I say. 'I can make it a B because the second half shows an understanding of utilitarianism, or have it re-marked by someone else. What would you prefer?'

'I suppose a B is acceptable.' She lowers her head and my attention is caught by the slope of her neck.

'It's a first year ethics paper, Kim, you're well beyond this – just try not to think too hard.'

It might seem dodgy as hell, but the way I treated Kim is the way I would treat any student – you're reading between the lines, I know. You can tell that I'm sexually frustrated, you're just waiting for me to slip up. Overtly, I would have acted in generally the same way if it had been Bruce, the six-foot, overweight mature student who sits in the front row. Honestly. I wouldn't have perved at his neck, of course, there's not much to see on that front, but don't get the wrong idea. Nothing's going to happen.

I go back to my lecture feeling more alive and it dawns on me: I've just had my best conversation all week with an undergrad about her bad mark. Elena has barely spoken to me in the last few days and when she does it's all about health and food and the baby. The realisation punctures my mood and I'm back to contemplating the secretary fantasy again.

Elena

I wind my finger around the purple thread and hook it back in with the needle. The clicking is supposed to be rhythmic but I'm not really good at knitting. Nan taught me when I was about five, but I forgot. My interest rekindled with pregnancy – something that is so clichéd that it almost goes the other way and becomes unlikely. I'm not sure what I'm making – it's supposed to be a blanket, but it's more like an uneven scarf. It's the thought that counts, I suppose, but it's the process I'm enjoying. It feels productive, somehow. In a life like mine, which has become so insular, I enjoy the tedium, not needing to think too much, the way it makes my mind go blank.

I've decided to let it go – everything Mum thinks about me, about the way I *should* be doing things. She can't help the way she is and it's not doing me any good getting pissed off at everything she says. I'm feeling very zen right now. I wonder if that's the pregnancy hormones too? Maybe they alternate between making me volatile and blissfully calm. I'd rather skip the volatility. I screamed at Malcolm last night because he was up on Facebook really late and I couldn't get to sleep, knowing he'd eventually come into the bedroom and wake me up again anyway. He's yet to fully comprehend that what is in my best interests is in *both* of our best interests and I told him as much. He laughed of course, although there was a serious undertow. If he continues to be a slow learner it will be at his own peril.

I laugh at myself as I drop yet another stitch. There are so many silly things that we get upset about, so many things that are inconsequential in the long run. If the point of life is happiness – which I'm not quite convinced of, despite it being repeated ad-nauseam – then why is it always a future conception of happiness that we're chasing? Seeking out the things that we're told will make us happy: a career, a relationship, marriage, a house, children, a holiday home, retirement … Where is the chance to be happy? Where is the time for happiness? Happiness is only ever in the here and now – with every swish of wool, with every click, every row. I'm feeling quite enlightened. Perhaps we will solve the mysteries of the universe, this baby and I, as we cohabit this body, this space, this time.

I remember an idea I had for a blog post and discard my knitting on the window seat.

The expectant mother pack

I was rummaging under my bed this morning and I found what was left of the 'expectant mother pack'. When I visited my doctor to confirm my pregnancy he handed me this folder filled with rubbish. There was propaganda from baby formula companies about what to feed babies, (as if such a vested interest is even capable of giving good, balanced advice), vouchers for various brands of disposable nappies, and a booklet about the stages my baby was going through each week – I gave up reading that when it was the size of a bean. There are a number of pamphlets: ableist information about how ultrasounds are safe because they've been routine for fifty years, Down syndrome awareness, (as if I don't already have enough to worry about in my life need to medicalise my baby further with invasive testing on the off-chance that I'd abort an 'imperfect' child), brochures from midwives and samples of baby wipes and special anti-stretch mark oils.

I was initially intrigued by these, but after reading the ingredients I was certain I would not buy them. I don't put petrochemicals on my skin – no Vaseline or 'mineral oil' for me. I thought companies who produced products for pregnant woman would realise that by-products of gasoline production are bound to be bad news. They're very bad for the skin and are toxic. They cause allergy reactions, skin irritation and smother the skin keeping it from functioning properly.

I'm a curious sort of person so I rip the small plastic packet open and squeezed some of the oil onto my hand. I figure if people use this sort of thing every day a small amount won't hurt me. I spread the greasy substance around. It feels weird to me, so unlike the vegetable oils I'm used to: almond, wheat germ, rose-hip, all nourishing my skin.

After about thirty seconds my hands start to tingle. Even after using soap and warm water to wash them they still feel peculiar. My skin is too soft, too sensitive, vulnerable. Obviously I threw the rest of the packet and the pamphlet away. I'm not sure if there are clinical trials to prove it but I will hedge my bets with plant based oils and the properties that I trust to help my skin stretch more easily over this baby as it grows. I'm making my own balm:

Luscious lavender skin balm

1 Tbsp beeswax

1 tsp cocoa butter

4 Tbsp almond oil

2 Tbsp wheat germ oil

1 Tbsp jojoba oil

10 drops lavender essential oil

Melt beeswax on a low heat in a small pot. Remove from heat. Add in almond and wheat germ oils slowly while stirring. Add lavender oil last. Pour into jars and allow to set.

You can swap these oils for others like apricot kernel, olive or avocado, depending on what you like or what you have at home. Use less oil if you want a firmer balm and more if you want a softer one. You can also use different essential oils for fragrance.

Aromatherapists advise against using essential oils while pregnant, but I'm not convinced. What do you guys think?

Have any of you used the kinds of 'pregnancy' products I mentioned earlier? What are your experiences? Do you have any recommendations for natural skincare during pregnancy?

Comments:

Sharonq:
Hi Elena, I enjoy reading your blog and hearing about your pregnancy. I've just found out that I'm three months pregnant and I'm so excited! After years of trying the conventional way, going through doctors and trying to 'eat right' I discovered Nourishing Traditions and started eating wholesome traditional foods (lots of butter fat!). I'm convinced that this is what has helped me conceive. Your balm recipe looks great – I must try it!

Elena:
Hi Sharon, so glad you like my blog and congratulations!

Mary Sand:

I just checked the ingredients of the anti-stretch mark cream my mother-in-law bought me – lo and behold: petrochemicals! What are they thinking, marketing this stuff to pregnant women?

Michael

The trimester is almost over and when it is I'll hit the surf and I won't come back 'til March. It's the best thing about uni: the long breaks. Mum wants me to get a summer job but I doubt that will happen. I just want to get amongst it – to be in Gizzy for New Year's, for the awesome roots festival I went to last year. My mates are all coming and it's going to be fuckin' BOSS.

Evie is gone again. 'Down south,' she said. I'm not sure when she will be back and it bothers me sometimes. All of my past girlfriends were way too clingy and now I have one who is the opposite. I never know where she is or when she'll be back. I guess that's why I never get tired of her.

I light a joint and listen to the surf below – too choppy. I hope it will improve by this afternoon.

I'm hungry so I drive into town for a feed. I feel like a pie or fish 'n' chips, or something. Elena criticises me for eating crap food – my 'lack of good nutrition' she calls it, but it's none of her business. She gets a bit anal over food. Last Sunday she wouldn't eat the salad Mum made because it had some kind of 'processed' dressing with dodgy ingredients. You'd think Mum would know better than Elena, she's the doctor, but Elena gets all high and mighty and eats only the meat and roasted vegetables. At least she didn't storm out that time like she did the first time Evie came and Mum made a vegan salad with tofu.

I grab a couple of steak pies from the bakery – I'm too hungry to wait for fish 'n' chips, then I cruise to Dave's place. He's still asleep. After all, it is technically still morning at 11.30. I grab his laptop and check Facebook:

Nico: Hey cobba how's shit been goin? What're you gettin up to? Hope alls well Cob

I message him back: Sup Grommie, just hitting the surf and the pies – gots ta hav sum balance eh? Wot u up to this wknd?

Georgia: yo wots up u stealth mutha fuckah was wonderin if ud b keen for car pooling sometimes to uni. giz a text

Georgia is Dave's ex. Uni's almost over so I don't message her back. She's always bitching and moaning anyway.

Matty: Hey there stranger watsup seen your hari hari hari hari krishna zoom past this morn goin to uni

This message is old, but it makes me laugh anyway. I'm just about to sign out when Nico pops up online.

howzit, you were pretty off chops last night ay ha oh well at least you didn't put a hole in the wall

I've still got a bit of a bruise on my fist from the guy I punched in the face last night. He deserved it. He said something racist to my mate. I can't remember what it was, exactly. But I remember the look in his eyes, his creepy smile, as if he was superior to us. As my darker-skinned friends remind me, by calling me 'whitey', I could pass for white. But I'm not. It doesn't matter what you look like, it's who you are that's important – isn't that what everyone tells you? Well it's not true. Looks matter. In the real world they do, even if they shouldn't.

Racism in New Zealand is not in-your-face like in middle America or South Africa. It's tucked away in the corner of everyone's vision. Some don't want to see it. Some have no choice. Some wouldn't recognise it if it smacked them in the fucking face because they're too caught up in it to realise it. That's what makes a racist: ignorance and hatred. I know I have enough anger to deal with on my own, but I don't need anyone else to hate. I hate racists and the pigs. That's enough.

Mum always comments that the racists are coming out of the woodwork when she sees something on the news about 'those Māoris'. It's usually twisted so it looks like we're all out to rip everyone off. The news media are a bunch of racist fuckwits. I apologise to any media person who doesn't fit into this category. You know, they could slant it so that they show all the history; of us getting ripped off and treated like shit in the first place. But the average New Zealander apparently wants to sit in their La-Z-Boy, bitch and moan about 'those Māoris' and shake their heads when anything goes our way. Never mind that our youth are dropping out of school and landing in jail, illiterate, with no options. Never mind that we were once a proud, educated and wealthy people. All they see is the bad stuff; the brown-skinned criminals who need to be locked up to protect their white asses, the greedy tribes asking for more when they've already had their share.

Last week my mate, also called Dave, was complaining that he saw something on the news about the Māori university getting half a billion dollars. The Wo – nan – ga he called it. 'Wananga (Wah-nah-ngah),' I said, 'It's a soft 'g' like in going.'

He tries to say it a few times, 'N-gah … Nyah, yeah, whatevs, man. Anyway, why do they get that?'

'Did they say if it was standard government funding?' I asked. I didn't know anything about it. 'Did they say that only Māori could do the courses?' I was curious so I asked my mate Will – actually he's a cousin, but I knew him as a mate before I found out we were related – who works for Te Wānanga O Aotearoa (the 'university') and it turns out that my suspicions were bang on target. The money was standard funding that every official tertiary institution gets based on the number of students attending, and the Wānanga courses are open to everyone, not just the brown-skinned.

'Plus, bro, most of them are free,' Will said. 'We don't have an expensive campus to maintain so we run the courses as cheap as possible so that people can afford to do them.'

Now compare that information to what Dave heard on the news. How do they expect New Zealanders to grow out of their racism if all they hear is it echoed back to them?

No one wants to be labelled a racist, but I guess we all are in some ways. I have my own stereotypes of Asians, which I won't go into just now, and they're probably just as full of crap as the racism against Māori. Maybe it's a human condition to hate the people who don't look like us. I don't know. I heard somewhere that it's the reptilian part of the brain – that crocodile that snaps at anything different, anything that could be a threat – he's still inside our medulla oblongatas or what ever that part by the brain stem is called, causing me to punch that guy in the face for being a dick. It might be human nature, but I don't know if I believe in that anymore. I think we have a choice. We choose our nature. And I wouldn't take back that choice. If I had to make it again I'd do it just the same.

Valerie

When I can't sleep I pick up the book next to my bed. It's tiny, a pocket book with a faded green cover and no published date: George Eliot's *Scenes of Clerical Life*. She is one of my heroes. Any woman who can make it in a man's world is. She published under the name 'George' because she wanted to be taken seriously. I've sometimes wished in med school and various times in my career that I could so easily pretend to be a man and not be recognised only by my sex. As a sexual or profoundly unsexual object, as a joke, as someone to be judged rather than someone with a preordained right to be recognised as a person.

This is not the reason I read George Eliot when I can't sleep. I read her because in the 1800s the world seemed to be a much simpler place, without television, computers and cell phones. Sometimes I wish I could escape to that time and just exist.

I can't sleep tonight because I'm worried about Evie. I haven't heard from her in days, not since her results were sent. I asked Michael how she was doing and he said she's gone travelling again. He thinks everything is normal, no doubt.

I want to reassure her. Abnormal smears are common. They don't mean she is going to get cancer. Cervical cancer is slow to develop, it takes ten years usually. The good news is we caught it now and we can deal with it. We can stop the cells from spreading, from mutating into cancer. She's all alone out there and I feel terrible. My thoughts circle my head over and over.

I open the book to any page and read from the top.

'... *a handful on her pinafore; happier still, when they were spread out on the sheets to dry, so that she could sit down like a frog among them, and have them poured over her in fragrant showers ...*'

I vaguely recall she is speaking of rose petals and lavender.

'*A frequent pleasure was to take a journey with Mr Bates through the kitchen gardens to the hot houses, where the rich bunches of green and purple grapes hung from the roof, far out of reach of the tiny yellow hand that couldn't help stretching itself out towards them ...*'

And with drifting thoughts of lavender, rose, kitchen gardens and grape bunches, I let go the book and slide away into the land of sleep.

Elena

A fog descends on my brain and I know I need to eat. On the table sit the pastel iced cupcakes Theresa left this morning. She's always baking things full of sugar and crap, but right now I feel like Alice in Wonderland, staring at the magical cakes. I peel off the crinkled paper cup and devour one. It's so light that a moment after I've swallowed the last bite, it's just a pleasant vanilla memory.

I don't know why I feel guilty. I shouldn't. I need to eat. I need calories, but this food is exactly everything I can't stand. The cupcakes are probably baked with margarine (Theresa's healthier option – my version of hell!). I wish she would listen to me, but I can't help but feel grateful that something so delicious and easy exists. Empty calories. I empty my brain and proceed to devour the whole tray. I convince myself to forget that cupcakes are a gateway drug.

I feel bloated but still unsatisfied. That's what processed foods like white flour and sugar do to me. I go to the kitchen and pour my sourdough starter in its second stage into a mixing bowl. Sourdough banana bread – here I come. It's tricky to mix, the sticky globs of sourdough don't like being tamed, but I get there eventually. As soon as it's in the oven I start my blog post and by the time I'm finished writing up the recipe the smell of baking banana bread fills the whole house.

As I cut into the crusty loaf my mouth waters. I slather it in butter and eat three pieces before I remember to take a photo for my blog.

I put a single piece on a plain white plate with the loaf in the background, and focus on the melting butter so that everything else in the photo blurs. I take a few pictures until I'm satisfied, then upload them and publish the post. This one gets lots of replies very quickly, complementing me on my creative baking. If they knew what I'd eaten earlier, would they still read my blog and comment? Would they lose faith in me? I would be lying if I said the sourdough banana bread wasn't an attempt to compensate for my cupcake extravaganza. I feel like a priest who sins but cannot repent because there is no one to confess to. I'm being ridiculous I know. This is just food. I'm just starting to realise that I can't judge other people anymore – as ignorant or innocent or blatantly wrong. We all have to eat.

Henry sits at my kitchen table stuffing his face with banana bread. I called him as soon as it was baked and he arrived within ten minutes.

'Evie didn't like it when I said that veganism was an option only available to the privileged middleclass.'

Henry snorts but can't reply because his mouth is full, so I continue speaking.

'She's right that my diet is too, I don't have a problem with that. I just hate how self-righteous she is.'

'Vegetarianism is just another form of self-hatred.' I love Henry for his bizarre opinions.

'How, exactly, is it a form of self-hatred?'

'It's deprivation is all. *Those* people don't like food, they don't really enjoy it, they don't let themselves, the fucking puritans. People used to eat all kinds of things which would be considered disgusting by most people nowadays. How often do you eat fish eyes or chicken hearts? Some people won't even eat seafood because they are grossed out by it, but it's healthy. People have been eating these things for generations and it made them strong and robust, these are the foods that helped humanity to evolve. Now people are on a diet of processed crap, soy, corn flour and canola, white bread and white sugar. We're clearly going to devolve if we carry on this way.'

'So people hate themselves by finding slimy things icky?'

'Yes!' He gestures wildly. 'Icky sliminess is a part of life, people ooze, we are all naturally revolting – by those standards anyway. Why don't we embrace our organic state, rather than hide from it? What's wrong with a bit of slime?'

'I've never liked shellfish, even when I was little.'

'If you were in a primitive culture you'd have no choice.'

'Some people would consider going back to a primitive diet devolving.'

'My dear, there was nothing wrong with food to begin with. Our marvellous technology has only made a mess of things, think of how many cases there are of heart disease and diabetes that didn't exist on a primitive diet?'

'I know. You don't need to tell me that.'

'So you see, there's no reason to go all vegany on me.'

'I'm not. I know it doesn't suit me, but may suit some people.'

'You know there were no traditional cultures that were completely vegan.'

'There are some that were mostly vegetarian.'

'They tended to consume a lot of raw milk, sometimes even insects.'

'I know.' I looked down.

'So what?'

I hesitated, guessing his response. 'Do you think it might be morally superior?'

'Hah! That's a good one. Morals are just another human construction, aren't they?' He looked at me and decided that wasn't enough. 'For me it's a grey area. We are naturally predators, conquerors. But that doesn't mean I'd kill my pet dog because I was hungry. But life feeds on life.'

'I tried to be vegetarian once but my body resisted me. All I could think about was eating chicken rolls from the bakery up the road. I dreamt about them. Even the cat food started to smell good to me – that was when I decided to stop trying.'

'Ha! that's hilarious. I can imagine you scoffing back the cat food out of Serah's bowl. That's your body telling you something. I don't know why you bothered being vege in the first place.'

Hamilton is like a big small town. The arty and alternative subcultures seem to get mixed up. I have been to parties over-populated by goths, listening to metal, or folk music gigs where some of the same people showed up. I have seen Evie around for years, hiding in the corner at parties, fire dancing in the main street. I actually met her several times and she didn't remember me. I don't think she recognised me when she knocked on the door of our flat a few years ago selling Greenpeace. But I'm pretty sure she could pick me out of a crowd now.

I was curious about the things Evie had to say that night, even if I blatantly disagreed. I looked up the website she had given me: Veganoutreach.org. Most of it was about animal cruelty in factory farming, which I disagree with anyway. The information on health was from some medical associations, which usually have warped perspectives based on the research that is funded by people with agendas.

'What are you thinking about?' Henry asks, reaching for more banana bread.

'I like to think I'm an ethical person.' Henry nudges me in the ribs.

'Well, you only buy free-range eggs and go out of your way to buy organic, free-range meat. You're practically a saint compared to most people!'

'I just want to support those models of farming because I feel they are good.'

'That's exactly right, support what you feel is good. It does a lot more for the world than abstaining.' He scrunched up his nose at his own mention of abstinence, my dear friend the hedonist. 'The world doesn't need more martyrs.'

Malcolm

'We haven't had sex in months!' I erupt. It's probably not the best way to respond to Elena asking how I am, but it's really starting to bug me.

'I'm five-and-a-half months pregnant.' She glares at me.

'I know that. But it's not going to hurt the baby. And anyway, this has been going on since well before you were pregnant.'

'That's not true.' She folds her arms and I can tell by her tone that she feels a bit hurt.

'Never mind.' I say, and go back to what I was doing before – scanning my Facebook newsfeed.

'Well it's not like I feel attractive with this giant thing around my middle – you don't make me feel attractive.'

I sigh. 'Don't worry. Forget I said anything.'

'I'm so tired all the time, and my brain keeps working and I just want to sleep.'

'It's not important.'

'Obviously it is, or you wouldn't have brought it up.'

'Look. I love you and I find you incredibly attractive, always, and I miss having sex – that's all.'

'There's this little voice in my head that is always worried about the baby and thinks it's too much hassle and wants to sleep or do something productive – you know it's the same voice that's always telling me to accomplish things and finish things and stuff.'

'You put too much pressure on yourself.'

'Maybe.'

'You do.'

'Well, there's so much to do before the baby comes.'

'Maybe you're too tightly strung.'

'Maybe, well, how do I loosen my strings?'

'I don't know. Just relax – have a bath.'

'Yeah.'

'I can hear you at night – your breathing's irregular when you're thinking about things and getting wound up.'

'I'm busy writing blog posts in my head.'

'Yeah, I can tell. Look, just give it a rest – you don't need to blog, just relax!'

Valerie

'Evie!' She comes into my office without an appointment. I'm grateful that I have a no-show patient right before my lunch break. She looks so small and vulnerable, even more than usual, as she sits down in the chair next to my desk. She's wearing her 'Meat is Murder' T-shirt.

'How can I help you?' I want to keep things professional because I'm at work and this is obviously a sensitive subject.

'I just want to let you know that I'm okay.' She says in her little voice. 'So you don't worry.'

I nod and explain to her about the abnormal smear, about the colposcopy and what it will entail. I tell her, over and over again, not to worry.

'It's normal,' I say. 'It happens all the time.'

'But it's abnormal.' She looks puzzled.

'Now that we know about it we can put it right. Everything's going to be fine.'

I know she hasn't told Michael.

'I don't want him to worry.' She says. 'It's bad enough that you know.' She looks down. 'It's private. I don't want anyone else to know.'

After she leaves I rush into the staffroom and gulp down my lunch before my next client. The tuna salad gets stuck in my teeth and on my breath. I'm out of breath mints so I have to brush my teeth quickly before my next client comes in. All the while I'm thinking about Evie and doing the very thing I told her not to do. I'm worrying.

It is an odd kind of relationship that a parent has with their child's partner. I have met a few of Elena's ex-boyfriends, briefly. I know Malcolm quite well, and I like him enough but I don't feel emotionally close to him. Evie is different. She's the first girl Michael ever really brought home and that leads me to think she is serious. He's had scores of friends crashing at the house over the last few years, some of them female, but he never properly introduced them.

There is something about her that brings out the mother in me. She needs nurturing, she is fragile and sensitive and beautiful. I almost want to swaddle her like a baby and protect her from the world. I don't like to think about her and Michael breaking up. She feels like a surrogate child and I don't want to lose her.

Evie

There may be times when we are powerless to prevent injustice, but there must never be a time when we fail to protest.
ELIE WIESEL

No one ever talks about your cervix. It's not something you can ask someone about casually. 'Hey, how's your cervix treating ya?' It's silent, hidden, female. That is something about being a woman; you never see most of your genitalia. It's in there somewhere and you don't even know what it does or what it looks like, except from the stupid drawings in sex-ed class.

This is what a colposcopy is like, in case you don't already know: I'm looking at my cervix on a screen. It's enlarged on the monitor next to where I lie, my legs hoisted up in stirrups. It's pink. I don't know why but I think it's pretty. It reminds me of a soft toy or something.

It feels so strange lying here, not painful – it's more like excruciating discomfort to be in such an unnatural position.

'I'm going to apply some liquid,' the gynaecologist says, peering through the colposcopy.

'Vinegar, you mean?' I say. My voice sounds sharp, more certain than I am. Tara has done a lot of research. She told me that the 'liquid' they apply is acetic acid or vinegar.

'Yes,' she says, obviously a little uncomfortable with my knowledge. 'A weak solution, to make any abnormal cells show up.'

Doctors are experts, they have all the power and knowledge. They don't want you to have it.

She goes through the vinegar process, brushing the solution with a cotton bud that looks oversized on the screen. She can't tell if any of the cells are abnormal but that doesn't stop her from going further.

'I'm going to take a smear,' she says in a mechanical voice.

She takes a brush, which I can tell is made of wire because of the sound it makes as she picks it up. I see it on the screen as she scrapes away at my pretty, pink cervix, leaving it bloody and scratched. I feel assaulted.

Is this what Valerie did to me when I had my last smear? It's so strange.

I empathise with the cervix on the screen. I know what it's like to be roughed up. *Poor thing*, I think.

The worst is still to come.

'I'm just going to take a biopsy – a little pinch.' She says, holding something in her hands that looks like a long metal hole punch.

I grit my teeth as I watch it go in. I can feel it, internally, as she takes the 'pinch'. It's not exactly painful; there are no pain receptors there, but it's like chomping on numbed skin, like when you have your face anaesthetised by the dentist and accidentally bite the inside of your cheek.

Unsavoury.

There is some kind of pain – an ache – deeper than the tissue that was directly affected. It's as if my body realises it is being attacked.

The blood gushes out, seeming like much more than there actually is because the image is so enlarged. I want to cry.

'Now we will just cauterise the wound with silver nitrate to stop it from bleeding.'

Hasn't it been through enough?

I watch as she pokes the hot cauteriser around in there, leaving my cervix grey-black. So different from the healthy pink it had been before. Leaving silver residue inside me. A strange kind of bling. If it wasn't damaged then, it surely is now. It's been abused. We both have. And now there is only one person in the world I want to see, well, him and his mother.

Michael

When I get to Dave's he's still coma'd out on the couch so I check my email. A few people have posted on my Facebook wall. To be honest, I hate computers. I'd rather be surfing or skating than glued to a screen, but the surf is limp and I'm waiting for Dave to get up so we can skate, plus I guess it is a good way to keep in touch with friends.

Zarah: ello ello ello!!! whats up hun?? how you been … excited for this weeknd, clubbing satday night then we gonna do the mish back to ragz with you boys early hours of the mornig ahah … think we gonna be staying in ragz Sunday night to yay yay!! anywho hava good one … xxoo

Zarah and I go way back. We've been fuck-buddies, on and off, for years. Sometimes I think she wants more but we just don't have that vibe. I feel as emotionally attached to her as I do to my boyz. We're just friends. In her profile picture she looks hot, literally, in her bikini in the sun. It's an old picture, I remember being on that Gizzy beach with her and the boyz last summer. Good times.

Because Evie is away a lot we're not exactly exclusive. We don't hook up with other people when we are around each other – that would be weird – but we can do what we like when we're not together. We have two rules. The first is, as long as we're careful. The second is, don't ask, don't tell. It seems to work.

I don't fuck around a lot or anything but when the mood is right I can. I try not to think about what Evie does. I don't want to be the jealous, possessive boyfriend. This is the longest relationship I've ever had: almost a year. The only real relationship, I guess, because the others were over in a matter of weeks.

A couple of other girls I barely know have sent me messages.

Kelsey: Hey stranger! how r ya

Liz: Hey babe whats up … how you been??

I think these two are friends I met in town one night. I'm not sure why it's mostly chicks who message me on Facebook, maybe it's more of a girly thing to do. Just as I'm considering the possibilities of getting back to one of these girls I feel vibrations against my leg. Perfect timing – it's a text from Evie.

I'm back in town. Let me know if you want to catch up.

Suddenly I'm not sure. There are so many options. It's only been a couple of weeks since she left. Before I get a chance to think about it too much my phone vibrates again and it's Tobias, one of my best mates in Raglan.

Sup oi? Sk8 down da new subdivision. 1200

Dave, the master of perfect timing, chooses that moment to wake up. He looks up at me through unmistakably blurry eyes.

'Sup, Cobba?' Me and my mates speak our own language.

'Cruise to Raggas for a skate?'

'Trumps.' The mention of a skate always wakes him up – like the adrenaline from all those previous rides comes back with the thought. 'I'll hit the shower. You feel like Macca's?'

It looks strange, just some new dead-end streets with nothing around them but grass. In another few years this will be full of houses that all look the same. Fortunately for us, this development is carved into a beautiful hill, paved in brand-new concrete and tar-seal, and even better – no one cares if we skate here – at least for now.

I drop onto my longboard. Dave, Joel and Matty follow me – Tobias is up front with his camera out. We pick up speed, and I feel the rush as if the wind isn't just blowing over me but through me, stimulating my nerves. I feel so alive – so powerful – using my weight to steer the board. I'm going so fast now I couldn't stop if I tried. Then the curb comes up out of nowhere and I've bailed – in the air, completely free, completely terrified – there's a moment of nothing and then the hard smacking crunch accompanied by the feeling of having no fucking idea what just happened. I open my eyes and see a snatch of blurry sky and close them again.

'Fu-uck.'

'Holy shit, Gov.'

'That was out the gate.'

'You alright?'

The voices are murmurs in the dark. I open my eyes again and see the blood on my hand.

'You're lucky you can't see your face, Cobba,' Dave says.

I'm lucky, Mum says. My face is only bruised and grazed, and the only thing broken is a fracture in my forearm. Mum and John wait while the emergency room doctor does my cast. I'm gutted because I can't surf for the next six weeks, but at least until I get this piece of shit off. It covers half of my palm and when he sees it John says, 'Half-caste with a half cast.' I crack up and even Mum can't help smiling.

Later when I repeat the joke to Evie she looks surprised.

'You know, 'cause I'm half-Māori and half-Pākehā.' We're sitting on the couch at Mum's house. Well I'm lying down resting, and Evie is sitting next to me.

'Yeah, I know. I thought it was racist.'

'I guess,' I say and then I remember something from Culture Studies 101 and make an intelligent comment about how I don't have half an identity. I am Māori and I am Pākehā, it's not like my body is half-brown and half-white. 'But it's just a joke.'

She nods. 'So this is insider racism; one of those cases where you can joke about something if you're part of a group, be racist if you're part of that race?' She seems more serious than usual. I take that as a challenge.

'Yeah, I guess. Don't any of your friends make vegan jokes that don't piss you off because they are vegans?' She looks at me blankly.

'Oh wait,' I say. 'I forgot that vegans don't have a sense of humour.' That makes her smile and push me. 'Can't you see I'm injured? Jeez!'

'We do make vegan jokes.'

'Like what?'

'How many vegans does it take to change a light bulb? '

'How many?'

She grins. 'Two. One to change it and one to check for animal ingredients.'

'Hah, is that the best you can do?'

'What's the best way to keep milk fresh?' I shrug.

'Leave it in the cow.'

I do laugh at this one. 'That's even less funny. It's like a fucking protest sign or something. Wait a second, I've got one. What makes vegans go blind?' Evie rolls her eyes at me.

'I suppose you're going to say, 'Lack of nutrition'?'

'Nah – reading the tiny print of ingredients lists!' We both crack up. 'Although Elena has just as much chance of going blind from that. You're both food Nazis.' She elbows me in the ribs and goes into rant mode.

'I'm … she … she still eats meat! I suppose free-range eggs are understandable, maybe even milk if the cows are looked after – even though milk is made for *calves!* But meat? Dead animals? Seriously? Even if they're 'free-range' – whatever that means! Give them a nice life and then send them off to be slaughtered for dinner? It's *murder.* How can she say that is morally okay? I just don't get it.'

'Hey – I eat meat,' I say, pretending to be hurt.

'You're amoral, you don't even care if it's right or wrong.' I raise my eyebrows.

Evie glares at me. 'Don't get me started on you. But *her,* she thinks it's right!' I take the opportunity to release some gas that had been building up in my gut.

'Eww! Gross,' she says, squinting and trying to fan the fart away with her hand.

'It smells beautiful.' I inhale deeply.

'You are so disgusting! I can't believe I like you.' She has moved about a metre to get away from my stench.

'You know, it's a fact that everyone enjoys the smell of their own fart.'

'That's not true.'

'I read it somewhere.'

'Well, it's still disgusting.' She folds her arms, but I can see the smile twitch at the corner of her mouth.

John

Mr Johnson leans over the desk, his left eye droops making him look retarded. He breathes on me with his garlic breath and I want to vomit.

'Where were you yesterday?'

'Um,' I say, playing as stupid as he looks. 'I don't know.'

'You don't know?' he raises his eyebrows.

'Nah – think I had a headache.' I lean back in my chair – mostly to get away from his yuck breath – and put my arms behind my head.

'Are you too cool for school, Mr Joyce?' His voice is so nasal he might as well be speaking out of his ass. The class giggles – and I know they're not laughing at me – not that I would care.

'Do you have a note?'

I probably should have forged one, but I forgot this time. 'Nah, I'll bring one tomorrow, and some tic tacs for your breath, sir.' I couldn't help it, it's just too easy. Mr Johnson goes bright red and pulls at his collar as if he needs to release the pressure.

His voice comes out like it's breaking all over again: 'Principal's office.'

What the fuck is the point of that. I'd rather not sit on my ass and explain to a balding fat dude that my teacher is a twat and almost certainly get myself into more trouble. I'm not stupid – this system is. I don't buy any of it. I don't know where I'm going but it must be better than this.

I pull the fingers at Mr Johnson. 'Laterz,' I say as I gap it - out the door, out the gate, and out of school for good.

Valerie

It was Mr Hannigan, the principal, who called me to say that John had walked out of school – again, that he had been on his last warning and that they were going to ask him to leave. I was in shock. I said nothing. John came home.

'I just got off the phone with your principal.'

'I don't give a fuck.'

'Excuse me,' I said, getting upset. 'I'm your mother, you can't talk to me like that, in my house, where you eat my food, wearing the clothes I bought you!'

'Fine,' John smiled, but it was nasty. 'I'll get out of your house then.' And he walked straight back out the front door.

I've tried calling Elena but she was no use. I called Mum too, but she was out. So I call the only other non work-related number I know by heart – Audrey's. She and I haven't been as close since that strange church service where she found out my opinion of Down syndrome testing – but I'm running out of shoulders to cry on.

'Oh, Val … You poor thing … I'll be right over,' she says, her voice bursting with compassion. But the thought of her turning up with her kids – turning this place upside down – is enough to get me to pretend that everything isn't as bad as it really is.

'You will be in my prayers,' she says, and I remember God. Just in this moment, the adrenaline from the phone call with the principal and the fight with John is enough to get me to fall to my knees in the living room and pray for him. As my knees sink into the soft carpet I can almost feel Jesus' arms around me. I feel ridiculous. I feel safe. Everything will be fine.

Two hours later I get a call from Caleb. 'I'm coming to pick John up,' he says.

Thank God, I think. 'Wait – where are you taking him?'

'I've got him a job lined up on a dairy farm up here.'

Panic claws at my chest, 'What about school?'

'He's left – I talked to the principal. They won't let him back in and he won't go back anyway.'

So now Caleb decides to show some interest – great.

'Can't you at least talk to him? Convince him to give it another try? We could see if a different school would take him.'

'I can try Val, but I'm telling you now, it's not going to do any good.'

'But his education …'

'Education isn't everything.' There's a sharp edge to his voice. It was always one of our tensions (one of many) that I was so educated while he wasn't. I wonder why we were ever together at all. Of course it's worth it for the children – I'd never regret them – even at a time like this. I just hope everything's going to be alright. Caleb's still on the other end of the phone line.

'Anyway,' he says, 'School's almost over for the year. Let's see how he likes life on a farm doing real work – get him to harden up – or the reality will send him running back to you next year.'

I hang up the receiver, not sure about anything anymore. I do the mental check I've been doing since they were babies:

Elena: fine, healthy, pregnant, doesn't listen to anything I say, but she'll be alright. God knows how she'll handle labour. I get a twinge of crude joy at the thought that she'd probably last five minutes into her home birth before demanding to be taken to the hospital for pain relief.

Michael: busy with uni, not at terrible risk despite continuing to participate in dangerous activities. I hope that cast slows him down – the last thing I need is a child with a head injury right now.

John … oh, John. Why are you punishing me? Were you sent here to test me? Do you always have to cause this much trouble? Is it possible that you will settle down, and be a normal kid so that one day you can have a career, a normal life, a family – rather than the career criminal that Elena suspects you will become?

I move on. Rosa. There's nothing to worry about with Rosa, is there? She goes to school, she does her homework. She's a good girl. She does whine a lot but that's probably just the age. She needs to stop watching so much TV. It's all very minor.

My mind flicks to Evie, the new addition. She seemed okay, last I saw her. Medical procedures can be scary, I understand that. I deal with enough patients in the same situation, some of them stay calm, they go through the process and come out the other side, relieved that they don't have abnormal cells anymore. Some of them don't handle it well at all. A young woman I was treating recently was surprisingly angry about the whole process, she yelled and cried in my office and prompted a call from the Women's Outpatient Clinic when she went for her appointment.

Apparently she passed out and, after the treatment, sat curled in foetal position as if she was suffering post-traumatic shock. I hope Evie gets through this. I know she can. I know she's strong enough.

Elena

Mum calls me in tears. 'John's left school,' she sobs.

'What?' Although I know he has always had trouble with 'education', it's a surprise. 'You let him?' It's a stupid question. Obviously she doesn't approve, given her emotional state.

'No, but I couldn't stop him. He's gone.'

'Where is he?'

'With Caleb.'

'Dad? Why? Does he condone this?' My moral outrage shocks even me.

'I don't know,' Mum sighs. It sounds like she's given up.

'What is he going to do?' Suddenly I've surrendered to the situation – what choice do I have?

'Caleb's going to find him a job with a farmer.'

'Well that will suit him, I guess. He's a bit rough round the edges,' I joke, but Mum's not in the mood.

'I don't know, Elena. What else can I do? I do everything I can for you kids.'

'Well, I'm not the one dropping out of school, Mum.'

'I know. It's just, so hopeless. I'm hopeless.'

'You know John. He's got to find his own way.'

I run the bath. It is my favourite part of the day. My body is already starting to weigh on me, burdensome. I feel tired and heavy. I sometimes have several baths in a day just to feel weightless, to allow my muscles to relax. Undressing is becoming more difficult, even at five and a half months – just in the balancing-on-one-foot part. It's worth it as I sink my feet into the steaming water and tension melts away.

I was named after my great-grandmother. I barely remember her but sometimes think I inherited some of her old lady qualities. Henry always says I dress like a grandma. I know this doesn't really make any sense. She was only an old lady for a small part of her life. But we tend to think of the people we know as always existing in the age that we know them in. I can't imagine Mum as a kid, even though I've seen photos. The idea of her being a teenager seems implausible to me, although logically I know that she once was. I wonder if this child growing inside me is someone I will always think of in this way, as a bump where my waist once was. Will I always think of this baby as a two-year-old running towards me with open arms, as an eight-year-old slamming the bedroom door or making fart jokes? Will my understanding of this being evolve naturally as he or she does, or will it stay stuck at one stage? Stunted.

The water is too hot but I don't care. I lie on my back and kick with my feet so that I drift a little, back and forth, and let the water lap at my sides. The baby kicks and it feels like I'm being nudged from the inside by this invisible creature. It often gives me butterflies. I lie there with my hand on the round of my tummy, waiting for more. The baby continues to kick into my open palm. My mind struggles to wrap itself around the concept of my belly kicking my hand. It's surreal.

My mind jumps to thoughts of John dropping out of school.

I don't have a lot of faith in the high school system. I learnt a lot more from my own volition, from discussions with friends, from the internet and good old fashioned books then I ever did from high school. It's a gateway, I suppose: a gateway drug to higher education and the addiction it can become. Dropping out can mean seriously limiting your options. The baby kicks inside me. Am I growing a delinquent? A saint? A murderer? There are so many questions that all mothers must surely lose sleep over, and I'm just beginning to ask them: will my baby live? Will she die before I do? Is she even alive now? I don't even know the gender. I never had a scan – I just couldn't trust that the radiation wasn't detrimental. Will he become a religious zealot, a politician, a street cleaner?

For the first two months of my pregnancy I kept repeating the startling fact in my mind. 'We're having a baby,' I'd say to Malcolm.

After about the tenth time he got over it. 'Yes, yes, I know.' He replied this way in a bored voice until I stopped repeating myself to him, but I just couldn't get over it. It was so strange. So huge. There are so many parts of my mind and each part needed to realise this important development. And so it went. I would wake up in the morning to the exciting revelation. *I'm having a baby*. As my pants slowly began to feel tighter around my waist the pregnancy was more obvious to me but it still seemed newsworthy. *This child is made of my DNA and Malcolm's*. I felt like a five-year-old discovering the solar system. *This baby is growing inside me*. It was obvious but still somehow out of my mental grasp. *I am creating life*.

I catch myself thinking this way at times and I wonder if this will ever become less extraordinary, if I will ever get used to this massive change, if I will ever really become a mother.

'Most people think giving birth is hard, painful and awful,' Zena says, her voice calm as usual.

'Isn't it?' I say. That's about all I've ever heard about labour.

'It can be for some women.' Zena is tactful. 'For many it is a mental struggle, but not always.' That's the first I've heard of it. My look of surprise gives me away.

'Some women have birthing experiences that are amazing, beautiful events.'

'Really?' I sound incredulous.

'It can be a real mental struggle for some women, they want to be in control but all you need to do is let your body do it. Your body knows what to do. It's what it's designed for.'

I nod.

'All you have to do is let go. Giving birth is about surrender.'

When I first started to think about having this baby the only thing I was sure of was that I didn't want to do it in a hospital.

'Hospitals are for sick people,' I said to Mum, although she insisted that new technologies could help with difficult births.

'I don't want to think about that!' I was irritated that she always focuses on the worst scenario. 'My baby is going to be healthy.'

In my first meeting with Zena we discussed the options. I had been thinking about booking a room at a birthing centre; at least it wasn't a hospital.

'I'm a home birth midwife,' she said. And then I knew that

I was going to have a home birth. This woman had the power to make me feel calm and relaxed with her mere presence, something that will be invaluable to me when I'm in labour.

'Birthing centres aren't equipped with anything you can't have at home. They don't have doctors, they send complicated cases up to the hospital. I have a kit that I bring with me with everything that could be needed in a healthy birth. I have birthing pools you can use.'

The more I thought about it the better it sounded, despite every TV show and movie depicting an awkward hospital birth. I want to bring my baby into the world in an environment that is safe and familiar to me. I don't want to have to worry about packing bags or when the right time is to leave the safety of my home and go into a sterile environment full of strangers and uncomfortable beds.

'When a birthing woman goes into an unfamiliar place like a hospital, her body produces stress hormones that slow the labour,' Zena says.

'Hospitals were having problems with this though, so they invented an artificial version of oxytocin, the main hormone used to give birth, Syntocinon.' She gives a disapproving look.

She gives me a book by an Australian GP who endorses home birth. It goes into more detail about the hormones and I find out that Syntocinon is different to the natural hormone in many ways; it doesn't provide the euphoric and pain relieving qualities that oxytocin does, so hospitals use epidurals, which some women claim are more painful than labour itself. Epidurals numb half of the body so women don't even know how to push, they can't feel their muscles. It all sounded a bit weird to me, weird and tragic. Because so many women had these awful disempowering experiences and then had to deal with the day-to-day trials of motherhood. It's no wonder post-natal depression is so common.

Got milk?

People are scared, they're ruled by fear. All I ever hear about raw milk from the mainstream media is scaremongering about its possible bacterial risk, never mind its health benefits.

Many children who are supposedly lactose intolerant can easily drink raw milk. I wouldn't recommend just any old milk. Many commercial farms are not careful with their milk because they know it will all be heated and crap gets in there (literally). Organic pasture farms that supply milk, legally, from the farm gate to the public are very careful about their milk and the milk also has ways of protecting itself. As a living food it is filled with enzymes and beneficial microorganisms. I have read about experiments where they put a pathogen into raw milk, left it overnight and by the morning the pathogen had been eliminated by the natural agents in the milk. Very few cases of food poisoning exist around milk. In the States they make a big deal about it in the media – of course. If someone gets sick and happens to have consumed raw milk the media have a field day, even when the tests come back clearing the milk of any fault. No one hears about that. The cases where the milk is to blame are usually linked to commercial, non-organic, feed-lot herds which are most likely contaminated with faeces, antibiotics and nasty chemicals used in farming practices. Never mind the fact that cows naturally eat grass, not corn, but that's another story.

Raw milk doesn't go rancid. Unlike its pasteurised cousin, those same protective enzymes change the consistency and composition until it is more like a yoghurt. The whey separates from the curd, which can be made into cream cheese. The adults of traditional herding tribes would consume their milk after it had soured because almost all adults lack the enzyme (lactase) that children have which breaks down the lactose sugar in milk that most human beings can't properly digest.

Raw milk herbed cream cheese

Ingredients:

1 litre raw, unpasteurised milk, left on the bench to sour overnight until it begins to separate into curds and whey

½ cup fresh herbs (oregano, thyme, basil, lemon balm,

Trust your own judgement with this. If the milk smells wrong – don't use it. I find after about five days in the fridge the milk begins to thicken and then separate anyway, so this is a good way to use it up. Sour milk smells a bit like a yoghurt. Make sure it is still white and doesn't have any strange mould growing in it.

Place a clean cheese cloth (or other fine-weave cloth) into a large bowl and spoon or pour the soured milk into it. Take the corners of the cloth, careful to keep the curds inside and tie them together. Find a way to suspend the cloth so that the whey can drip through it. Some people tie it to a wooden spoon and put that across the top of a bucket so the liquid can drain into said bucket. I hang mine from the kitchen cabinet handle and catch the drips in a bowl underneath. Leave overnight.

Scoop the curd out of the cloth into a bowl and add herbs and a generous pinch of salt. You can either stir to combine or get in there with your hands (which I find more effective). At this point you can taste the mixture and then add more salt to suit your tastes. If you want to be fancy, you can use a small container as a cheese mould – line it with waxed paper and refrigerate. This simple, delicious cheese should keep for five days in the fridge – if it lasts that long!

Remember to save the whey. It is great for digestion and is also high in protein (like the whey powder that athletes use). You can add it to smoothies or even dilute it and use as a fertiliser on your garden.

Malcolm

Facebook is the most soul-sucking device known to mankind. Well, it can be. It plays on our human need for validation – both to give and receive – by making it as easy as clicking the 'Like' button. You can request 'friends' you barely know or have your friendship requested by people you've never met. Your social world can be represented in just one tab on your internet browser. You can chat to your cousin studying politics in New York while face-stalking someone your girlfriend was talking about last night and be frustrated at their wisely strict privacy settings. Then you can send a message to Dan to see if he can bring the iPod he borrowed back when you see him at Doug's party tonight. You can check the Facebook invite to the party to make sure it is tonight. You can scroll down your news feed and read what your 'friends' have been up to – watch the funny YouTube videos they post and 'like' a few pages for political causes – gay marriage, Hipsters for Goldsmith, Oprah for president. Mark Zuckerberg could not possibly have foreseen the monster he was to create.

Obviously I love it, more and more these days, where I'm either working or hanging out at home with Elena, feeling too guilty to go out partying all the time when she can't drink because of our baby. We don't have TV so I get my news from Facebook, mostly courtesy of a couple of old uni friends who are now journalists.

I'm watching a video of the Occupy Melbourne protesters

who, after being evicted in Melbourne, are dressing themselves in fully erected tents – hiding inside them to attract police and then popping out and running around as tent monsters. It's funny before the police brutality kicks in. Elena would be upset. She cries at anything these days. She never used to cry at all.

I see a notification pop up. New friend requests are always mildly exciting. From Kim Saunders. Strange that a student would 'friend' me. None have before. I suppose it's not a bad thing to have a student as a Facebook friend. It's not like I'm doing anything to be ashamed of these days. There are no embarrassing photo opportunities for me to be tagged in. Sure, why not. I click 'Accept' then wonder why she wants to be my 'friend'. There was that tension in my office a while back. The slight anxiety makes me contemplate 'unfriending'. She probably wouldn't notice. Nah, I know lecturers who have done far worse things with their students. Besides. The trimester is officially over. She's no longer even a student – just a 'friend'.

Elena wants me to go out to get milk and the blueberry chocolate she's been craving. She will want to come too and proceed to attempt purchase every calorific item in the supermarket despite feeling guilty about every ingredient they contain. I am her partner in food crime. She would die of embarrassment if anyone else knew about the box of donuts she ate last night so it's kept a secret from her family – lest they accuse her of hypocrisy, and God knows what she'd do if her blogging audience found out. I sometimes fantasise about going into her logged on account and posting as her about what she's actually been up to. Of course I'd never do it, I'm not cruel, just bored. Hence the Facebook. I'm about to log off when a chat box pops up bottom right of the screen.

Kim: Hi Malcolm

I'm surprised at how excited I am.

Hi

Was it weird to friend you? Sorry.

Malcolm: Nah, it's fine

It is fine. Right?

I just wanted to thank you for your help last trimester, and to apologise for being so arrogant and emotional.

Haha, what ever happened to an apple for teacher?

Kim, you're not arrogant, you're fiery. It's refreshing.

Is this flirting? Either way it's harmless.

Thanks Malcolm, you're really cool for a lecturer – I mean, you're cool anyway …

Of course I am. Elena walks into the room and I'm tempted to close the conversation like a child caught with his hand in the cookie jar. Does this mean I'm doing something wrong? God. This is ridiculous.

Hey, I've got to go. Emergency supermarket mission. Catch you another time.

Rosa

Chardon looks over at me and smiles and I know there's something wrong. She never smiles at me. She hates me. It's not really a nice smile, anyway, it's a mean smile and I want to get away from her, but she's coming over to my desk.

'Hi, Rosa.' It sounds like she's trying to be nice. 'Your hair looks good today.'

I glare at her.

'What?'

'Do you want to have lunch with us?'

'Why?'

'Well, you're Aroha's friend, and she's my friend, so, really it makes sense that we should all be friends.' I don't trust her but she's really pretty and she wears make up and her hair is all shiny and blonde. If I was her friend it would make things different and maybe Johnny wouldn't call me a *loser with no friends*.

I feel nervous; like when you have to go to the dental nurse even though you know she's going to give you a new toothbrush and she's really nice. My handwriting gets messy and Mrs Mills tells me to start again on my project, which is really dumb.

When the bell rings Chardon grabs my arm – not hard – but like we're friends. She pulls me over to where they usually sit – the bitchy pretty girls – under the big trees that drop those spiky brown things that the boys throw at each-other and it make me wonder why they plant those trees at a school anyway. I hope she doesn't want to share lunches because I already ate my tweezels and cookies at playtime and I only have the jam sandwiches Mum made which are always soggy and yuck.

'We're going to start a club,' Chardon says, after we all sit down. She is on one side of me and Aroha is on the other side and Christen and Melissa are in front of me in the circle.

'Why am I here?' I ask.

'We need five people to start a club, and like I already told you, you're Aroha's friend so you get to join.' I still don't trust her because I know she's really a bitch.

'Are you in?' She asks.

'Okay.' I shrug my shoulders like I don't care.

'So now we need special club names. I want to be *Jewel* because it's my middle name.' She looks around at us.

'I want to be Crystal,' Christen says. 'Because it's like my name.'

'No, it's too much like Jewel,' Chardon says. 'You can be …'

'No. I want to be Crystal,'

'Fine,' Chardon says. 'Be Crystal.' She looks at Aroha 'You can be Love, because it's what your name means in English and it's better than Māori.'

Aroha looks angry but she doesn't say anything. I can tell she's as scared of Chardon as I am.

'Can I be Ocean?' Melissa asks. She sounds like she might be a bit scared too. 'It's my middle name.'

'Yes.' Chardon looks at me, 'And Rosa, you can be Blossom – like a rose blossom.'

'Okay,' I don't care about her stupid name club anyway, but it does feel cool to be better than everyone else that doesn't have a stupid name and isn't part of the club.

'Now, sisters,' Chardon looks around at all of us. 'To seal the deal we have to tell each other a secret.'

I feel strange. Chardon keeps talking.

'We need to all trust each other, so we have to tell each other which boy in the class we have a crush on.'

'Okay,' Christen says. She's not scared of the queen bitch. 'You go first.'

'I will,' Chardon says. 'You just all need to promise that you will too.'

No one says anything.

'Good,' Chardon says. 'I have a crush on Derek.'

Of course, he's the most popular boy.

Chardon looks at Christen.

'You already know I like Cameron.'

'Still? That's so gross. He has braces!'

Christen looks down, 'Derek is poor.'

'What?' Chardon is shocked.

'He said he only gets one present for Christmas.'

'It doesn't matter. He's perfect.' Chardon crosses her arms.

Melissa says she likes Frankie Massey, who is really tall and good at sports. Aroha doesn't want to say who she has a crush on but she writes it down on a piece of paper that she ripped out of her writing book.

'You've got to be kidding me!' Chardon looks at her. 'Thomas Benedict? He's chubby and has long hair.'

Aroha goes bright red.

'You don't have to be mean,' I say.

'Well, which boy do *you* have a crush on?' Chardon asks. 'You have to tell us or you're out of the club.'

'I don't have a crush on any boy,' I say. 'And I don't like your stupid club.'

Chardon is really angry now. 'I knew you were a weirdo, Rosa. You don't like boys. That makes you a lesbian and that's really yuck. You have a crush on Aroha, don't you?' I get a sick feeling. 'Rosa and Aroha up a tree K-I-S-S-I-N-G.'

I get up and run back to the classroom, past all the desks, past the cloakroom with the bags and into the toilets. I lock the door and sit down on the seat even though I don't have to go. I put my head in my hands. I'm feeling too many things at once and it's too much to feel so the tears come out and take the feelings away with them. I want to be at home with Mum cuddling me, but Mum is never home when I need her. She's too busy looking after people who are sick. I wish I was sick. I don't want to ever have to see Chardon again. Maybe I will just go to the sickbay and say I have a headache and need to lie down for a while. Maybe if I'm sick, Mum will care and she'll come and pick me up and look after me.

Evie

A life without cause is a life without effect.
PAULO COELHO

The supermarket is crowded. I hate it. I hate people looking at me. I pick up a basket and grab some almost ripe avocados. I remind myself to get crackers to have with them. I check the ingredients on everything to make sure there's no milk or egg, honey, meat, gelatine or other animal products. I choose the cheapest loaf bread with no milk solids. It's the one I usually get. I pick up two jars of Marmite in case the rumours of a shortage are true. Apparently the earthquake in Christchurch a while back shut the factory down and I need the reserves of vitamin B12 to keep me going.

I look at the 'normal' customers all around me. They probably judge me for my piercings and my clothes. On a good day I can handle it, I can throw it in their faces. I can be proud of who I am. Right now I'm down. Right now I just need to be alone. I feel out of place in this world. I just want to hide. I wish my body didn't need to be fed. I buy some butter-free cookies and some milk-free chocolate. Brace myself all through the checkouts. The operator looks as though she'd rather not serve me – but I bet she'd rather not be here at all. My bank account just stretches to buying another pouch of Drum, papers and filters. I get out the door and feel like I can breathe again – even if it is only the muggy air of a typical overcast Hamilton day. I walk the three kilometres back to Tara's.

She's whipped up some leftover lentil casserole for lunch with home-made bread.

'Thank God for real food!' I take my bowl to the rug-covered couch and dig in.

'You're welcome,' Tara smiles. 'It's not often people call me by my real name.' She pokes her tongue out. I elbow her gently in the ribs.

'I can't wait for the day, if I ever live to see it, where food this good is available everywhere.' Supermarkets are horrible; cafes and restaurants are pathetic when it comes to vegan food. Fast food is nigh impossible.

'You'll live,' Tara responds, serious all of a sudden. 'Hey, how was that smear thing?'

I'm feeling surprisingly relaxed about it.

I put on a posh accent. 'Oh, you mean, the colposcopy.' I gesture excessively, flicking my fingers out and raise my eyebrows then drop them and the accent simultaneously. 'It was … it was surreal.' I start. Then I remember the cervix that went from pink to white to scratched to bleeding to grey. 'I feel violated.'

'I bet.' Tara puts her arm around me and I nestle in, relaxing in the comfort of easy intimacy. I think of my mother. She would never make me feel this safe; no one in my family would. All I have are my friends and Valerie … and Michael, I suppose, although that's different. Sexual intimacy is never as safe, never as nurturing. There's too much power – too much potential to cause pain. I know that Tara will always be here, and that I am here for her. It's equal; it's mutual, balanced. I can't say the same for Michael, or any of my past boyfriends or girlfriends. I don't really understand why, it's just the way it is, I suppose, and that risk of pain keeps me on guard. Michael could leave even though it's me who usually leaves him; he could put up a wall or remove the metaphoric bridge that connects us at the moment; he could fall madly in love with someone else, a blonde, probably, who smells like apricots and wears make-up. Would that be love, or just desire? Either way, it would mean our ties would be severed and I would be drifting again, with no family, because I couldn't rely on Val, as a mother, if her son wasn't in my life. I would have no excuse to see her unless it was for a check-up. There would be no place for me in her busy life. I suppose that makes relying on her just as dangerous as on Michael, except I wouldn't feel rejected by her. That's the difference.

I'm lost in thought but slowly find myself listening to the beat of Tara's drum.

'Oh,' She says. 'I'm not sure if you want to know, but there's another letter for you from the hospital.'

Fuck.

I tear open the envelope with the green District Health Board logo in the corner.

'Abnormal.'

Tara wraps her arms around me and absorbs the tears.

'It's okay, honey. We will get through this. It's only been a few weeks since your smear … Of course the results are the same. I've been through this, I can help you through this too.'

'It must be quite common …' I realise. 'Valerie says it happens all the time. Why does no one talk about it?'

'I guess it's personal.'

'Damn right it's personal. It's my cervix … but do you think the fact that no one talks about it just makes it kind of like a dirty little secret? I mean, I know I'm not making any sense, but if there's this medical thing that happens all the time – but no one talks about it. What if they're treating it wrong? What if something really dodgy is going on and no one says anything so no one knows?'

'You mean, like the Unfortunate Experiment?' Tara asks.

I shrug.

'You know, in the 80s, where all those women had cervical cancer and didn't even know about it.'

'I was born in the 80s.' She elbows me.

'I know, so was I. I just keep up with New Zealand history better than you do.'

'Whatever. I bet your grandma told you all about it.' Tara's grandma is a feminist academic.

'So? Anyway. It was at some women's hospital in Auckland. It's pretty dodgy. All these women weren't treated for cervical cancer, or even told about it. Apparently it was some kind of experiment to see if the cancer went away by itself. It got leaked in the media. Some of the women died. It looked really bad for the hospital – for our whole medical system.'

'I wonder if that's why they're so anal about getting smears these days.'

'Probably. The whole system now is all about getting as many people treated as possible, whether they need it or not.'

I sigh. 'I hate hospitals.'

'I know.' She pats my back.

'So, what next?' I ask her, even though I've read the letter myself.

Tara pulls away, still holding my shoulders. She looks me in the eye in her infinite wisdom and experience in this topic. 'Next, you actually quit smoking, do a juice fast with me, stop eating all that disgusting white bread, and we'll see if we can reverse these abnormal cells.'

Thank God for Tara.

Michael

I thought the six weeks would drag but with the end of the uni trimester and all those assignments I hardly noticed my cast. Lucky it wasn't my right hand. I got all the assignments in. I'm even pretty sure that I passed everything.

When the doctor cracked the cast it stunk to high heaven and exposed scungy white skin underneath. A small price to pay to have my freedom back. Now I'm heading back out to Raglan, but I swing by Tara's to see if Evie wants to come with. Tara's place is like hippie paradise – but what else would you expect from the ultimate hippie child? She's pretty cool though, I guess, with her crazy dreads full of beads. That's got to be uncomfortable, right? She's even got a little pouch sewn into one of them where she can stash a joint, although it's a pretty obvious place for a pig to look.

Tara is standing on the porch when I arrive.

'Take good care of her,' she says. It sounds pretty heavy and there's a strange look in her eyes. Something's up. I'll have to remember to ask Evie about it when we're alone. She seems fine, smiling, dragging her backpack behind her as she walks into my arms. For a second I realise how different we are – her in her silk rags and me in my surf labels; her with her activism and strong beliefs and me with, well, surfing, I guess, skating, uni ... What else do I have?

Evie is sitting on the bed in my room at Mum's – looking

through my old art folder from primary school while I'm grabbing some clothes.

'This one's great,' she says, pulling out a bright yellow and red painting of the sun. 'You should frame it.'

I don't really get her sometimes. 'Who, apart from parents – have that kind of shit on their walls?' She shrugs. 'Besides, it would clash with my surfing posters and all the naked chicks with big tits.' She kicks at me from across the room but misses. I go over to her and put my arm around her waist, taking the rough piece of cartridge paper.

'It's Māui conquering the sun,' I explain, pointing to a little black stick figure. 'At school it was my favourite legend.'

'Why?' she asks. 'Did it fit with your delusions of grandeur?' I tickle her 'til she shrieks, then let go.

'It's just a strange concept – that the days used to be so short because the sun raced across the sky so no one could get any work done. So what do you do?'

'Write a letter?'

'You bloody Pākehā,' I tease. 'Nah, you have a hui of course, get your bros together and discuss the situation, come up with an action plan.'

Evie giggles. 'These days guys like to sit around making zombie attack plans, but back in those times they had real problems to solve, like how to slow the sun!'

'Exactly! So Māui has an idea: "Let's make some ropes out of harakeke, cobbas," and everyone goes along with it. They cruise out to where the sun lives – and they know they're getting close because it gets really fucking hot and the ground is all cracked and dry. They find the hole that the sun sleeps in …' Evie giggles. 'Bear with me – and set a kick-ass trap. The sun starts to rise and Māui signals his brothers to throw the ropes to catch it, then he smacks it in the nose with his magic jawbone 'til it agrees to travel more slowly in the future. Mission accomplished. The sun limps across the sky and everything's sweet.'

'So violence solves all your problems?' Evie jabs me in the ribs. 'Poor sun.'

I should have known she would take the sun's side.

I'm just pulling out of the driveway at Mum's house. Turning left. Looking right. I accelerate and something huge hits the windscreen with a loud thud. Evie, sitting next to me, screams. It's a horrible sound I've never heard before.

I'm reaching for my cell and Evie is already out of the car, asking the woman if she's okay. I'm ready to dial 111 when she assures us she is. Other cars have stopped on the street and moved her bike off the road. I'm freaking out. A fucking cyclist. I hit a cyclist.

My windscreen is fucked. It will need to be replaced completely. Evie writes down my name and contact details on a piece of paper and hands it to the woman. She has grey hair, I notice, and an American accent. I can't fucking believe it. She seems okay. She's walking and talking and probably bruised, but I'm hoping that's all that's wrong with her.

Evie has her hand over her mouth, recovering from shock. I'm feeling guilty as hell. I can't believe it.

'I can't believe it.' Evie mirrors my thoughts.

'I know, I know,' the woman says. 'I was just coming down the road and I looked at you,' she gestures to Evie, 'and we smiled and then –'

Oh my God. I didn't even look.

'I'm so sorry,' I say.

Her bike is ruined. 'Can I leave it here?' she asks.

I take it into the carport for her. All the while I'm wondering when was the last time I renewed my car insurance. It seems like ages ago.

It was. The insurance company has since changed ownership.

'We sent your renewal out at the beginning of the year,' the woman on the phone says.

'To what address?' I wonder if it was Mum's or Nan's.

'42 Berely Street, Frankton, Hamilton.'

'What? I've never heard of that address.' I didn't even know that street existed.

'Would you please hold the line?'

So it turns out that the previous owners of the insurance company got my address wrong and there's nothing I can do about it because – well, hey – it's my responsibility to renew my insurance. Fuck.

I call Mum at work.

'Michael?'

'I hit a cyclist!'

'Is he okay?' She sounds as shocked as I feel.

'She's fine.'

'What happened?'

'I was just pulling out of your driveway and I hit her.'

'You were turning right?'

'No. Left.'

'Left?'

'Yes.' There's a pause from Mum. 'Was she on the wrong side of the road?' It's my turn to think about it. After a few minutes I realise that she in fact was on the wrong side of the road.

'She was American, so maybe she didn't know?'

'Well, Mike, it would have been pretty obvious if all the cars were going the other way.'

'I guess so. So it's her fault.'

'Well, the important thing is that she's alright.'

'Yeah, she's alright, but my windscreen is fucked and I don't have insurance.'

'You don't?' She doesn't even notice my language. I explain about the insurance company fuck-up.

'Well, I guess you just need to get it fixed then. Call some of the companies in the Yellow Pages. Get quotes.' Mum is always making sure we don't get ripped off. Sure enough the first company I call, a big national one, quotes me $460 and say they can't do it 'til Monday. Today is Friday and I am in major need of a good surf this weekend. They say it will be a couple of hundred extra dollars if they do it in the weekend. Fuck that. The second company is a local one and the guy takes pity on my lack of insurance. $340. A much better deal, and they'll do it tomorrow morning. Perfect. Okay, so it's hardly been a perfect day, and I still have to spend a few hundred bucks, but it's still a much better deal.

The more I thought about it, the more it pissed me off. What the fuck was she doing on the wrong side of the road? Did she have a death wish? Why do I have to deal with the consequences?

I don't have her contact details, so I make sure I'm at Mum's on Monday when she said she would pick her bike up. I guess I still feel kind of bad because my anger disappears as soon as I see her.

'I got my windscreen fixed,' I say.

'Oh good.' I'm glad she is still alright and has no serious injury, but I really think she should pay for it, because if she wasn't on the wrong side of the road, none of this would have happened in the first place.

'Did you realise you were on the wrong side of the road?' I ask her.

'Yeah, I know. I was just going down the street to the coffee shop and I didn't feel like crossing over.' Well, that's just great.

'So how does this work?' She asks. 'We were both at fault so we split the cost? Is that right?'

Her accusing me of being at fault makes my blood boil, but I keep my cool. I guess she is offering to pay for half of the windscreen, which is better than nothing. I get her details so I can call her later and let her know how much it cost. I'm not prepared to have that conversation just yet.

I call her a week later. I ask how she is and express my relief that she's still alright. She says she just has bruises and her bike is wrecked. I tell her how much it cost to fix the windscreen and that I'm a student so it's a lot of money to me. I suggest that if she wants to make a contribution …

'No, you know. The way I see it, we both were wrong so we both have to pay for our own damage.' This really pisses me off. I try to explain that although I feel bad about hitting her, actually, she was on the wrong side of the road, so she was at fault.

'But you're supposed to look both ways before you pull out.'

'I was looking for the cars and the traffic that were supposed to be there – not on the wrong side of the road.' I'm surprised I'm not yelling by now. 'An insurance company would find you at fault and ask you to pay.'

'Well, that's because they are just after money. I'm sorry. I have an appointment. Would you like to call me back later and we can discuss this?'

I'm over it. 'No. I've said what I needed to say. If you want to make a contribution, you can. That's all.' I'm still pissed off but I give up. Putting more pressure on her isn't going to help and I've wasted enough time and energy on this already. Of course I could take it to Small Claims court and win, but I've watched enough televised court cases to avoid subjecting myself to that crap. So I'm cool. I'm letting it go. Just watch me.

Elena

It's impossible to find a park, so I double-park, blocking a driveway. Surely no one will need to enter or leave in the next ten minutes. I'm in sight of the gates. I hear that familiar bell and watch as the swarm of children emerges and then disperses in various directions. I'm looking out for the familiar dark hair, tanned skin, cheeky smile, SpongeBob school bag. Where is she?

I watch a girl in a sun hat dragging her feet. Obviously not excited about what the rest of the day holds. She looks up and I realise it's Rosa. I wave and her face lights up.

'Hey. Want to come hang out at my place for a bit?'

'Sure!' Like it's Christmas. 'Will Malcolm be there?' She sounds more cautious.

'No, he's at work. Just us girls.' She relaxes and begins chatting excessively about the movie they're watching in school. She has that uncomfortability with men that I had as a child. I blame Dad for being a despicable human being. She's okay with Michael. John is a pig to her, taking out all his issues about being displaced as the youngest child, even though it's not her fault she was born.

'You looked sad when you came out, hun,' I comment as we pull into the driveway. 'What usually happens after school?'

'I wait for Mum for ages if she says she's gonna be early or I walk home and it takes ages and I get tired and then no one is home so I watch TV or play Sims.' I should have known.

I have been so absorbed in my own world that I didn't notice my little sister was suffering neglect as serious as I did as a child. As an older sibling you really notice when your younger brother or sister has it easier and the stereotype of the spoilt youngest child seems to often be accurate. Rosa has a lot more stuff than I had. Mum spends more on her clothes and presents, she buys her DVDs and games. Mum didn't have any money when I was a kid, so I suppose, now that she does, that is to be expected. Rosa doesn't have to live with Dad, either, which is a bonus. She doesn't have to listen to all the arguing, she only has to see him on holidays. When we all lived together it was a nightmare. She doesn't have the nuisance of younger siblings either – that's a definite bonus. My childhood would have been a whole lot easier without John and Michael.

I let Rosa into the house and she looks around, remembering we don't have a TV.

'Can I go on your computer?' she asks, the default of any bored child of the technology age. I try not to judge. I was exactly the same, except I was playing Sonic the Hedgehog instead of Second Life. I'm probably still the same, escaping into the net to avoid my relationship dramas, my family dramas, my friends being too busy with their own lives to hang out with me, my lack of meaningful paid work.

'How about …' What can I possibly suggest? 'We walk down to the greengrocer and buy cherries and then I will French-plait your hair.'

Rosa's eyes light up like Christmas again.

John

Every morning is the same. There's the loud knock on the door.

'Get up!'

'Fuck.' Milking time. I'm out of bed with my gumboots on before I've really thought about it. It's too early to think. This is more like sleepwalking. I take the quad down to the shed and go through the motions – put the cups on, take them off – watch out for the mighty shit that pours out of a cow's ass. Stay out of the way of their hooves. Such a big, dumb animal, but they can really fuck you up if you get on the wrong side.

I have to say, this is better than school. What does that tell you about high school? Probably nothing you didn't already know. At least here I get some money – even if it's piss all. At least I'm not in a stupid classroom with a twat teacher all day.

Michael can piss off with his lectures on uni – about expanding your mind and getting somewhere in life. What would he know? He studies sports. I'm doing something useful. Something real.

The farmer's wife, Lou, makes real food – roasts, steak, bacon and eggs. It's not like at Mum's where everything's low-fat except when Elena's around. I haven't heard from Elena since I've been here. I don't care. She's a know-it-all bitch anyway. People like her shouldn't be allowed to breed.

After milking there are always more things to do: fences to fix, feed to dish out, animals to move.

Bill says he will help me to get a hunting dog so I can take her pig hunting. We went out last weekend and Bill's favourite pup got mauled by a boar. Had to put her down – two thousand dollars down the drain – but we got the pig in the end. It was a good weekend.

Sometimes I think I was born in the wrong family. I've never liked town, all I've ever wanted to do was go hunting and fishing. Do real things, not just read books and learn maths and study bullshit that I won't ever need in the real world. The world that human beings have made is just a delusion full of wankers. It's just built to make the weak feel better about themselves. I see right through it.

Michael

I open my eyes to the brightest sunlight. It's warm but I can tell it's still morning and some kind of tropical scent blows through the mosquito net on the door. Gorse flowers and magic. No matter how much I'm hanging out for it, summer always sneaks up on me. I'm on the phone to Dave before I even know it.

'It's tiiime.'

'What's the tiiiiime?'

'Parteeeeeeeeee tiiime.' I've got to cut loose before I have to face the whole family for Christmas. They don't understand – but then again, neither do my mates. Everything is coming together now. I can see the future lighting up in front of me. Everything is finally making sense in a way that I can't even explain, but I know it has everything to do with Māui, and everything to do with me.

Valerie

The smell of roasting turkey wafts through the house. I wonder how this Americanism came to be part of our family tradition. Certainly there was no turkey when I was growing up. There was ham or pork, maybe lamb. It must have been Caleb, his obsession with department store hire-purchase deals that came with a free festive turkey, that started it. The thought makes me want to call off the whole thing. I'd rather not think about him today, although he's bound to show up to see his kids. I take another swig out of the flute in my hand. The bubbles tickle my nose and make me smile involuntarily.

I can hear Rosa chattering away to Malcolm in the computer room about her new video game. They've been getting on famously since Elena miraculously started picking Rosa up from school and having her until I finish work, a practice that both alleviates my parental guilt and gives her practice at caring for a child. Elena is in the kitchen, mashing potatoes. She thinks I haven't noticed the horrendous amount of butter she's put in. She brought two blocks – that's a whole kilo! I bet she will try to feed us all of it before the day is up. She may be eating for two but the rest of us aren't.

Christmas should really be about Jesus but in our family it's about getting through the day. The first time Caleb left was on Christmas day when John was a baby. He took off after I yelled at him when he turned up empty handed after a hard night of 'Christmas shopping', reeking of the familiar TAB, beer and cigarette cologne. Needless to say, it's an anniversary I'd rather forget. The champagne cocktail I just downed has added a certain jolliness to my mood. I swagger into the kitchen to pour another one. It's a long-standing family tradition to get through Christmas by consuming liberal amounts of alcohol. The combination of cherry brandy and bubbly goes straight to my head.

'Too bad you can't have one of these,' I say to Elena's back. She jumps, she must not have noticed my grand entrance. She's trying to conceal that she's already used half a block of butter.

'I'll probably need one by the end of the day,' she laughs.

'Have you thought about Evie?' I gesture to the golden-coloured mash.

'Actually, I have.' She shoves a small bowel of boiled potatoes at me, seasoned with what I can only imagine is kelp salt and olive oil.

'That's very sweet of you, love.' I put my hands on her shoulders and feel her relax.

'Someone's gotta feed her up. Being vegan is no excuse for being emaciated.' Elena says and I smile. I know she's trying.

'You know, with the Down syndrome test …' Despite my mild inebriation I feel like I need to clear the air. Bad move. The mere mention of our little conflict brings the tension back to her shoulders.

'Yes.' Her voice is as rigid as her stance.

'I just want to say … you're right.' It's the easiest way – to blatantly placate – to wave the white flag. There is no use arguing with a hormonal, pregnant woman. I should know that. 'It's your baby, your choice. I respect that.'

Elena is hesitant. 'Thanks.' Her voice sounds odd, out of place.

'I was just worried about you – as any mother would be.' She should understand that.

'Thanks.' Her voice is more certain now, deeper and resonant. 'Thanks, Mum.'

I feel like we've finally made some common ground. It was that easy. All I had to do was admit defeat. I'm reminded of what Michael said the other day. *You're always right, Mum – you always have to be right.*

I can't even remember the conversation. It doesn't matter now anyway. I grab a bowl of cherries from the kitchen counter and carry them through to Mum on the couch, who's watching an old Christmas movie on TV.

'Ta, Bub,' she says. Needless to say, she's the only person in the world who calls me Bub – the most hideously unsuitable nickname for a middle-aged GP.

I do the mental list. Michael should be arriving soon with John and Evie. It's the first time she's come for Christmas. My sister, Claire, and her partner, Maurice, will be here later. We have nothing in common. They're obsessed with car racing, rugby, golf; well, any sport really. I've never had time for watching sport. They got on famously with Caleb. Maybe they will turn up at the same time as him and entertain each other. One can only hope. I remember I've misplaced my cocktail and go in search of it.

The front door bursts open and Michael comes in, armed with

presents. There's something not quite right about him.

'You're drunk,' I say. He's swaying like trees in a breeze.

'Nah. Just had a couple of beers.'

'You were driving.'

John is standing in the door way. 'I was driving.'

'You drove all the way back from the farm? You don't have a licence!' I'm so full of surprise I don't even know if I can fit any anger in. I put my hand up to my forehead. I need another drink.

'Where's Evie?'

'Whadaya mean?' Michael hiccups.

'You were supposed to pick her up after you got back from the farm.'

'She'll be fine.'

'I don't believe you! This is the second time you've forgotten to bring her. How can you be so irresponsible?'

'She's not even family,' Michael slurs.

'You invited her.' I want to say she is family, or as good as. Obviously he has no idea what she's been through and I can't tell him.

I instinctively move closer to Michael and soften my voice, 'Look, sweetheart.' This is mother's magic. 'I'm really worried about Evie. She doesn't see her family. No one should be alone on Christmas.'

'She's got plenty of friends. She's at Tara's.'

'I'll get her.' John's out the door before I can stop him. Michael runs after him. They've taken off in Michael's station wagon before I get to the door. *Jesus, I know I'm supposed to be celebrating your birth, but what is going on with my family?* I look up at the sky and wait for the answer. *Have faith.* It echoes, heavenly, in my mind.

I feel Elena put her arm around my shoulder. She passes me a strawberry daiquiri.

'I figure if I can't drink I might as well make the cocktails,' she chortles. 'John will be fine, Mum. He is the most cunning of all of us. If he can't take care of himself there's no hope for any of us.'

'Did I do that?' I wonder aloud. 'Did I just get my drunk son and my underage, unlicensed son to get back into the car?'

'No, Mum. They have their own legs. You didn't carry them.'

I sigh. *Let it go. Have faith.* I let the cool, refreshing alcoholic strawberry ice drink calm me. After all, family is easier to tolerate with a little alcohol.

John

'Fuck. Pigs.' Mike sees them a mile off. It's like how they say bright insects are poisonous, tigers have stripes, the police have the blue and yellow patterned white sedans that give me that reaction. They're predators. I'm not scared. I just don't want to get into more shit. It's not right that I'm not allowed to drive. I can drive better than most people I know – a truck, motorbike, tractor. I'm probably the best driver I know of. I can drive Mike's station wagon better than he can. I just don't have the card that makes it legal.

'Fuck.' I'm not scared but I can feel my heart beating in my chest. It's nature. I need to pay attention. I need to relax. I can bluff my way through this. Easy.

'It's alright. I've got this covered,' Mike says, passing me his wallet as we pull closer to the check point. I roll down the window.

'Can I see your licence?'

I pull open Mike's wallet and flick the licence out. Mike is facing the other way, trying not to look like himself. Time has slowed down. The cop stares at the card. This is taking too long. We're fucked. We are their target market: young, male, a bit rough looking, at least we don't look too Māori. I could do without being drug-searched as well. The cop looks back at me and then back at the card. I try to stay calm.

'Please state your name and address,' he says, holding up a

breathalyser. I'm about to say my own name automatically when Michael coughs.

'Michael Joyce, 43 Rawhiti Road.' *It's gotta pass. I haven't even had one beer.*

The machine beeps and the light goes green. Sweet. He's about to hand me the card but he looks down again at the picture. This dude must have a sixth sense or something. The picture on the card was taken two years ago and looks more like me than like Michael, even if my hair is darker, but he knows something's up. His suspicious eyes gaze at Michael and so do I.

Michael's head is on a strange angle and his eyes look like they're about to pop out of his head. He pulls up his elbows and jiggles one back and forward. This is not normal.

'Are you alright, mate?' the cop asks.

'Tat tat tah,' Michael says.

'What's wrong with him?' he asks me.

'Oh, just a bit of autism.' I try to keep myself from cracking up, to keep my voice serious as if I'm almost offended.

The cop looks down and I see his face go red. Sweet satisfaction.

'Drive safe, gentlemen,' he waves.

'Merry Christmas!' Mike calls in a jolly voice as I pull away, as fast as I can without looking suspicious.

'That was fucking weird,' I say.

'Nah. Just my Jedi mind tricks.'

'Just your Jedi ability to look like a retard, you mean. We're lucky he didn't see through that bullshit acting job of yours.'

Michael cracks up. 'Yeah, you're lucky that picture was taken two years ago and I was clean-shaven.' Mike is talking too fast, probably because of the alcohol and the buzz of almost being caught.

'Lucky I shaved this morning and you've got some mangy pubes growing on your chin to disguise your true identity,' I say. Michael punches me in the arm.

'We'll go the long way home.'

I nod. 'That's the smartest thing you've said all day.'

Rosa

I'm bored 'cause Dad is on the couch watching golf even though it's the morning and he was here all night and he's asleep, but when I change the channel to cartoons he wakes up and grumbles and changes it back. He picked me up after Christmas and took me to Janine's house. She's at work and her kids are at their dad's house, which is good because they're annoying and pull my hair.

Christmas was better when I was younger. This year it was mostly just the grown-ups fighting and drinking alcohol. It was okay because I got presents. Mum bought me a new PlayStation but she wouldn't let me get *Grand Theft Auto* and John took his copy to the farm with the old PlayStation and Mum says it's way too violent and R18 for me to play and I liked to play it but not to be that violent anyway. I just liked to steal the cars and run away from the cops and stuff because it's exciting. Mum bought me *The Sims 3* instead which is a bit dumb because it's mostly just made up people in a house but it is also cool because you get to make up the people and the house yourself. Mine has a pool in the lounge and a fridge in the bedroom. But after I made the house and a lady who looks a bit like me when I'm old but like Barbie as well I got bored because she just needed to eat all the time and I had been playing for too long and I had to eat too so I stopped. Malcolm played with me for a while on Christmas which was cool. He doesn't like all the fighting either.

I go outside and sit on the steps and look at the grass with bugs in it. After a while ants start to crawl on my toes and it tickles. I wonder if Dad will take me to the beach later if I ask him enough. He will probably want to go fishing if the tide is right and the sea is flat. I stand on my tippy-toes to look at the sea. I can't tell if it's flat, it just looks blue from here. I got some new togs for Christmas. They have pink and blue polka dots.

Mum says that we don't pretend in Santa because Christmas is about Jesus being born but I think Santa is a bit better because he brings presents and Jesus is just a stupid baby but now he's really old and dead even though he came back from the dead at Easter and he doesn't look that old. I guess it's okay because I still got presents and I got to feel Elena's tummy kick because of the baby and I'm going to be an aunty when it's born but Elena says I can't call the baby 'it' because it's not a thing it's a human but she doesn't know if it's a girl or a boy so no one knows what else to call it anyway and I wonder why everyone has to be girls or boys anyway.

It was cool because Evie came to Christmas even though Michael was drunk and it made them all fight a bit. Michael used to be more fun and play with me but now he is acting weird, and he told me he is the carnation of Māui, like in the books at school, which sounds pretty crazy because carnations are flowers and I tried to tell Mum, but she is still angry with him and says she doesn't know why Evie puts up with him. Evie is nice to me and she gave me a little flute thing that I don't know how to play but she said her friend made it and she will teach me to play it if I like and it reminds me of Narnia and Mr Tumnus.

It was dumb because John came back from the farm and was mean to me. It's better when he's away because there's no one who's mean. John says if I wasn't born his life would be better and that makes me feel bad for making his life worse but it's not my fault that I was born, it's Mum's and she likes me most of the time.

Dad wakes up and goes into the toilet and shuts the door. I can hear him pick up one of the fishing magazines and I know it's going to take a long time. At least I can watch cartoons now.

Evie

Whenever people say, 'We mustn't be sentimental,' you can take it they are about to do something cruel. And if they add, 'We must be realistic,' they mean they are going to make money out of it.
BRIGID BROPHY

The Rainbow Gathering is tranquil by night. Just a bunch of hippies sitting around the fire making music any way they know how. I open the bottle, releasing its familiar kero fumes, pour the fuel into a jar and dip the wicks of my poi in, trying not to breathe too deeply.

I don't know where I fit anymore. It's sad that I was looking forward to having a real family Christmas but Michael was barely sober enough to talk. Val alternated between stressed and tipsy, and Elena was actually really nice to me for a change, which made me uncomfortable. It was awkward, but I guess that's what a real family Christmas is like. I don't know why I care anyway. It's sentimental bullshit. I'm not Christian by any stretch. I don't appreciate the capitalist holiday season; in fact I'd rather not do any of it. I'm glad I'm here now, with my rainbow family, even if I'm over the under-salted food and the hand-holding, song singing. Every day here I go through cycles of being more or less at home. This morning everything was beautiful. The sunlight sparkled off the creek surface enticing me to dive in. I embraced the refreshing rebirth. The low point of the day came when

Hemp, the most feral of us all, started telling me I needed to wear more colourful clothing and less black.

'I'll wear what I like, thanks, brother.'

But he was insistent. Too many egos here; just like anywhere else I suppose. Sometimes everything is perfect and harmonious, as it can only be in this beautiful forest with no 'electrickery' or junk food or meat; sometimes it's just a game of my tipi is bigger than your tipi. We pass the talking stick, we sit around the campfire, we workshop, we play our music and dance. Could I live like this all the time? I probably couldn't live like anything most of the time. Chaos is too much a part of me. I have to transform and grow. I have to keep running away from my demons because they're too terrifying to face.

The fire roars around me and I'm lifted to a different level. My poi loop in figure eights chasing each other, over my head, behind my back. I know people are watching but right now they don't exist. I don't even exist. Just this trance, this fire. The wick begins to gutter. My time is up. I swing the poi fast to put them out properly then collapse into the ground.

'That fuel smells noxious, man.' A tall guy with matted hair and a tie-dyed T-shirt calls out. 'What is that? Kerosene? It's not natural.'

Fuck it. I'm out of here.

Michael

All I feel is the beat, the bass, the rain …
Shaping me.
Transforming me.

Dubstep so deep it takes me over. My body becomes the beat, the base, the rain. I close my eyes and I'm alone in a world of darkness. I open them, I'm part of the crowd, all moving, contorting, swelling like the ocean. We are one human organism. I lose myself and find myself again, again, again. I don't remember the last time I ate. I'm starved. I wade through the puddles back to our campsite and grab a packet of salt and vinegar chips. They taste amazing. Matty comes up, soaked. He has this kebab he waited in line for half an hour to buy. He gives me a bite – that's friendship for you. It tastes delicious. I'm still starving but can't face the queues. I grab a ciggie off Matty and a V drink out of my backpack. That will stave off the hunger.

'Mix us some vodka in with that brew,' Matty yells. He pulls out an empty Coke bottle and we mix the V and vodka, half-and-half.

'That's out the gate.'

'Yeah, that'll sort you, Gov.'

Dave and his missus come back, wearing rubbish bags with holes cut in them. She looks pissed. He looks tired.

'Got the mean steez,' I comment on their stylish attire.

'We're gonna cruise back to Hamz.'

'Back to Hammies.' It's only New Year's Eve. It's not even dark yet. 'Sweet, Guv.' I shake his hand. 'Laterz.' That's what girlfriends do. I'm glad Evie's not like that.

I down the drink we just made and make another one for Matty.

'Gentlemen.' Nico is rising from his afternoon tent siesta just as the sun sets.

'You missed it, Grom.'

'Whaa?' He rubs his eyes.

'S'all ova, rova. Happy New Year.'

'What time izzit?'

'What tiiiiiem.' This is all part of our language.

'Nah, you're sweet, Killer. It's only nine o'clock.'

'Shut the frickin' gate.' Nico is easy to bullshit when he's still half asleep.

'Crack the beers.' Matty brings out a box of Steinies and passes them around.

'Cheers, Govna.'

'Trumps.' This is the best thing about summer. Not the festivals or the music. Just the time with the boyz, and this feeling that time doesn't really exist. Only the colour of the sky tells us that any time has passed at all. We could be doing this all day – and we do. Matty starts telling us this exaggerated story about his experience out in the crowd while the first DJ was playing his set.

'I went flying – ten feet into the air.' We crack up.

'Serious. True story. You should have seen the size of this guy.' This is one of our pastimes. Nico joins in with one of his stories from last New Year's. It's even more ridiculous than the last time.

'Where's Jake?' I ask. I'm sure we are camping with more people than this.

'Oh, Gov. He's chasing hornets.' Our word for hot chicks.

'The usual,' I sigh. 'Bet he gets stung.'

This set is sounding good. It won't be long 'til we're back amongst it. Swimming in the music. I sit back in my folding chair and feel the base pulsing through me like fuckin' destiny and it's here – now. It hits me right in the chest like my life spreading out before me – everything past condensing into now … Everything in the future reeling me into my own legend.

Malcolm

I fold up the newspaper, finish the dregs of my latte and look out across the campus. A dark-haired girl walks towards me carrying a pile of books. Ironically it seems out of place at a university. These days electronic journals are all the rage, but that's not why I'm paying attention. For a moment I thought it might be Kim, and even though every shadow of doubt has been removed – this woman is too curvaceous, too much make up, her clothes are too mainstream – I keep watching until she gives me a strange look. *Why is it not polite to stare at people?* Because it feels awkward to be stared at, I suppose. It's the golden rule: Do unto others.

Technically, she's not my student anymore – that role ended when the trimester ended months ago. So why is it so wrong that I can't stop thinking about Kim? Well, there's the small matter of my pregnant girlfriend, of course. I feel terrible, but Elena has lost all interest in sex, she's lost all interest in me and everything other than her stupid blog. It's like this pregnancy has taken over her body and all her other energy goes into feeding this child, this child that is also mine. I feel trapped. Yeah, typical male, I know. I should suck it up. I've been watching Kim's Facebook all summer; her status updates about crazy parties, the pictures of those parties and camping trips, messages her friends write on her wall. She's not likely to be on campus. She's about to go to a big music festival where they play young-people music, which I probably don't understand anymore, being thirty-five and clearly over the hill.

I love Elena. I do, but there's something missing from my life at the moment and it's freedom. It's like when people get married, which I don't ever want to do because it's an expensive and silly outdated ritual about property transfer, and Elena is with me on this. She would add, 'And, honestly, how can you make a promise about the rest of your life when you don't even know who you will be in ten years' time, let alone who the other person will be.'

Anyway. At least when people get married, incorporated into that ritual is this one last night of freedom where you get to go out and get drunk and dance with strippers. If you get your girlfriend pregnant, which wasn't exactly accidental, there's none of that. You just get on with it.

I do want to be a father. I don't want to miss out on that. I feel like it's every parent's responsibility to provide their child with a more interesting and less damaging childhood than their own, so that, as a species, we are actually evolving. Basically, I want to be a good dad. I'm not a prick, even though I know it sounds like I am. I just feel my life closing in on me; my options becoming more limited, my youth disappearing before I've really had a chance to enjoy it. I was always studying, married to the university, as Elena says. I've got a few close friends, Rewi and Jim who I've known since high school, who've both travelled and let loose a lot more than I have. I suppose freedom is one of those 'nothing' things, like air, you barely notice it until it's not there when you need it. I don't really know what I want. I just don't know how long I can put up with things as they are, and I have a feeling it's only going to get worse.

197

Elena

It's such a hot day that I can barely breathe, barely move under all this weight. Summer is the worst kind of punishment for pregnant women. Malcolm's car is like a Sauna. Henry is in the passenger seat babbling incessantly about some conspiracy theory thing he's into but I can hardly concentrate. I park, badly, and attempt to climb out, hefting my bulbous belly upwards and squeezing through the gap the car door allows between my car and a more expensive looking one. I'm finally free. I slam the door behind me and simultaneously feel a trickle running down my leg. Panic. Is this a miscarriage? It's a public place, I can't very well lift my skirt to find out. Breathe. I bend over and run my hand up my leg 'til it reaches the trickle. It's clear. Sigh. Just sweat.

'God, I'm sweating so much I thought it could be my water breaking.'

Henry laughs, totally unaware of my brief anxiety and how awful the situation almost was in my mind.

Straight through the door I notice a 'healthy options' magazine with a cover claiming to expose the sneaky places that bad fats hide and for a moment I wonder whether they've finally got it right. Alas, page twenty-two reveals only information about saturated fats.

'You expect too much,' says Henry.

'Maybe one day they'll catch on,' I sigh. 'Or maybe I'm just a crazy conspiracy theorist.' Henry pats me on the shoulder.

'Being your best friend and knowing you as well as I do, I have no doubts that you're crazy …' He links his arm through mine. 'But that's more to do with the way you arrange your soft toy collection than it is to do with food.' I gently push him away.

'Leave the toys out of this!' We get to the second aisle and I put back the bags of chips as Henry tries to place them discreetly in his basket.

'I take it back – you are crazy when it comes to food!' Further down the aisle I'm examining the cans of coconut cream, wondering what it was I read about cans recently … was it the plastic lining that had something … BPAs? I scoff at the cans of 'lite' coconut cream just as a small woman with short hair bends down and scoops one up.

'What on earth is the point of buying lite coconut cream?' I ask Henry, rather loudly.

'It has less fat in it,' the woman responds.

'What about your fat soluble vitamins?' I ask her, not sure whether I'm actually trying to pass on information in this brief encounter or just soothe my own ego.

'There's plenty of other places to get them from,' she says with a wink and she's off, down the aisle to drop soft drinks into her trolley. I scope out its other contents and notice margarine, packets of chips and other heavily processed foods. Not a lot of vitamins where those come from.

'Get off your bloody soapbox, love. Let the woman shop in peace!' Henry nudges me.

'It seems so counter-intuitive!' I say in exasperation. Henry, still beside me, pats me on the shoulder again. I don't mind his patronising affections.

'This is what our ancestors thrived on! Yet, everyone today is worried about saturated fat. I don't get it! The islanders who eat their traditional diet of coconut and fish aren't the ones on the cardio operation waiting lists, it's the people who eat modern food – these are modern epidemics. Has the whole world gone mad?' I do my best Gomez Addams impersonation. Henry comes out of his trance to converse with me. 'We know that it's the trans fats that are really dangerous, but it takes the pleb population a while to catch up.'

'Your alienating language doesn't help,' Henry smirks.

I poke my tongue out at him. I find the coconut cream with the most fat content and, realising that this is actually a food that Evie and I can both eat, I pick up an extra can. It's strange that there are such vastly different versions of ethical eating.

I studied ethics at uni. That was how I met Malcolm. He was my tutor in first year. I liked to watch him pontificate about the virtues and downfalls of various moral approaches. I liked the way his eyes would light up when he was passionate about something, and the way he would tousle his dirty blond hair. I got to the point where I would think about him more than my papers and I decided to do something about it.

I used to fantasise about meeting him at the café by the lake, by chance. I would make a fascinating comment about the book he was reading and we would get into a deep, meaningful conversation which would inevitably lead to more.

It just so happened that I stumbled across him one day, on

a good hair day, when I had a break between classes. He was exactly where I had imagined him to be and it gave me shivers. I almost walked straight past but then I figured that I had put all this energy into dreaming up this situation, it would be a shame to waste it. I walked closer to him with some kind of electrical current running through me. He looked up just as I was about to walk right past him and our eyes met.

'Hi, Elena,' he said, with that lazy smile on his face. I was stumped. I didn't think he would remember my name outside of class.

'Hey,' I said, trying to sound casual. I had come to a standstill and was fidgeting with my folder. I looked down at his book and realised I couldn't make a witty comment. It was Sudoku.

'Oh,' I said. Too loud. Half surprised, half disappointed.

He gave me a quizzical look. I looked down and blushed.

'It's just that … I can't do those.' I gestured to his book. 'I'm no good with numbers.' I felt incredibly stupid. Everyone else in the known universe could do Sudoku.

'Sure you can,' he said. 'Pull up a seat.'

And so he became my impromptu Sudoku tutor.

'It's not maths or anything, the numbers are just symbols.'

I nodded.

'Each line and each box can only have one of each number, so you can eliminate the numbers that can't be there, based on the numbers that already are.'

I messed up my first two attempts. But I gradually figured it out and I gradually figured *him* out. He really liked to teach.

The next time I saw him outside of class I had questions ready about my essays, about the philosophers we'd studied and others we hadn't. It got to be a habit, talking to him by the lake. He always seemed to be there. And then one day he asked me if I wanted to go to a film – it was part of a film festival, in French, subtitles, something about philosophy. I hardly remember it. My heart was beating so fast with all the possibilities of union or rejection. I could hardly believe my plan had worked, or that he would be interested in me, a naïve undergraduate.

One date turned into movie night every Thursday – holding hands in the theatre progressed, ever so slowly, into snuggling on the couch at his flat or mine. I felt, the whole time like I was holding my breath, waiting, never certain if he actually liked me or was just passing the time. What was he waiting for? One night, after we had driven out into the country and drunk a bottle of apple wine, sitting on the bonnet of his old Volvo, I summoned the guts to ask him.

'Me?' he asked surprised. 'I was waiting for you.'

Gayle

'Nan, have you heard of attachment parenting?' Elena asks as we sit on my deck eating roast beef sandwiches made with her home-made sourdough bread which is very tough to chew, especially with false teeth. It reminds me a bit of my Māmā's rēwana bread. She has driven out here for lunch without Malcolm. Something's not right with them. I can almost hear the warning bells ringing.

I listen to my granddaughter's sweet voice as she talks about baby slings and never putting them down – about sleeping in the same bed with them and leaving them on the breast 'til they get sick of it. She has her work cut out for her. She's handing over her life to the child and he probably won't thank her for it for a very long time, if ever. Something about her kaupapa makes sense, even if it's not the way I raised my babies. It's more like the way I was raised.

I thought I was doing the right thing at the time. But the more I think about it, in my old age, the more guilty I feel. Then I just have to let it go. I know the guilt's not going to do an old woman any good. I raised my children in the way I was told to by the Plunket nurse. I breastfed every four hours and didn't cuddle them in between, even though it hurt me to let them cry. I weaned them and switched to bottles when they were six weeks old. I made them sleep in their own cots because I was scared they would get cot death in our bed if Charles or I rolled over on them. I always followed the doctor's orders and now my oldest daughter is the doctor and I'm not sure if I can keep following orders anymore. It probably doesn't matter what an old lady like me thinks or does. The world has this way of forgetting their elders.

'Can you pass the salt, love?' Elena looks at the salt as if there's something wrong with normal table salt but doesn't say anything, just like I don't say any of what I'm actually thinking to her, because she doesn't really want to listen. Most people don't want to listen they just want to be heard. She wants my approval. I nod every now and then and she smiles at me gratefully. Valerie would argue. Elena needs reassurance from me.

The more I think about it, the more I treasure my own childhood. I think back over those old memories, my earliest ones, and I remember the feel of my mother, her warmth, as if I was always near her. I think I was. I remember she was always around, always there, always with a baby on her breast and a toddler on her lap. I think we all slept in the same bed until I was ten. It might sound strange to you, maybe even wrong, but I guess that was just life on our marae. Mum used to say we were lucky to have a bed. When she was a kid she slept on a mat on the floor with the rest of her family. I don't remember ever feeling lonely, not in the whole time I was growing up. The first loneliness I remember was after I left and moved to town. I was sixteen, working at the button factory. It was during the war and buttons were in high demand so we worked twelve-hour days but even so, when I got back to my cot in the boarding house, I was alone for the first time in my life.

Elena is still nattering away and I nod every now and then while my thoughts drift back in time. Those evenings seemed to drag on and on and I was so homesick, I actually felt physically sick. That was probably why I married Charles so young. When I met him I felt that loneliness lift, I felt connected to someone. I was at the post office, sending money from my wages home to the whānau, and I bumped into him, literally. He had his leg in a cast and I felt sorry for him, especially after I had bowled him over. I helped him up and we started talking. His eyes lit up and I felt this magical feeling come over me. It probably wasn't very sensible, but we thought we were in love.

After we got married we moved into a suburb in West Auckland. I was so proud to live in our own house. All the houses looked the same and all the gardens were neat and tidy. It was so different from the marae where I had grown up. I had no one to talk to all day and I hoped and prayed for a baby to keep me company. Unfortunately, when my babies did come, they weren't very good conversation. I spent my days gardening, cooking, cleaning and changing nappies. I spent my evenings ironing, bathing my babies and soothing them to sleep in the rocking chair. That was the only time I broke the rules. In the evening I would cuddle them and rock them, just so they would get to sleep and we would all be better for it. Maybe that was one thing I did right. I'm not sure anymore.

Michael

My car rocks along the gravel avoiding the pot-holes. I've driven this road so many times I barely have to think about it. I have enough on my mind. Evie is hiding something from me, I can tell. I don't know what it is, but I have the feeling everyone else knows except me. I hope it's not some serious medical thing. I just wish someone would let me in on the big secret. It makes me nervous. Then there's Dave. I see his red hatchback as I pull up outside Nan's house. I feel weird all of a sudden. I know I shouldn't. He's been staying for a while since his missus kicked him out. Nan says she doesn't mind. She likes the company. It's fine. I walk up the steps to the house, ducking under the fern fronds as usual. I hear laughter but I know something's wrong. I open the door and see Dave, red T-shirt, in the kitchen with his back to me. He's telling the joke he always tells about the nun and the monk that goes on for ages and he can never tell it without laughing. Nan is laughing too from over on her chair and even though I know the joke I'm left out.

'Dave,' I say, my voice is probably stronger than it needs to be. He turns around.

'Hey, Mike.' He's smiling until he sees my serious expression.

'Sup, Gov?' he asks, but using our words won't help.

'I need to talk to you,' I say. What do I need to talk about? I need to let him know that it's not okay. It's wrong. Everything's wrong. That doesn't make sense. I'm tired. I rub my eyes. Dave goes up to my room and I'm left in the kitchen with Nan.

'What is it, boy?' She knows. She knows something is wrong. Of course she does. She's wise. I need to get her back on my side.

'Nothing,' I lie, and she knows it. Why did I have to do that? She nods and I walk out the door. The sunlight is so bright, the cicadas are deafening. I must have left my sunnies in the car. I'll get them later. I get up to my room. As soon as Dave sees me he shoves his hands behind his back. I know he's hiding something.

'What is it?' I demand.

'What?' He looks freaked out.

'Show me what it is or get out!' He stalls. I duck behind him in time to see a little white packet.

'P. You had P at my house. Get the fuck out of here!' He looks shocked.

'It's not.'

'Just get the fuck out.' I push him and he moves back towards the door. 'I never want to see you again.' I watch his red T-shirt disappear down the steps. What a relief. Now everything is finally falling into place.

Elena

This morning Malcolm has left for work early. I stay in bed, enjoying the cosiness of its warmth in comparison to the frost outside. Serah nudges the door open with her nose and prowls into the room, her tabby fur is ruffled from her night outside, Malcolm must have let her in as he left. She springs effortlessly onto the bed, mocking my diminishing mobility.

She is silent as she investigates me. She creeps up to the top of the bed and I hold the covers open and let her in. She snuggles up next to my thighs. It's been a while since she's done this, she is still adjusting to the move. Her purring is soothing. It continues to lull me like ocean waves until a car backfires in the street and startles her. She climbs out, ears raised in attention.

'Go catch a mouse,' I say, letting my hand brush her soft fur as she walks away. I lie in bed for a few minutes more, in the vain hope that I will get more sleep. Eventually I give up and go out in search of breakfast. My life has become so simple, so easy and yet confined. I spend most days at home, reading, blogging, resting. I sit in the garden, I prepare food and eat it, I drink copious cups of peppermint tea. I text Henry and ask him to visit me. Occasionally I go out and shop, I sit in cafés, catch up with friends, see movies. I don't drink and there's not much socialising I can do at night. Most evenings Malcolm and I sit in and watch TV, sometimes we hire a movie or copy them from the hard drives of friends. We buy box sets of the shows we like, his sci-fi and my comedy and the occasional drama. Malcolm wants to get into his collection of *Babylon 5* but I'm hesitant; he gets mortally offended when I laugh at it in all its space soap opera glory.

Zena, my midwife, comes this morning. She hugs me when she arrives and I feel momentarily self-conscious.

I never wear perfume, not even deodorant. Malcolm teases me but he also says he likes the way I always smell like a French pastry. If I eat too much starch I end up smelling more like a sourdough loaf, or worse, yeast wine. It is just another reminder that I need to be careful with what I eat. Zena doesn't seem to notice.

She checks my blood pressure and gets me to pee on a stick to make sure I don't have sugars or proteins in my urine. I can't remember what those things indicate but my levels are low. She asks gentle questions. She is a lovely woman, an old hippie with her drooping skirts and shawls in earthy tones. She's always wearing beads and her long hair hangs in silver dreads.

I enjoy the company, it breaks up my lonely day. 'I have been getting cravings,' I admit, a little guilty. 'For unhealthy food.'

'You just carry on with that wonderful healthy diet of yours and you will be absolutely fine,' Zena tries to reassure me.

I want to confess that my diet has been far from healthy for the past few days but I let her words comfort me instead.

'Is it normal?' I ask. 'I'm craving calories, I guess the baby needs energy, I just hope I don't have any deficiencies.'

'You know, every pregnancy is different,' she says gently. 'There is no real normal to measure yourself to, just in the same way that every baby is different. You'll know if there is something wrong.' She gives me a meaningful look and I nod. I know that it's true, I can tell this intuitively. My baby is healthy.

Malcolm and I are not married, which doesn't bother me but I think his parents would like us to be. Malcolm's mum, Theresa, pops over in the afternoon when I'm on my way to the farmers' market. I let her in and tell her to make herself at home. Big mistake.

She's always trying to help us. She buys sugary muesli bars and processed corn snacks that I can't and won't eat and leaves them surreptitiously in the pantry. She buys ghastly baby clothes with all sorts of frills and lace and peculiarly shaped designs. She offers to clean the house, something that I'm not enthusiastic about myself but feel strange about someone else doing, but I let her, partly in selfishness, partly in kindness. I allow her to help and she spends two hours vacuuming one room.

'I took the liberty of cleaning out the fridge,' Theresa says. I can tell from her voice she expects me to be pleased with her, but it just makes me slightly anxious.

I pull the door towards me and reveal the sparkling white interior. It looks decidedly emptier than it did this morning. Of course, she's thrown out my kombucha.

'Oh, that,' she says when I confront her, trying to censor my irritation.

'Something was growing in it, it looked vile.'

'It's supposed to grow! It's a culture.' I grit my teeth and watch her smile fade into the kind of mystified stare I'm starting to think she reserves for me and my eccentricities.

'Oh, sorry, Elena.' Her eyes are downcast and I realise she means it.

'You were only trying to help,' I console her half-heartedly, although I'm not sure she's understood the enormity of her mistake. 'It was quite hard for me to get it, I'll have to see if anyone I know has a spare kombucha mushroom.'

Now she looks truly repentant and I feel guilty. To compensate I google kombucha and give her some more information. At least this way she won't make the same mistake twice.

Tea and culture

Kombucha is a colony of symbiotic bacteria and yeast that is cultured with tea and sugar to produce a delicious beverage. When I first smelled brewing kombucha in a friend's kitchen I thought she was making vinegar – and if you leave it fermenting too long it does go quite vinegary, but I prefer to drink it earlier, when it's a bit like a ginger beer.

Kombucha is a fermented tea drink. To make it you will need to get some of the culture, called a kombucha mushroom, from someone who has it. All you have to do is add it to cooled, sweetened tea. I leave it out at room temperature for a week and then seal it and put it in the fridge. After a few days it starts to go fizzy. I think of it as a healthy alternative to soft drink.

Nourishing Traditions recommends Kombucha (despite usually warning against its two main ingredients – sugar and tea) because it's so good for digestion. It also contains B vitamins as well as glucuronic acid, which boosts the immune system and helps the body to detox. The caffeine also makes it a natural energy drink – much better than that yucky stuff you get in a can!

As I write I'm tempted to mention something snarky about my mother-in-law but I resist. Not that Theresa is interested enough to read my blog, I'd just rather not come across as bitchy. Blogging, for me, is about sharing information and building community through shared interests. I'd rather stay focused. I know if goes deeper than that. There is some part of me that clings to this one external part of my life that remains untarnished by personal grievance. If I can keep this pure and simple, and not weigh it down with all the emotion I'm drowning in every day, maybe I can hold my head above water. Maybe I can get through this.

Malcolm

Rewi gets up from the couch and stumbles towards the stereo, knocking three beers off the coffee table in the process. I feel so out of place. The music changes from AC/DC to Johnny Cash and gets louder as everyone joins in. I've been here so many times – at a party at my mate's flat. But now it's different. Now I'm different. I haven't been out in such a long time. It's just work, home, Elena, Facebook. That's my life right now. There's nothing else. But now I'm feeling guilty for leaving Elena at home and going out, even though she doesn't care. She'd rather be knitting or blogging or preserving or chatting to Henry on the phone. She doesn't need me at all. She never has.

'Beer.' Jim thrusts a cold green can at me.

'Cheers.'

'You finally been let out of the house?' He elbows me and chuckles.

'So it would seem.' I like to think my friends are too mature for sexist clichés, but they're not above any kind of ridicule. Neither am I: 'You finally put some Rogaine on your face?'

Jim scratches his attempt at a moustache, which looks more like teenage pubes.

'Movember is over, dude. Shave it off,' Rewi chimes in, exaggerating his drunken slur.

This is what I've been missing. Well, not really. Five minutes ago I was lost in a sea of drunken idiots, convinced I wasn't missing much, but now I can feel the love. It's emanating from Rewi dry-humping Jim's leg. Okay. These are my friends. This is how we roll. Sorry for being embarrassing.

'Loving the homoeroticism, guys – let it all out.'

I turn away from their stunned faces, laughing and walk straight into someone with dark hair.

'Malcolm?'

'Kim.' Oh God. What a surprise. I'm cool. Take a deep breath.

'What are you doing here?' we ask at the same time, the awkwardly attempt to explain, our words overlapping.

'These are my friends.'

'This is Sasha's 21st.' True. It is. I gave Rewi's little sister a bottle of expensive vodka and a ridiculous hat for her birthday. I haven't seen her since.

I can tell Kim is tipsy by the way she leans into me. I don't believe in determinism, but there's an air of pre-destination about this whole scenario. Maybe it's the beer going to my head. I take a deep scull and finish the can.

PART TWO

The storm

Late summer 2012

Michael

Lucky I didn't just clean my car. It would be coated in dust from the gravel road. I pass about six fat lazy-looking cows and pull up to the farmhouse. John comes outside with a beer.

'Hey.'

'Howzit?' I ask.

'Alright.'

I know it's not really. Dad told me that John's working fourteen-hour days for $200 a week. He's not even old enough to leave school so he doesn't have any rights. It's bullshit.

'I've come to pick you up,' I say. 'Nan's invited us to a pōwhiri.'

'Why would I want to go to something Māori when I'm not even a real one?' He's wearing his cheeky smile, so I know not to punch him for that comment. He's just trying to rark me up. I grab him by the shoulder instead – in a brotherly way – and then push him away.

'They won't let me leave.'

I have to get him out of here. This place is all wrong. I look up at the old pine trees. A cloud passes over the sun and everything looks like it could be out of a horror movie. 'Where's the boss?'

The boss is away for the weekend so I go up the hill to his dad's house instead.

'Excuse me, sir.'

'Hey, mate,' the old man says, grasping my hand, and I know he's someone to be trusted.

'Look, I've come to pick John up. There's an important family reunion. My grandmother wants him to be there.' I automatically know which lines to spin. The old man scratches his head.

'Oh, mate. Bad timing. We've just lost some milk.'

How do you lose milk?

'Wait a minute. I think I heard something about that – yes, I'm receiving some information about that right now. Yep. I'll sort that out for you.'

He squints at me. There's a moment where neither of us speak. I know this is where I have to stand my ground and wait for him to give way.

'Alright. You take the boy. Have him back before milking.'

'Yes I will.'

'What the fuck?' John asks, cracking up in the passenger seat as we take off back down the driveway in a cloud of dust.

'I'll get you back to work, if you want.'

'It's only a five-hour drive.'

'Is that all?'

'What's wrong with you, oi? You've lost it.'

'Nah. It will be sweet. You'll see.'

Gayle

I hear the wail of the karanga and watch as the manuhiri walk slowly onto the marae, stopping every few paces. Through the crowd, I catch a glimpse of my grandsons. I feel awash with pride at how tall and handsome they look, their young skin glowing with summer tans. Michael's face looks serious, John looks bored. Maybe he's too young for all this. I feel like I should be walking next to them but this is my marae, I am tangata whenua, and although they belong here by blood, they've never been here before. This is protocol. The men file into the front seats, the women sit behind. This is how Tainui do it. Michael and John are in the second row, behind the rangatira who will be the speakers. Old Hone, from our side, gets up first to speak. He talks about the land, the ancestors and current events. He welcomes the guests. He pays respect to the ancestors and to the recently departed and to the kaumātua who are with us. I watch Michael's face, solemn, taking everything in. His Māori has become quite good, he's understanding at least part of Hone's whaikōrero. The next speaker is from the manuhiri side, Erik Kingi. He's pale-faced and for a moment I think he's going to start speaking in Pākehā but his reo flows flawlessly. It's a song, this language, my language, with its even syllables and the absence of the harsher sounds that English is loaded with. It's earthy and strong, so full of reverence and life and movement, especially in this ritual of pōwhiri which is so much like a dance.

The whaikōrero echoes all around us, washing over everyone like water. He speaks of his ancestors, tracing his whakapapa back to common ground as he paces the marae ātea. He is from Pōneke and I feel as if I should recognise him, but I was disconnected from te āo Māori for so long, I feel like a stranger here, sometimes, even on this marae where I was born. My language is only just now starting to sound like it's really mine again. For a while it sounded alien, I had kept it so close to my heart, wrapped so tightly lest someone try to take it from me again, but the world has changed and I'm allowed my culture in a way that I once wasn't. My grandchildren can learn te reo in school instead of being punished for speaking it the way my generation were. My, how things have changed.

The next speaker from our side is Mataira Thompson. He's a cocky young man, in his late forties probably – but that's young to me. He likes to blow his own horn. I watch his oily black hair as he struts up and down like a rooster. He speaks of myth and legend, of Māui Tikitiki and how he tamed the sun, of how we must look to our leaders for greatness, of how the old must pass unto Hine-nui-te-pō and new leaders must rise in their place, brave enough to take on responsibility, with enough mana, and so on. It is obvious to me that he's talking about himself. The ladies in the kitchen told me he was going for a job in Pōneke and probably wants to impress Erik with his grand tales. I glance at Michael and am surprised to see his eyes are lit up with excitement. John is texting on his cell phone.

I look back to Michael and try to figure out what's so appealing about Mataira's whaikōrero. It must be the legends. Michael is so fascinated by those old stories of Māui.

Just as Mataira goes to sit down I hear the sound of a throat being cleared and look across to see Michael stand up. My heart begins to race. Everything seems to be moving slowly and I have the urge, pulling at my heart, to go to him, to cross the marae ātea and hold my grandson who is breaking protocol by interrupting the flow of speakers. He stands there, in front of all these kaumātua with much more mana than him and he opens his mouth. His voice is loud and clear and as it hits me I feel myself crumbling inside; every failure, every weak link, snaps and I feel tremendous grief for my family and what I wasn't able to give them.

Michael

Everything is falling into place. Pre-destination. That's the word. I don't know what's coming but I have this sense that everything happening now is meant to be this way. Something's coming and it's big.

I can see Nan looking at me. I know she understands. I know this is where I'm meant to be but there's something I need to do. Māui conquered the sun. Would he stand here and let this man wank all over his name? I have to say something. It takes all my courage to stand, to step forward, but the momentum gives me strength. I clear my throat and speak from my heart.

The whaikōrero flows out of me like a river meeting the ocean. I don't even know where it's coming from. It feel like my ancestors are speaking through me, so fast I can't even understand what they say. I look around at my audience. I see a mixture of fear and respect in their eyes. Nan looks shocked. Doesn't she realise this is for her, this is for our whole family. It's right. I know it is.

I sit back down, the adrenaline still pumping through my veins like after a surf or skate. I could get used to that. Something has shifted. The people around me move uncomfortably in the silence. The dickhead I interrupted looks really pissed. Oh well.

Gayle

The whakamā chills me to the bone. I've never felt so embarrassed. It was such a breach of protocol for Michael to speak. The kaumātua are all older, more experienced, well-respected members of their communities. For a little sprat to stand up and challenge one of our own – well, it was wrong. That he was my grandson reflected on me. I know I haven't lived a perfect life. I know there was something missing, something broken in my family, the way I raised my daughters, and that it's been passed on, like a disease, through to Michael. Now he's not the only one suffering.

When he kisses me on the cheek after the pōwhiri I want to yell. But I don't. It's something we can work through later. He doesn't even seem to realise what happened – how out of turn he was. I don't know how to tell him. John comes next. Even though he's never taken an interest in Māoritanga I can tell, from his eyes that he knows – that there's something wrong. I begin to realise this goes a lot deeper, and that it's something I can't fix. I better call Valerie.

Elena

As I walk in the gate I notice something is out of place. I see it out of the corner of my eye. The grey-and-black pattern that is so familiar to me. Serah. I don't recognise her at first because she's not really there. It might as well be a soft toy or discarded sweater lying on the grass next to the driveway. I don't have to check to see if she's breathing. She's never lay in that way, with her legs slightly sticking up. Rigid. I'm in some kind of shock and I can't deal with it. Not now. I walk right past and let myself into the house. I pretend I didn't see anything.

Malcolm's not home and I can't deal with this by myself. I've never had to. When I was growing up I had Dad to flush my goldfish down the toilet. When he wasn't around I had brothers who were old enough to bury my guinea pig before I even got back from school camp and then harass me about it. I don't know how to deal with death.

It doesn't feel real. I sit in the office and play Sudoku until my head hurts. Malcolm won't be home for an hour. I start to wonder if maybe she was just napping. I peek out from behind the curtains and snatch a glance at what I can see of her, in the same position.

I thought cats usually crawled away to die, under the house or otherwise out of sight. Maybe she didn't get a chance. She's too young to die of old age. I feel the dread creep up on me again. I have to deal with this. She is – was – my cat, my responsibility.

I go out the back door and stand in the sun. The grass is too wet to sit in. I walk around, winding my way between the sculptured figures. Perfect and whole. Never alive, never dead. That would be a safer world: constant, consistent, peaceful. I slowly make my way around to the front to face the mottled furry corpse.

Now I can see red mingled with the grey and white. She must have run out of our gate and been hit by a car and the driver had the decency to return her to our garden. I'm furious but it doesn't help. I picture her running out in front of a car, the tyres screeching before the thud. I picture a confused, alarmed guilty driver pulling over and using a plastic bag to move her somewhere less exposed, more dignified. I suppose I would do the same.

Maybe he, or she, knocked on our door and got no answer, contemplated leaving a note, but what's the point? There's nothing to say. 'Sorry' doesn't mean much to me now.

I get a shovel from the garden shed and begin to dig up a flower bed near where she is lying. I'll have to tell Malcolm when he gets home but I don't know what I'll say; I don't even know if he'll care – with his pragmatic indifferent utilitarianism. My rage flares again.

The earth is moist and soft from the previous week of rain. Tears stream down my face as I dig. I remember Serah as a tiny kitten, playing with my shoelaces, darting about the room in hot pursuit of Henry's laser pointer. I remember her prowling under the covers and then settling down, tucked in next to me, a purring hot water bottle.

It's not the same as losing a person, but it still hurts. I've still lost something precious. She's not in that body anymore. It's just the shell that she formerly animated. I'm too tired to dig anymore. The hole is barely deep enough but I'm panting and exhausted. In this sweltering, muggy climate I find my throat dry and raspy.

I can't bear the thought of shovelling her into the ground so I find a cardboard box of peaches in the kitchen that Theresa brought over. I tip them all onto the bench and take the box outside. I scoop her up with the shovel and place her, as gracefully as I can, into the box. I lower the box into the shallow grave and scrape the loose dirt back over it.

'Goodbye, Serah,' I say. It sounds wrong to say it to the grave. She isn't in there. I don't know where she is. 'You have lived a good life as yourself. You have been all you needed to be.'

And that was all I had to say.

The knock at the door startles me. The shadowy figure behind the frosted, dimpled glass is tall and sinister. As I turn the lock I wonder if the glass really protects me from sight or if it would be better to see and be seen. My pulse races as I pull the door towards me. I let out a sigh of relief to find it's only Michael.

'Can I use your phone?' He is stooping slightly, looking at me as if he'd rather not bother me.

'Hi,' I say. 'It's nice to see you too.'

'Wow, look at you,' he says, taking in the growing round of my belly. 'Hi, baby,' he says, with a warm smile, pressing his palm briefly to my navel as he walks past and I think, not for the first time, that he likes this unborn child much more than he ever liked me.

His eyes become serious again, 'I just need to make a couple of quick calls.'

'Sure,' I say, nonplussed. Michael hardly ever shows up here, I'm not surprised that he needs something.

He picks up the cordless phone and takes it out to the back porch. I hear his voice, muffled through the walls. He sounds more serious than usual. Angry.

When he comes back in I'm making tea in the kitchen.

'Do you want a hot drink?' I ask, out of politeness more than anything. I almost drop my cup when he accepts.

'Tea? Coffee? Cocoa? Herbal tea?'

'Coffee.' I vaguely remember he likes it with milk and lots of sugar. We don't keep instant in the house so I get out the coffee plunger and I see him tense slightly, as if he hates to burden me.

'It's fine,' I reassure him. He looks at me puzzled and then his eyes cloud over slightly.

'Yes,' he says. 'Yes, it is.' He drinks his coffee quickly and then he gets up from the kitchen table, restless. I watch him fidget with his pockets.

'Is everything okay?' I ask.

'It is. It will be.' He looks around the room, his gaze is anxious. Mine is inquiring.

'Have you seen my wallet?' he asks.

'No, I don't think so.'

He goes to the kitchen counter. 'I put it just here. Now it's gone.'

I'm a bit confused, because Michael only came into the kitchen a minute ago to have a drink. I didn't notice him near the counter. 'Did you leave it in your car?' I ask.

'No,' he says. 'I had it here.'

'Outside?' He retraces his footsteps and then returns to the kitchen and begins to pace in an agitated way.

'Do you want me to help you look?'

'No. It's fine.'

'It really isn't in your car?'

'No.'

I sigh at his stubbornness.

'I think I would have seen it if it was in here, Mike.'

'You think you would, but you'd be surprised.'

'Are you alright?'

'Yeah. I just really need my wallet.' He walks around the kitchen. 'Has anyone been here?' he asks me, casually.

'Malcolm was here earlier.'

'Malcolm – what would he want with my wallet?'

Now I'm really confused. 'He left well before you even came here.' I take a closer look at my little brother who towers over me. His eyes are slightly bloodshot, his hands tremble a little. 'Have you been smoking?' I ask. I don't mean to accuse him, I just wish he'd make sense.

'No. Not for ages.' But I can smell something on him. My enhanced pregnancy senses are picking up the sweet, familiar, herby scent. He shrugs. 'Was Dave here?'

'Dave?' I'm wondering why on earth his best friend would be in my house. 'Of course not. That's ridiculous.'

'Ridiculous,' he smiles, tight lipped, his eyes crinkle. 'You'd think so. But it's not.'

'What do you mean?' I'm starting to think we're on different planets.

'Never mind,' he says, and he's out the door before I can stop him.

The next few hours whir past in a blur. The phone rings and Theresa wants to know how I'm doing, how Malcolm is, and when we're coming around for dinner next.

'Dinner.' It reminds me I need to think of something to have tonight and get started on it. Malcolm is a terrible grump on an empty stomach. When he walks through the door my eyes are streaming from the onions I'm chopping and I suddenly remember Serah, which only makes me really cry. The tears wash away the bizarre discomfort caused by Michael's visit, and all the other tensions and worries from my mind leaving me present and clear again.

Valerie

'Val?' Walter, our only male receptionist pops his head into view through my office door.

'Yes?' I'm in between clients. He usually doesn't bother me with my messages until my break.

'There's someone on the phone for you. He says it's urgent.'

'Right, put them through then.' I briefly wonder what could be so urgent that someone would dare to ring me at work and suddenly I'm full of fear. *Is it one of the kids?* It's always the worst thought that comes to mind in these situations when only part of the information has been provided.

'Hello?' My heart is racing as I speak into the handset.

'Mum?'

'Michael. Are you alright?'

'I'm fine.' I exhale. Thank God.

'Mum, I need to talk to you.'

'I'd like that very much, sweetheart, it's been a while since we talked. I'm really busy right now at work. You know how it is here. Why don't you pop around this evening and I'll make us some dinner.'

'Yeah … okay.' He sounds alright, maybe a bit tired. Nothing serious.

Twenty-four hours later we're at the hospital.

Michael

Mum won't listen. No one will because no one understands. 'I've got to get out of here,' I tell her. I'm trying to spell it out real clear, to make it simple, because to tell the truth would be too much.

'It's okay,' Mum says, 'I'll take you home.' She looks worried and checks my head for a fever, but she doesn't know the half of it. I have to protect her. I have to protect all of them: Rosa, Elena's baby, the others. Even John can't save himself from what's coming.

On the drive back to Mum's I can tell they are watching. 'Faster,' I tell her. I try to grab the wheel – to trick them – but she pushed my hand away.

'Jesus, Michael! What has got into you?'

'Into me?' I ask, and then it hits me – they've gotten to her too. No one is safe. I have to get to Nan first. Nan will know. She understands the Wairua – the second kind of water, the spirit and soul that are the essence of everything. Evie knows too, that's why she won't eat animals or buy new clothes. She's outside the system. We have to stick together. Elena knows too – she knows it's all fucked, but her fuckin' boyfriend is one of them: the enemy. They system is killing us all, and if they find out about me and what I know now we might lose our only hope.

'It's okay,' I tell Mum. 'It's all going to be okay.' She doesn't believe me. They are too powerful, more powerful than I realised.

'Where's Rosa?' I ask.

'She's at the holiday programme,' Mum says, but that sounds wrong.

'No, she's not.' I tell her. Rosa knows, though. She's showed me pictures she draws of other worlds, of doorways into them. She understands because they haven't gotten to her yet, she might even know the greater truth – that this world is make-believe too – that we have all been brought here. It's a test and I know how to outsmart it.

Mum pulls into the drive and gets out of the car. I follow her inside, but I check first to make sure no one is watching. Just the birds, the birds are friends until they trick you – until they laugh. The house feels different.

'Let's have some tea.' Mum flicks on the jug but I can tell there's something wrong. When she leaves the room to go to the toilet I pour the water out of the jug. I rinse it out three times with fresh water from the tap and ten refill it before she comes back. I don't want to freak her out but I know they did something to the water. Who are they? You ask. If you have to ask that then maybe they've already gotten to you so you can't even see how fucked we all are.

Mum is back and pouring the water into cups, making tea. I hate tea but she probably can't remember because they messed with her brain. That's what I think until she passes me a Milo, just how Nan makes it. Just how I like it. My head drifts back to that night on the deck at Nan's and the story of creation, how it flew so perfectly out of my mouth, like magic. It's a sign. She's on our side still. They are going to hate this.

'We need to figure out the next step,' I tell Mum, because now she should understand.

'Maybe you could lie down for a while, love, and see if you feel better.'

'No!' that is not going to help. 'Hang on.' I close my eyes, I can hear a sound like the sea at Indicators, crashing waves, just waiting for me, or is it a trap? No. I tune in, deeper. 'Just hang on –' I say, 'I'm getting a message from Nan.'

'A message?' She is confused for a minute, but I can't waste my time. I keep my eyes closed and when I open them Mum is gone. I go to her room and she's on the phone, she's calling THEM.

'He's just acting very strange,' I hear her say, 'and I'm a doctor – I should know … yes … yes. Exactly … okay.'

'Exactly.' I say.

I look at Mum and I know it's too late.

'Michael,' she says gently, even though I know it's all a lie, 'Mikey,' she reaches out her arm towards me. 'Honey, we are going for a drive, okay?'

'That's just what THEY want you to do,' I say.

'We are just going to get you checked out at the hospital, and maybe stay there for a little while.'

'Exactly. Exactly. Kia ora,' I say. My instinct it to run but I'm so sick and tired of running. Running is what they want me to do, when I'm running away they think they have me scared. No. Time to face them. Time to fight. I look Mum in the eye.

'Ae.' I tell her, 'I will come with you, but you won't win. They will never win. You'll see.'

Māui was the original trickster. He would set up a whole situation, go to heaps of trouble, just so he could figure something out. One day he was staring at an open fire and wondered where it came from. All the fires in the village were lit from one another, but what was their origin? Only one way to find out – put them all out. The villagers were pretty pissed when he owned up to what he'd done. They sent him to Mahuika, the fire goddess, who also happened to be his aunty. His only real friends were the native birds, tūī, kererū, pīwakawaka – so they went along for the mission. When he got to the epic volcano that was Mahuika's pad he went in alone. She was a freaky chick, surrounded by fire with magical flames for fingernails. He told her all the fires had gone out in the village and she generously gifted him the taonga of her pinkie nail flame. On his way out of the volcano, Māui wondered what would happen if all the nails went out so he dropped his in the stream and went back, time and time again, making all kinds of excuses: 'A bird stole it,' 'The dog ate it,' etc. Anyway, by the time Mahuika got to the last nail she was mightily pissed. She threw the flame at Māui, who ducked, and it landed on the kaikōmako tree instead. So Māui grabbed some twigs and took them back to the village to show people how they could use this tree, imbued with the fire goddess's magic; how they could rub the branches together to make fire any time they wanted.

This is the story I tell to Mum in the car, but she doesn't get it. She doesn't see that I am the trickster, that this is all part of the game. She just looks worried. That's how I know that she is the one who has something to learn. I can't tell her, I can't show her. She always thinks she's right. She thinks she's in control. But things are just becoming clear to me now, and everything is about to change.

The double doors slam shut behind me and I realise the seriousness of the situation. I walked in here a free man and now I'm a prisoner. Mum did this. She brought me here. A loud moan comes from one of the rooms. A woman walks down the hallway with greasy hair, food on her shirt, her eyes are blank. This is a place for crazy people and I'm not crazy. I'm only just beginning to realise everything and this is some kind of test. I start to worry because I don't know what the rules are in this sick game they're playing. Fucking with my head. I realise I'm sane and I know they expect me to be crazy. I don't want to give them the advantage. I don't want them to think I'm wasting their time. I let my left leg relax and start dragging it behind me when I walk, I lean my head to the right. I hear Mum gasp behind me and that gives me a sense of satisfaction. After all, she's the one who brought me here. If it weren't for her I'd never be here at all. She just kept arguing with me. She never stops.

An ugly nurse takes me to my room. It's like a prison cell. Single bed, grey-blue bedding that matches the carpet and walls. It's all the same here. The first thing I do is look up. They don't even try to disguise the cameras. The blinking red light warns me that I am always being watched. I better put on a good show. Mum is standing in the doorway.

'It's okay, love.' I don't know what role she is playing in all this but I can't trust her. I can't trust anyone. She is the one who brought me here. I know she's scared of me. They all are. I know why, too. I know too much. I've figured it out. This is a test. There is something big coming.

I sit down on the bed and put my head in my hands. All the links keep going through my head. Dave – what does he have to do with it? He's been smoking P, or maybe that's all part of their big plan. They wanted something to set me off – to bring me here.

The nurse comes in with a pamphlet, *All About Psychosis*. I smile. This just keeps getting better. 'Feelings of superhuman power', it says. I laugh. I know I'm not a superhero. I'm not about to fly or attack anyone with laser vision. Mum looks worried so I start to read the pamphlet out aloud. Pausing after every word to make sure I know exactly what it means. I'm not going to let anything get past me.

'I know I'm not a superhero,' I say. I've never sounded so convinced of anything in my life. It would be funny – but I'm too serious for that.

'I know, love,' Mum says. 'Don't worry about that.'

'But it's not true. They're all wrong.' I wonder if I'm giving too much away. Being here is wrong. I need to be home. I need to be in the surf. But I have to play their game until they let me go.

Elena

It's 7:30am when I get the text message. I don't really want to check it. I think it's probably just Henry in one of his manic states. He texts me at all hours sometimes. I snuggle under the covers, tucking my knees behind Malcolm's. My phone beeps every five minutes to make sure I know there's a message waiting and after the second time I give in.

MICHAEL SICK. AT HOSPITAL. HENRY BENNETT'S.

My mind does a double take. The Henry Bennett Centre is the psychiatric unit. I know this because my high school was nearby and we occasionally had the pleasure of escapee patients masturbating naked on our school field.

Michael? In there? It's such a foreign concept to me and I try to figure it out. A suicide attempt could get someone admitted, maybe he's depressed or something. I'm frustrated that Mum doesn't give me more information.

What's wrong?

My fingers are so nervous they slip on the keys. Two minutes later I get a text back. This one I check straight away, my heart still racing from the first.

PSYCHOSIS

Her capital letters make it even more ominous than it would otherwise be. Her phone is so old that it doesn't correct the case for her. *Psychosis*. My mind spins.

Michael was fine. Wasn't he? How did this happen? I remember the wallet incident. He was so convinced that Dave had been at my house. That was weird. I'm out of bed, pacing the room.

'Calm down,' Malcolm says. 'It will be fine.'

His words mean nothing. He doesn't know anything.

'Can you take me to the hospital.'

'I guess.'

I know he doesn't understand. His family isn't that close. I guess ours isn't either. Michael and I aren't ever on the same wavelength but I feel it, when something's wrong it affects me, the way twins feel each other's pain, the way one appliance can blow the fuse for the whole circuit.

Caleb

Avoid, ignore … it's not easy, life is hard. That's how it is. The truck bumps along the gravel. *Stay awake.* But there's a clear stretch of tar-seal as soon as I hit the main road. I need to pull over, before it's too late. I was going to come down to see Rosa last week but Janine had a hissy fit and said her kids needed me more right now. When I got the call from Val I expected her to rip into me again about Rosa, but instead her voice was tight and quiet. It's not Rosa who needs me now, it's Michael.

Last time I saw Mike it was Christmas, he was cracking beers and jokes. Now he's in the psych ward and I'm panicking about what might be going on. My uncle had a serious mental illness. He was always babbling nonsense and I just can't believe that it could happen to one of my kids, least of all Michael. He's always been so happy and active with a chilled-out personality. The thought of him in psychosis is enough to keep me wide awake 'til the bright lights of Auckland and a servo coffee drags me the hour and a half from here.

Janine expects so much from me – more than she even tells me. It's always, 'Why weren't you?' 'Why aren't you?' 'Why are you?' It's never-ending. As if I don't feel bad enough for my first failed marriage, for leaving my kids, for failing them all the time even when I was around. This was supposed be easier: escape up north with a new woman to a new life. Start afresh. Get it right this time.

I scoff down a pie, also courtesy of the servo. Every hope that I've had has turned to shit, washed up downriver like a corpse. Every time I try, I fail. It doesn't stop me from trying.

My childhood was a white version of *Once Were Warriors*. Mum always had to work. She never had any time for me. My dad only ever had time to give me a hiding. My brothers and sisters were all in the same boat which is why we always picked on each other like a pack of wild dogs.

I've always looked to people better than me. Val with her med degree couldn't save me. Her parents never accepted me. When they guarantored our mortgage they made me sign a no-claims agreement, even though I did double courier shifts to help cover it. I have no claims, no rights. Nothing. I'm not feeling sorry for myself, just telling it how it is. I never had the opportunity to amount to anything, even though God knows, I've tried. It's all I ever do – try and fail – story of my life.

My kids are the only blessings even if John's dropped out of school and always getting into trouble, Elena won't talk to me and most of the time, when I have Rosa, all she does is whine that she's bored and hungry. 'Try having real problems,' I tell her. Try being nothing. 'You kids have got it good,' I always told them. Fed, clothed, educated, money for holidays and PlayStations. What I wouldn't have given for luxuries in my childhood.

I remember when I was about six our old Kingswood breaking down once when me and Dad were on the way back from his brother's place in Taupō. We were helped by a rich family in a new Mercedes. They took us to their house nearby. It was the first time I'd ever had a bed to myself, the first time I'd stayed in nice white linen sheets, in the guest room! I remember thinking this must be how normal people sleep every night, people that aren't poor like us, six kids to a dirty mattress on the floor with scratchy, mouldy wool blankets. Damp house.

If the pub in Taupiri is still open I'll pull over and have a break, have a beer, have a breather, maybe have a bet. You never know when it might be your lucky day. I get a twinge of guilt. Part of me feels bad that my son is in hospital – is crazy – and yet I'm thinking of gambling. That's probably Val's voice, years of hearing her complain anchored into my brain on some deep level. It didn't come from my childhood, that's for sure. Mum loves the pokies as much as Dad loves horse racing. Pokies are open late. Michael will be asleep by the time I get there anyway. He won't notice if I'm half an hour late. I look out into the distance but the pub lights are off. Disappointing. I should be used to that feeling by now.

Valerie

The sitting room is full of chairs that look like the ones in the waiting room at work, but this place has an atmosphere that you wouldn't want your young children exposed to. I can hear the hum of the air conditioning. There are strange noises coming from every direction, some people scream, others yell but the noises are intermittent. For the most part it's silent, they seem to lurk, these mentally ill people. It horrifies me to think that my son is one of them.

There's a man sitting in a chair on the other side of the room with his knees tucked under his chin. He stares at the TV screen but occasionally mutters things, and I don't know if he expects us to reply.

Caleb sits next to me but we hardly speak. We don't have much to say to each other after all these years. I wish he would go home to Nancy and let me be alone, but part of me would feel unsafe with these sick people all around. There's a girl who walks up and down the hallway, her eyes dazed. Two men are playing pool, one of them keeps repeating the same words over and over.

'Yeah, yeah, yeah,' he says, followed by, 'My son, my son.' Every now and then he says something like, 'Marr he pie terra.' It takes me a while to realise he's speaking Māori, but still I don't comprehend.

I can't believe my child is in here, with these people.

Thank God Rosa was staying with my sister Claire last night after watching the cricket with her cousins. Now she's safe at the school holiday programme, oblivious. I'm not looking forward to picking her up and having to explain all of this to her eight-year-old brain. 'Your brother is crazy.'

He really didn't seem crazy, not on the phone, but he showed up yesterday afternoon at the surgery. He'd never done that before. He walked right up to reception and asked to see me; he said it was urgent.

I'm ashamed to admit that I was angry with him when he came to me at work. I didn't know. I told him I was busy but he really didn't want me to go back to work. I left him in the staffroom with a sandwich and coffee while I went to see a patient, five minutes later he was knocking on the door of my office asking if I was ready to go.

It was about then that I realised there was something strange going on. He should have known better than to disturb me with a patient; he would have known better if he was himself.

I took the rest of the afternoon off. It's the first time I've done that. Even when the kids were sick, I always found a babysitter or got Caleb to stay home with them. I plan my time off meticulously.

I took him out to the car. I started the engine, not knowing where I was going. I just knew I couldn't stay there. What would my patients think?

Elena

It's creepy, this whole thing. When I arrive at the hospital I have to wander around for half an hour trying to find the building. It's modern, probably late 90s. The doors are closed and there's no one at the desk so I push the buzzer and wait for what feels like ages, while anxiety bubbles in my chest, until a woman walks out. I barely look at her, my mind is so overloaded, but I take the opportunity and walk through the two sets of sliding doors left open in her wake. The lobby looks like it could have been corporate offices or a hotel, but it smells sterile, which gives it that hospital feeling.

I take the elevator to the third floor and then wait at the doors to the ward for a nurse to come and let me in with her swipe card.

I hate institutions and this is the worst kind. In my passage down the long hallway I can hear strange noises, some angry, some unearthly.

I remember the social science paper that I took at university years ago. Society locks people up who are different, who are dysfunctional, who are unable to work. It you have physical symptoms then you see a doctor, a specialist; take some medication, have an operation. If your symptoms are not physical, if they can't work out what's wrong with you, they call it 'mental illness'.

Shame hangs, heavy, over the room. Michael is in bed, facing the other way. He looks smaller than usual, lying there with a sheet pulled over his body, like he's lost everything he once was. The gravity of the situation hits me.

'Mickey,' Mum says in her gentle voice. 'Elena is here, isn't that nice?'

'Yes,' He mumbles, nodding his head slightly. I'm relieved. Michael and I have never exactly been close.

Mum leaves the room.

'I need a haircut,' he says, reaching up to his slightly overgrown hair, passing his palm through it. 'Zoom,' he says.

'Okay,' I say. I didn't know what to expect, but this is bizarre.

Then he goes quiet. I sit there silently, resting my hand on my swollen belly.

'I'm here for you, Michael,' I say softly. 'If you need me.'

'Kia ora,' he says, his voice is hoarse, not his own. He sounds like an old Māori man, the kind you might see speaking on a marae. That makes me wonder if this could be some kind of curse.

Michael identifies as Māori. I don't. I don't need labels. I don't want an ethnicity. I make my own culture. I live it. It is about wellbeing and wisdom, friendship and sharing. This is what I want my baby to be brought up in.

'Hungry,' Michael says. Mum asks the nurse about food.

'Lunch is in twenty minutes. We can bring you some sandwiches.'

'Do you have any baked beans?' Michael has always loved baked beans on toast.

'No, sorry, we don't.' I have this strange urge to go out and get him some, bring him whatever he wants, in the vain hope that it will make everything better. It's the rescuer in me trying to come out, but I know there's nothing I can do.

The sandwiches arrive and I frown at them. So does Michael. Little triangles of white, processed bread spread thick with margarine and some watery tomato that looks like it's out of season (although it's not). Michael bites into the first one and spits it out.

'That's disgusting.'

I agree. I can't believe they feed these people, most of whom probably haven't been eating properly before they came in, this kind of crap. Surely there's a nutritional component to mental health. There is with depression, with most things. Why don't they start treatment with the basics, the solid foundations like food, sunlight and exercise … and community, the basic human needs. This is ridiculous. I'm so angry I want to cry.

'What do you want to eat, Mike? I'll bring you something.' Despite being pregnant and not having a car, I'm determined.

'Baked beans.' I look over at Mum, standing by the door. She shakes her head.

Dad is in the hallway ringing his hands. It's the first time I've seen him in months. He kisses me on the cheek and asks the obligatory greeting questions.

'I'm fine.' Whatever.

He seems anxious. I don't really care. As far as I'm concerned he stopped being family when he left us, and maybe a long time before that. In my teenage years all he ever did was yell at me. Mum said he was depressed. I think he was useless and still is. He tried harder with the boys, took them to sports games and fishing, but we never really had anything in common. He hated the way I argued with him and Mum; he hated the way I dressed and after a while I stopped seeking approval from him and focused on giving it to myself, instead. Now I'm apathetic. If he wants to pretend to be part of this family, it's not my place to stop him.

Dad goes out to get takeaways for lunch with money he borrowed from Mum. Michael is resting. Mum and I sit on the chairs in the waiting area and try to piece things together to make the world make sense again.

'He came to my surgery – he never does that,' Mum sighs, 'but it seems so sudden. I keep wondering how this happened. How did I miss the signs?' I can tell she is blaming herself. She always does this – even when she is blaming us kids she's also blaming herself for everything we do wrong at the same time. I make a mental note never to become this kind of parent.

'It's not your fault, Mum. Michael seemed really normal … well except for that time he thought he lost his wallet at my house. He got really paranoid.'

'That's it – that's what your Nan said too. She called me up the other day and told me he kicked his mate out of her house – you know, the one who was staying there … and she said something funny happened at the marae. Michael spoke out of turn or something. She sounded so embarrassed. She knew there was something wrong. She was trying to tell me. I should have realised!' Her face creases in pain and she cups it with both hands.

We sit for a moment in silence before Mum remembers more. 'Rosa told me there was something wrong – that Michael was being weird – so did John. Something strange happened at Christmas, I don't know what – and at the farm when Michael went to pick him up last week … Michael said he was receiving messages.'

Slowly the pieces come together and we realise we missed all the signs along the way because we had been so determined to make sense out of something that didn't – we'd explained them away.

Rosa

When the school bell rings I feel tired because my bag is heavy and I know I have to walk home by myself and it will be boring. I don't feel excited like the other kids. But at least school's over and I don't have to see any more bitches 'til tomorrow. I walk out the gate and then I hear a strange noise.

'Rosa!' I look over and it's Mum calling to me and I'm so surprised because she's never there after school and she's never on time. I go over to the car and I feel nervous because Mum has her serious look and I wonder if she knows about the cookies under my pillow or the rotten orange in the bag in my wardrobe or her pretty dangly purple earrings that I stole and broke and so I threw them away.

I get into the front seat and put my legs up on the dusty glove box that has that wavy grey plastic on it. I look down.

'Rosa. There's something I'd like to talk to you about.' Mum is already driving but she doesn't go far. She stops outside the park with the little kids' playground in it that we used to go to when I was little. I bite my tongue to stop it talking. I don't want to admit to anything.

'Michael is sick.'

'Does he have cancers?' I wonder if he's going to die like Grandad.

'No. It's a different kind of sick. His body isn't sick. It's his head that's not well.'

'Can't you fix his head? You're the doctor.' That's what Dad used to always say.

'I'm not the right kind of doctor.' She sighs.

'Is he crazy?'

'Yes … No. He's just not thinking like a normal person. He's in the hospital.' She looks at me. 'Would you like to visit him?'

I nod my head. Yes.

'I just want to warn you that he's saying funny things. But don't worry. There are lots of doctors there who are going to make him better.'

I don't like the hospital because it smells like toilets but the place where Michael is looks like the hotel we stayed in on holiday. There are lots of pictures on the walls and everything is blue and the lift is shiny, like the one in my story, and for a minute I want it to take me to another world but I know that I'm not allowed to go.

Michael is lying in bed with his arm above his head. He moves a tiny bit when we come in but he doesn't look at us. Mum uses her gentle voice.

'Mikey, it's just me – Mum – and Rosa.'

He turns around and it looks like he's just waking up.

'Rosa.' He nods and then he looks at the ceiling. 'Good,' he says and then he's quiet.

'I need a haircut,' he says and he moves his hand through his hair like a shaver thing and says, 'Zroom zroom.'

I laugh, and Mum gives me her shut-up look so I put my hand on my mouth and bite it.

'Rosa,' he says.

'What?'

'Kia ora.'

Mum goes to get a drink of water from the nurse.

'Are you really crazy?' I ask him.

'Nah – I'm just pretending,' he says. And I know he's telling the truth because he doesn't have that bullshit look that him and John and Dad get when they try to trick me.

'Why?'

'Because she just won't listen,' he says and he sounds mad and I know what he means because no one ever listens to me and it pisses me off.

'Well, now that you're crazy she might listen,' I say, because I want to say something nice. But in my head I think: she won't believe anything you say. And then Michael closes his eyes and makes funny noises and laughs and then I know he actually is crazy, and he just doesn't know that he is.

Mum comes back in and Michael looks at her.

'I know you think I'm crazy,' he says. His voice is slow and serious. 'But I'm not. My mind's not broken, Mum – it's our family. Our whānau is broken.'

Mum just shakes her head and cries.

Caleb

I tried to talk to Michael but there's no point. He doesn't answer at all, and when he does it's in Māori. I wonder if this is all an act, if he's trying to teach me a lesson for being a shitty father. Maybe that's my own paranoia.

I'm standing in the hallway outside his room. Val is off having lunch at the café across the road with Elena who flinched when I tried to give her a kiss on the cheek. They couldn't get away from me fast enough, neither of them.

I look down the hallway. Everything is grey. That's depressing. Did they ever think about that when they designed this place? I can see a woman, clutching the doorway to her room, her chin moves up towards the ceiling, her eyes roll back and she moans. I wonder if she knows where she is. Michael's not that bad. He's fine. He'll be alright.

A middle-aged Māori man comes down the hallway, his knees bend out to the side, he tips his imaginary hat at each door and at me and at people who aren't there. 'G'day, g'day, g'day,' he smiles, cheerfully. He reminds me of something out of *Mary Poppins* – that old kids' classic that Michael and Elena used to watch over and over on VCR when they were little. They had a good childhood, really.

I watch as a doctor in a white coat comes out of an office. He looks around, sees me and heads towards me. 'You're Michael's dad?'

'Yep.' I don't know whether to feel proud or ashamed, so I feel both.

'We have assessed his condition. This is a fairly common form of psychosis for young men. Do you know if he's been taking any drugs?'

'How would I know?' I didn't mean to say that out loud. It makes me sound like an idiot, like a bad parent.

'Well, the drug tests will show that sooner or later.' He looks down at his clipboard. I hadn't even noticed he was holding one.

'Look,' he says. 'The typical procedure is to medicate him with antipsychotics.'

'Makes sense,' I nod, sounding like an idiot.

'We just want to make sure we can follow through with the treatment.' He pauses, and I'm waiting for something bad.

'This is a form. If you sign here we will get a court order so that we can medicate him, even if he refuses.' The doctor looks a bit flustered. 'This is standard procedure.' Didn't he say that before, maybe he's new. 'People in Michael's condition can be unpredictable. We just want to make sure we have the power to help him.'

'That makes perfect sense.' I sign. They're the doctors of course, it's what they think is best.

I don't think about it again until Val and Elena get back from lunch. When I tell her, Val is pissed.

'You never would have agreed if I had thought it was best.' She always snaps at me.

'I can't believe you did that.' Elena won't even look me in the eye. 'Mum says he's getting better. He's better now than he was last night. Can't we just wait and see if he can get over this himself before rushing in with pharmaceuticals?' She sighs. I should have expected this. She hates medicine, doesn't she? I wonder why she always takes Val's side.

'This is the standard treatment,' I say, knowing that that won't be good enough for her. Little miss-know-it-all.

'Now he's got even more reason to be paranoid. We're all going to have to convince him to take these drugs or they will force him. That experience would really mess him up!' She walks off in the direction of the lounge. Val follows.

I thought I was doing the right thing, stepping up. Turns out I'm still a failure.

I left because I was never good enough for her, or any of them. I don't know why she ever expected me to be, or why she still expects more.

I walk past where they're sitting but don't look in their direction on my way downstairs to the Whānau Room. The nurse told us about it before; it's basically a room for families to sleep in with a TV, a bathroom and a kitchen. I find the remote. Choice. They've got Sky. I flick to ESPN and settle down to watch the golf.

Michael

Mum comes into the little room with that look of worry in her eyes. Her smile is warm. She wants me to be happy and I trust her. She is trying to help. I don't feel the need to sit up so I just lie in bed. I tell Mum I need a haircut. I tell her that Elena should be here. I tell her that I didn't used to think Elena knew much but now I know. Now I think Elena is very wise. I tell Mum that I'm happy about the baby, that I'm going to be here for the baby and look after it. I'm going to be a good uncle.

Elena comes in but I think I'm asleep. She talks to me from the other side of the bed and she says she's here for me. 'Kia ora,' I say, 'I need a haircut.' The first time I asked about this Mum was so surprised that I figured it sounded crazy and that's what I'm supposed to be in here. So I ask for a haircut every hour, just so they don't think I'm faking. I even make sound effects. 'zroom'. I try not to laugh although it's pretty funny.

They are all standing around my bed like it's Christmas: the doctor and nurse and my family: Mum, Elena, John, Rosa, even Dad. It's a small room and I feel claustrophobic. I ask if they can all leave. I need some private time.

'We will,' Mum says. 'But first we need you to agree to take this medication.'

'What if I don't?' I look at Elena, her eyes are downcast. I know it's something bad.

They hand me forms and I read through them, line by line.

I'm making sure they make sense, that I'm not being tricked.

'If you don't agree,' Elena says. 'They already have a court order to make you. This stuff – it might help you.' She doesn't sound convinced, so what makes her think that she will convince me. 'If you don't …' Her voice is small, breaking. 'They will make you, and that will be a lot worse for everyone. Especially you.' She lowers her voice.

'I don't believe in this stuff,' she gestures at the little yellow flake. 'But maybe the alternative is worse.'

I weigh it up in my mind. I can play along with their little game. I can make them think that I'm 'getting better'. It won't make any difference to me anyway. I know that. I can stop acting crazy. It's the path of least resistance and I have probably caused them enough grief already. Part of me wants to know what these drugs are like, whether they can affect me at all. But something inside me still feels yuck. I continue reading through the court mandate.

'You can go now,' I say to the nurse and the doctor. But they insist they have to wait until I've taken their drugs. I carry on reading to waste more of their time. Eventually the doctor leaves. He looks pissed off and it makes me feel pleased.

'Just take it,' Dad says. Not that he is an authority. 'It will help you.'

'Please,' Mum says and I can see the worry in her eyes. That's what finally makes me do it. Not the cramped room full of people, not the doctor or the nurse who are hanging around, pressuring me. I hate it when Mum worries so I take the damn medication. Half an hour later I'm drowsy, drifting, barely human.

Elena

We sit at the hospital café. Not the cafeteria, the proper café across the street that serves almost-decent coffee and semi-gourmet sandwiches. Mum stirs her soy latte and looks across at me, eyeing me warily.

'You're still eating eggs?'

Did I mention my mother thinks I'm crazy? Michael and I were raised on margarine and skimmed milk; we ate lean meat, low-fat everything. Now I cook in butter and coconut oil because I have learnt that processing vegetable oils, hydrogenating them into margarine creates trans fats which are damaging to the body. The more I looked into it; the more information I found indicating that saturated fat wasn't bad at all. Lots of traditional cultures have followed diets that are high in fat and haven't gotten heart disease. I also found information linking the consumption of margarine, or trans fats, with heart disease.

Mum only believes things she reads on PubMed. She thinks I've been brainwashed by a crazy hippie food cult. She takes every opportunity to ensure I'm following the correct nutritional guidelines. Me being pregnant just makes her more pushy; but honestly, I have a good idea of what my body needs and what it doesn't.

'Yes, Mum.'

'Not the raw yolks, I hope.'

I look down into my decaf flat white, avoiding her gaze. I

hate the texture of cooked yolks. I only eat free-range eggs and I drink rosemary tea, when I feel the need, to cleanse my body of any parasites.

'You know, you're not supposed to eat sea food either, and I'd switch to soy if I were you.' She looked at my milky coffee as though it was a possible danger. 'Milk is prone to listeria infection.'

I sigh. 'Soy is disgusting, and it's not even healthy. I was reading about it online and –'

She cuts me off. 'Don't believe everything you read on the internet. There are conspiracy theories, you know anyone can put things on there if they want to.'

'Well, as it happens I was reading something written by a doctor who has been published in peer-reviewed journals.' It's a requirement – to back up all my claims with something she would take seriously. 'Anyway, apparently soy contains phytates that bind to nutrients in the digestive system and make people deficient in all sorts of micronutrients.'

'Well, soy is high in nutrients, protein, and it's usually fortified with calcium and iron. Are you getting enough of those?'

'I'm eating red meat, and dairy has calcium, so do almonds. It's actually in a lot of leafy vegetables. I can absorb it, too, because I don't fill my body up with that stuff.' I gesture at her cup. I don't tell her that I had Twisties and black forest chocolate for a midnight snack, that I made Malcolm drive to the late night supermarket to fulfil my craving rather than face my hormonal wrath.

'I hope you're cutting the fat off your meat.' She should know by now what I think of fat. I can tell she's had enough of our little conversation. She never listens to me anyway. 'Since when are you the medical expert?' She throws her qualifications in my face all the time, as if it makes her God.

'Your brother's up there in that building because of God knows what and you're trying to lecture me about my latte?' There goes the guilt trip.

'What do you think happened?' I ask her, deliberately taking up the new subject.

'Drugs. The doctors say it happens a lot to young men. Of course he denies taking anything other than cannabis.'

'What kind of drugs?' I wonder what could send my perfect little brother over the edge of sanity.

'I don't know, methamphetamines, LSD, Ecstasy, maybe P …'

'P is methamphetamines.'

'I know that,' she snaps. She always has to be right.

Michael

The medication I take is about the size of my thumbnail. It's yellow and tastes like banana. It melts in my mouth and I know that's because it makes it impossible to hide under my tongue and then spit out and hide. Once it's in my mouth I have to take it, but I spit out as much as I can when no one's looking.

I never wanted to take medication. I don't need it. It makes me drowsy and stupid. Everyone's already looking at me strangely, looking closely for any crazy behaviour, what do they expect when they give me that stuff? I'm a walking zombie.

Did I ever tell you how Māui got his magic jawbone? This is the weirdest story, the only one I hated in school. He tricked his grandmother – starved her of food – until she surrendered her own jaw to him. That's some freaky shit. The images from the book come back to me and I feel like I'm slipping into that world and into Māui's body.

'Is this a trick, Mikaere?' I'm startled back into the white room. Nan is sitting on the end of my bed. She asks me, using the Māori version of my name. I don't know how to answer. It is one of those trick questions. If I admit it's a trick she will be disappointed in me. If I say it isn't, then she'll worry that I really am crazy.

'Everything's a trick,' I say.

She nods, and just for a moment I realise that she understands everything. She is in this too. But I don't say anything, I keep quiet. No one else can know. They might lock her up too.

'It was a revelation to me!' the girl next to me is saying. We are having a 'support meeting' with the other patients in my ward. 'To realise that my condition had a name, that there were others like me.' Her eyes look crazy.

I'm not, I think. *I'm not like you. I'm not crazy.*

'Now …' she says, with tears welling up in her eyes, 'I realise that those dark, terrible moments could be doorways to love.'

I can't help myself, laughter just overcomes me; I struggle to turn it into a strange sounding cough.

'It was like I was falling through an endless dark tunnel,' the man across from me says. I like that. I can relate to it. Drawing time is next and I draw a picture of a hill with crayons. I feel like a little kid. On top of the hill are trees, on the other side is the sun. I draw a dark pit on the opposite side to the sun.

'That's where I was,' I explain to Mum. 'And that's where I am now. I point to the forest, halfway between the pit and the sun.' I feel silly doing this but they expect me to be crazy and I don't want to disappoint them.

When I first came in here I felt like I was the only sane one. I was important and that was why they were trying to lock me up. I could see the blinking lights in the ceiling and I was sure 'they' were watching me. People would ask me who 'they' are and I wouldn't know what to say because 'they' are so secretive. There isn't much I can know about them, but I knew that they were all working together: the hospital and the police and other more secret organisations. I knew they were trying to stop me because I could see through them, because I knew too much. Now I'm not so sure, but I still think I'm the only sane one here. I'm saner than my family anyway.

Valerie

For the first few nights we stayed here – the whole family – except Elena, who had to get home to Malcolm. He's never set foot in this place. I suppose it would make him uncomfortable. This is the first night I've spent at home. Rosa is staying with her friend Aroha. John's probably with Caleb or off with friends. I have the house all to myself. I feel like a free agent.

It's the first time in years that I've taken an unscheduled work break. There's no way I could be at work right now, telling other people how to be healthy when I can't even heal my own son. He is responding well to the medication. The doctors tell me that. He mostly seems a bit dazed and sleeps all the time.

I pick my pyjamas up from the end of my bed. They feel limp. They will need to be washed soon. Water has this way of replenishing things. I shower and let the water run over me. I turn the faucet off, automatically, and then wonder why the water has stopped. I wish I could stay in that flowing world where nothing else exists. I put my pyjamas on. They smell musky. Yes, I will have to wash them tomorrow. In the water clothes are renewed, revived, refreshed, replenished, re-everything: resurrected. And every time they lose a little something. They sacrifice their specialness and their newness is diminished.

I've always dreamed of everlasting clothes. I don't care about style as long as I look presentable, professional for work and passable at all other times. I don't want to be noticed. I don't want men to look at me with lust or women to judge me. I don't want even to be seen as a woman. I'm a doctor. And most of the time that is all my clients ever see: doctor, professional, expert. Being a woman makes me approachable, sensitive, safe. Outside of work, I'm just a woman. A frumpy, slightly overweight woman with bags under her eyes. At home I'm just Mum. Just the person who is responsible for everything and also to blame for everything. Sometimes I wish I could take that professional mask and wear it everywhere I go. I could wear a medical costume, a stethoscope and white coat. But that would only draw attention to me. I would be the crazy one, not Michael. I probably am.

When I arrive back at the hospital Michael is alone. I don't know where anyone else is, but I don't care. This is an opportunity to spend some time alone together. Michael is eating breakfast. Since he's been here the thing he has complained the most about is the bland hospital food. I'm inclined to agree. They follow certain health regulations; low-fat, low-salt, but the food seems so lifeless. It's one thing even Elena and I agree on. I even bought Burger King for Michael the other day just so I could see him enjoying his food. He's just about finished his toast before he acknowledges me. He's been like this the whole time, like there's only room in his head for one thing at a time. Everything is very deliberate and focused – eating, reading, talking – he takes time over every word, as if he's turning it over in his head suspiciously, checking to see if it's safe.

'Hi, Mum.' He seems almost cheerful, but dazed. I think that's the medication.

'Hi, sweetheart. How are you feeling today?'

'Feeling …' he says with a sarcastic smile. 'I'm not feeling. I can't really feel with this … with this stuff.'

'You seem better,' I offer, hopefully.

'Nothing's better. We're still broken, the world's still broken.'

I've been longing to communicate with him, to reach out to him, but I can't seem to get through, I can't find the words.

'We're here for you,' I say. Then I remember. I have to tell Evie.

Michael

Tupou leans against the pool table. He's always looking at me funny. I wonder why he's here. He seems pretty messed up, this middle-aged Māori guy who never stops talking. Maybe he's acting – like I am. If he is, I have no way of knowing whose side he's on, so I play it strategically. I smile, shake his hand, agree. If he thinks I'm on his side it will be easier for both of us. I sit on the bench seat out in the courtyard, which is completely fenced off, and he comes and sits down next to me. I wish he wouldn't, I'd like some peace.

'You got a girlfriend, bro?'

'Yeah … maybe.' I think of Evie. Does she still count? Why would I tell him, anyway? Why does he want to know?

'It's like that is it?' he winks. 'She mad at you. That's always the way with ladies. Don't you worry, boy. There's an easy way to fix that – buy her some roses – nah some Roses chocolates. That works every time.'

I laugh, imagining trying to give Roses to Evie.

'Wha?' He stares at me, as if he's amazed at my laughter.

'She doesn't eat milk chocolates. She's a vegan.'

'Who doesn't like chocolates? Jeez, if someone giz me some chocolates I'd eat them all right now, bro.'

'My girlfriend thinks eating animal products is wrong, my sister thinks eating normal food is unhealthy.'

'Man, youse must be rich if youse can afford to eat all that special food – caviar and champagne – eh? My whānau eats everything, and we're always hungry too. You eat everything on your plate and don't complain, 'cause you never know when there ain't gonna be food around, eh? A man's gotta eat. It's pretty sweet in here that they feed us our three meals, eh? With the little butter and the nice trays. Last time I went home all I could think about was those little butters and the food that just comes to you – every meal. It made me want to come back a bit, eh? Even though the nurses are bitches and the doctors are so far up their asses they can hardly walk straight, even though it's boring as Hades and I miss my son …'

I turn and look at Tupou. Suddenly everything makes sense. This guy makes sense. He has real problems. I don't. I'm just pretending. I've been born and raised in a middle-class bubble where there really is no problem, where there's so much food and nothing to worry about so all everyone does – Mum, Elena, Evie – all they do is worry about food, when they should just be grateful they can eat. If, by a twist of fate we had been born into Tupou's family, we would be starving – actually starving – without the luxury to be moral about food, just this desperate hunger. So much hunger we go mad, just so we can get in here to get fed, or get into prison to get our three square meals. That's when it hits me: this is why I'm in here. Because I need to know these things. I need to wake the world up and show them their insanity.

Valerie

I can't believe it's already the end of the week. It seems to have gone by without me even noticing, and yet when I think back to Monday it seems like an eternity ago. I don't know how time can do that, be so fast and yet so slow. When I get into the car I find it hard to believe the same song is playing as this morning. Of course it is, the CD player does that, but it's surreal, like time stopped while I was visiting Michael at the hospital. It's something by U2, from the mixtape Elena made me which she labelled: songs that happen to be on my computer that Mum won't mind, and that John calls 'easy listening pussy music'. I would tell him off but I've given up. Elena complains that I'm much less strict with the boys then I was with her. She's right of course. I only have so much energy to go around and I have learnt to pick my battles. In a way she got the better deal, although she'd argue with me about that. I believe that having firm boundaries is better for children, even if I don't exactly live up to my own value. Parents aren't perfect. Elena will figure that out soon enough.

The nurse's fake cough interrupts me from my occupation of staring blankly at the newspaper in the sitting room, not really invested enough in any of the headlines to read the stories.

'It might be good for Mike to take him out today, just for a walk or something. The doctor will sign him out when he gets here.'

It hits me, as if from nowhere. What have I done wrong, to be in this position? How did this happen to my son, to my family? I snap out of it. The nurse is still there.

'Okay.' I nod excessively. 'We can do that.'

Where would we walk to? To the lake, to feed the ducks like we did when the kids were little? I peep through the door of Michael's room. He's lying on his side, kicking his feet off the bed. He could be any normal kid, but knowing he's in this state – in this institution – makes me look for the unusual. I knock and enter. He looks at me and emotion flashes across his face for a moment: confusion, recognition, and then suspicion, all replaced by a blank, hazy stare. He knows it too. He knows we are watching him, waiting for strange behaviour.

Every day since the breakdown Michael has asked for a haircut. His hair had grown about two inches longer than usual. Now I watch as it falls in clumps onto the lino at the shopping mall hairdresser where you don't need appointments. Rosa, John and I are sitting on the waiting bench. I'm trying not to look anxious. It's our first trip out of the hospital with him and I can tell he's putting on an act of being normal. Perhaps too normal.

'My name's John,' he tells the hairdresser as she slings a black cloak around his neck. 'I work on a farm.'

John has the most amused smile on his face and the three of us are trying desperately not to laugh.

'Why did he lie, Mum?' Rosa asks me.

'I don't know,' I admit. *Maybe he's paranoid.* 'Maybe he was playing a game.' I lie. *If only.*

Rosa

'Mum?' We are in the Whānau Room and Mum is making coffee that smells yuck and tastes like burnt toast and medicine. 'How do you know if your mind is sick?'

'Well, people usually start seeing things that aren't there or they act funny and then people guess that there's something wrong,' she says. 'No one can see inside a person's mind.'

'What if they opened up their skull and looked at their brain?'

'They still wouldn't know,' she says. 'They can see the brain, but not what the person's thinking. No one can see a mind.'

'How do you know it exists?'

Mum puts her head in her hands like when she gets her headaches and I know not to talk anymore.

'We just know, Rosa,' she says. She sounds angry. 'Otherwise nothing would make any sense.'

And I wonder if a mind is like God because I'm supposed to believe it but I can't see it and then I wonder if anything exists because maybe it's just a dream and I pinch myself to wake up because I don't want to be here. And then I get bored so I lie down on the blue carpet that smells like pencil shavings and stare at the wall and wait for a door to appear.

'Mum?' I ask. She's staring at the wall and she doesn't hear me.

'Mum, Mum, Mu-um?'

'What?' She sounds annoyed.

'What if Michael's not crazy? What if he's found out the

secrets to another world?' I wonder if his mind has gone to a different place and it's only his body left behind with us.

'Don't be ridiculous, Rosa!' She yells and her voice is sharp and stabs me in the chest and the tears start coming out from behind my eyes and the world feels wobbly. Mum puts her arms around me.

'I'm sorry, bub,' she says.

The tears are hot and soak into Mum's jacket. I think about all the times I have to be by myself 'cause Mum's always working and my brother's crazy and everything's hard in my life and it makes me cry harder. I want to tell her that I need her but I can't because my throat's tight from crying and then I'm sleepy so I lie down next to Mum and she pats my back and I wonder if she will ever understand.

Evie

Truly man is the king of beasts, for his brutality exceeds them. We live by the death of others. We are burial places.
LEONARDO DA VINCI

The meeting is upstairs, above the main street in town. We sit on old mismatched couches with dusty cushions. Dharma is playing his drum in the corner. It's relaxing for me but Tara looks annoyed. She responds to the question in my eyes.

'I've got a headache.'

A couple of new people come in. They're wearing normal clothes. I wonder for a minute whether they are cops. They look too young.

The meeting goes on but I'm not really listening. In my mind I'm with Michael, sitting outside his room in Raglan, listening to the bird calls through the trees with my legs propped up against his. I miss him now more than ever. Three days ago he texted that he didn't want to see me anymore and when my phone smashed against the wall it felt like someone else had thrown it. I felt nothing but rage. It's subsided now and I'm left with this empty feeling. It seems only now that he's really gone from my life.

My thought process is interrupted by the sound of my phone, cracked but still functioning in the bottom of my bag. I feel relieved to have an excuse to leave the meeting. Outside in the dark mildewed hallway I read the text from Valerie.

Oh shit. Does he really want to see me or not? He told me to get out of his life. Should I stay away and respect his wishes. I text Valerie back, *He doesn't want to see me.*

Five agonising minutes later the reply comes: *He's asking for you, love.*

The grey-blue walls are imitating neutral, but they feel institutional. This place reminds me of hell. I was thirteen when my parents started to realise I wasn't interested in my food. I would push it around my plate, avoid eating the meat entirely and only take small bites of the vegetables. The doctor told them to monitor me. He asked me lots of questions that I didn't want to answer.

'Do you feel fat?' I felt like dying.

Hardly anyone even knows about this, I never talk about it. I'd rather forget it ever happened. Of course I was a stupid twelve-year-old. My friend Johanna and I would read *Girlfriend* magazines and want to look like the skinny models and celebrities. We would want all the stupid make up and fantasise about the adult world that seemed so exciting to us at the time. I would stare at the heroine-chic girls for hours on end, envying the freedom they seemed to possess, but it wasn't about them. I don't think it was really about body image at all. Not for me.

Johanna was bulimic for a while. Now she's fat and works in advertising.

I hated my life and my family and the way they hurt animals. Every day was so hard and horrible. My dad would yell at me for everything I did, my mum would nag me for everything I didn't do. There was no good side.

I had no control over the outside world so I took control of my body instead. I would cut the broccoli into equal squares, avoiding eye contact at the dinner table. I would make sure everything was perfect on my plate before I put anything in my mouth, and when I did, I would see how long it would take for the starch of the potato to dissolve on my tongue; how many bites it took for the carrot to be completely puréed.

They say it's an addiction. I didn't think about it at the time. My mother would nag me to eat and my dad would yell at me for not eating, but it didn't matter. They couldn't control this one small part of my life, and I wasn't about to let them.

I remember Mum calling me into the kitchen and telling me about a new, experimental treatment place for people with my 'condition'. I wanted to slap her. I was so pissed off. It wasn't a condition to me, it was something I chose. She said she had no choice, but what she really meant was I had no choice.

I was fourteen by then and the youngest one there. They usually send under sixteens with severe eating disorders to Starship Hospital, but this place was new and I wasn't at the point of hospitalisation. I was weak and tired, but I felt light, sometimes dizzy – like I could float away, and other times my emotion was so strong my body could barely contain it. I did hate myself. I hated everything, especially that place. It reminded me of a school, where strangers tell you what to do all the time. I was in a room with five other girls, all of them older than me. Some of them would try to exercise when no one was looking or make themselves throw up at night, and they would usually get caught the next morning when we had the inspections. I've never felt more humiliated in my life. It was the most invasive, degrading, thing I've ever been through, but I didn't have the words to describe it at the time.

We were forced to eat three meals a day. We had to eat everything on our plates: fish 'n' chips, lasagne, fettuccine. There was no vegetarian option. I remember the posters all over the walls: 'Love Your Body', 'Love Yourself', 'You Are Beautiful Just the Way You Are.'

Every 'love' was automatically turned into 'hate' inside my head. Every inch of my body wanted to rebel against those horrible people, that horrible place.

They say anorexia is like alcoholism. That there is no cure, only an ongoing recovery. That place didn't cure me. It made me conform just so I could get out of there, but it made me hate my life more than ever.

I went home and everything was the same. I had learnt tricks from the other girls, things that I wouldn't have gotten away with at the centre, but that my parents, who wanted to believe that it was all over, didn't bother to check. I wore long sleeves at the dinner table and hid my food in them when no one was looking. I fed it to the dogs later. I'm no good at bingeing and so purging never appealed to me, which saved me from burning the enamel off my teeth with my stomach acid, like the bulimics I had met.

I would probably have stayed in the exact same pattern. I might have even starved myself to death, if it wasn't for my cousin Audi. He was staying with us at the time. He had seen my sleeve trick and knew I wasn't eating properly and he had been reading about the LSD experiments they'd done in the 1960s.

'It's an addiction, right?' He'd seemed really excited.

'I guess.'

'So, I can cure it.' It's really no wonder he went on to med school.

'Right,' I said, sarcastically. We were in the barn. I sat down on an old chair and crossed my arms. He held out his hand and revealed a small, square piece of paper.

'Here is your cure,' he said. I turned my head away. 'So, Evelyn. You really have to ask yourself the question: What do you want more, to destroy yourself or to save the world?' I looked up at him and he smiled. 'You're no good to us dead.'

It just so happened that Audi had not only been reading up on LSD's potential to cure addiction, he had also been reading a lot about anorexia nervosa. He spent five hours with me in the barn, just talking. He never once told me what to do, he just wanted to hear what I had to say. No one had ever really listened to me before, and I suppose the LSD, doing its thing in my brain, rewired me in a better way. I could step out of myself and see myself, see my limitations and how pathetic I was being. I realised I did want to save the world. I still do. It's the most disillusioning goal at times, but it's the only goal that's worthwhile.

Audi is an eating disorder consultant in Christchurch now.

The last time I saw him he said he wished it was legal to use my treatment on his patients, then he winked at me.

Michael's door has a little window in it. I look through it and I can see him, propped up on the bed, reading. I hold my breath as I open the door.

'It's *Stupid White Men*,' He smiles. 'Elena brought it for me.' I nod. 'I need something to do in this mental place.' We both laugh.

I can't help feeling injured, like I've been slighted by him, but I know there's a lot more going on here.

'What happened?' I ask. He seems so normal, too normal, softer than usual and calm, not bursting with the energy that drives him to stupid adrenaline seeking activities.

'Everything happened.' He sighs. 'I'm not crazy.' Although I never thought he was. 'It's Mum.'

'What?'

'She never listens.' Anger seems to pour out of him, his words become cruel and I feel protective of Valerie.

'She's just worried about you,' I say, trying to sound soothing.

'Yeah, well ...' He's frustrated. Evidently, I'm not listening either. 'You can go now,' he says. It sounds so final and my heart breaks but I pause.

'Get out!'

John

I'm sick of this place, but I was sick of the farm too. Michael fucked that up for me. He probably did me a favour. At least that's what everyone else is saying. I don't know what I'll do now, but there's no way in hell I'll ever go back to school. This is like a holiday – in a hotel where everyone's crazy except my own brother, our whole reason for being here. I don't know why he's doing it but I know Michael's acting. He knows that I know. I've said so about fifty times and every time he agrees with me. I don't even know why we're here at all. What is he trying to pull? Maybe his life wasn't perfect enough already. He should try being me. Try being the kid that always fucks up because, when I don't, no one notices. He's had an easy life. Mr Popular, good at everything, even school, Dad's favourite, Mum's favourite boy.

My life was okay while I was the baby. I got some attention, but then Rosa, the little shit head, was born and I pretty much had to look after myself.

I'm probably the smartest one in the family, but I was just never good at school – not at maths or writing or anything. It doesn't mean shit anyway.

Now I'm babysitting my big brother. Giving him all the attention he needs while Mum is out having lunch with Elena and Dad is out with Rosa.

It's the first time we've been alone together for more than a few minutes.

'I don't get it,' I say. 'Why are you even doing this?'

'You wouldn't understand,' he says. He always has to know better than me.

'I'd understand more than you think,' I say. 'You've cruised through your life. You've had it easy.'

'No. You've got it wrong.' His voice is so sure, like he's the boss. 'You wouldn't know.' This sounds like the old Mike. Then something changes in his face. He's quiet for a while.

'My life has all been a dream.' He sounds like he's making a speech now, like he could be Martin Luther King Jr up on a stage. 'You see, I make it seem easy. It's never easy.'

'Bullshit.' There's no point in talking anymore. There never was. Michael has always been in his own world. He's never been able to understand anyone else's. He's probably never cared enough, so why should I care about him?

I guess he is my brother. He's about the closest person to me in my family, the least crazy of the lot of them, or at least he used to be. When he turned up at the farm I was happy to see him. I was relieved. I needed to get the hell outta there. I should have known something was up when he insisted on going to that boring Māori thing. I should have known when he stood up and started talking in front of all those people. I was just trying not to laugh.

Michael is acting, but he's just acting because he doesn't know how to be real anymore. He's lost in all that university crap, all those ideas. He's always been obsessed with being more Māori than he actually is, but now he's taken it too far. It's taken over his mind. It's like when you smoke too much weed and get lost in the loop. Your thoughts go around and around inside your head and you don't know if you will ever come out again. It's like that for him, but he's been in there for too long. We don't even know if he will come out.

Evie

As long as men massacre animals, they will kill each other. Indeed, he who sows the seeds of murder and pain cannot reap the joy of love.
PYTHAGORAS

I frantically scramble with my bags and Tara throws me worried glances from the kitchen. The zip's stuck and it makes me want to scream and throw things at walls, but I don't. I grab tape from the cabinet and secure my belongings. This time I'm taking all my things from Tara's house and disowning everything that might be in Michael's possession.

I'm hitching down to Wellington. I'll crash at the marae for a few weeks and then maybe head down south. If there's still fruit picking work going I might be able to save enough money to go to India or maybe Nepal. I'll learn to play the local instruments and maybe even speak the language. Maybe I'll stay there for good. It's not a good way to leave, I know, but there's no place for me here. I feel the strange urge to curl up on Valerie's lap like a baby in foetal position, superseded by more anger. I feel like I've lost my family because of Michael's crisis. I'm not going to sit around and worry about him like Elena and Val are.

You might think it's callous to leave now but I know he'll be fine, I've seen enough friends with psychosis over the years in much worse states. It changes you, and for him that means there's no room for me anymore. I'm not going to wait around to see if he wants me back – it's not that kind of relationship, is it? I don't have 'that kind of relationship'.

Maybe I'll meet my soul mate in the slums of Rishikesh where vegetarianism is the law and alcohol is banned, where the doctors will have better things to do than poke and prod at my cervix. We'll make spellbinding music together and she'll feed me paneer made from the milk of cows that have been worshipped; I can probably justify eating that, if any, animal product. I'll send Valerie a postcard with a cheesy tourist picture of a sacred monument and pretend that I don't miss her.

Elena

Mum tells me she is praying for Michael. She says it in a whisper, as though she's confiding in me, there's a hint of desperation and I see how much this whole situation is hurting her.

'To get him back,' she says, and I wonder if he's really gone. It's a scary thought that this strangeness might become his normal. I don't believe it.

'You could pray too,' she suggests. I look at the ground. I don't want to upset her. She's always been spread too thin and this turn of events is pulling her so tightly I'm afraid she might be torn to pieces. For the first time, I'm actually glad she has religion, as bizarre as Christianity seems to me.

I remember one of my lecturers claiming that most New Zealanders, regardless of their religious affiliations, are practical atheists. 'Which means,' she explained, 'That although they claim to be Christian or Muslim or Jewish, et cetera, they usually behave as if God doesn't exist.' This is the category I'd put Mum in. She goes to church on Sunday but I think that is more to fill in the schedule of her weekend then out of religious piety. She might pray, I'm not sure, but her prayers would most likely be about the things she wants: more money, less body fat, her kids to be safe. Not that I'm complaining about that last one but it's not exactly selfless. I've known her to keep the money when someone gives her too much change, to covet the things that other people have, to swear, to talk about people behind their back, and definitely to hold a grudge. I don't think that makes her bad. No one's perfect, I just don't think she is as religious as she would like me to think. God is like a drug to her that keeps her going through the day, like an invisible version of her anti-depressants that she tries to keep secret from me. Jesus is someone to talk to when she gets lonely, who always cares and always forgives, absolving her from responsibility over her life. It's not real spirituality; it's a crutch.

I grew out of Christianity early. It didn't make sense to me that God knew everything that was going to happen. If he did, it didn't matter what I did because he would already know it was going to happen. It was a strange and repetitive thought that circled my mind: *He would know what I'm thinking now, and he would know that I just thought about what he was thinking about.* If he knew everything, the world would be boring for him, like watching a movie for the millionth time. If he knew everything then why would he bother letting it all play out? And, furthermore, if everything is predestined then there really is no free will and I might as well just do and think what I like because it's the way it's going to be, anyway.

As a child I wondered who God's mummy was. Mum said God didn't have a mummy, but I knew that wasn't possible. How could he be born without a mother? It's the sort of thing Rosa asks about now. I have hope for that girl. A few years later I graduated to asking why God wasn't a woman and Mum gave up on my religious education. I'd already made up my mind not to take anything at face value. I would decide for myself.

As a teenager I was angry at the stupidity of religion, of religious wars, of teaching people to believe rather than think for themselves. I would look up ridiculous quotes on a search engine and read them out over the dinner table. While Mum was serving crayfish or mussels I read Leviticus 11: 9–12:

9 These shall ye eat of all that are in the waters: whatsoever hath fins and scales in the waters, in the seas, and in the rivers, them shall ye eat.

10 And all that have not fins and scales in the seas, and in the rivers, of all that move in the waters, and of any living thing which is in the waters, they shall be an abomination unto you:

11 They shall be even an abomination unto you; ye shall not eat of their flesh, but ye shall have their carcasses in abomination.

12 Whatsoever hath no fins nor scales in the waters, that shall be an abomination unto you.

But it's not really about the Bible, is it? It's about having something, a bigger picture, a guiding force, a benevolent omnipotent being looking out for you. Faith is a mental cushion. I should know, I've always had it. I just don't understand why this particular form appeals to so many people. Why this religion? Why this god? Buddhism makes so much more sense, or Hinduism (without the vegetarianism of course), or just having your own religion, your own faith that there is a purpose, that there is meaning, that everything will work out, even if you don't know any more than that. A practical spirituality that helps you get through the day, that alleviates worry. But as Malcolm says: 'Yeah, yeah, Elena, you have all the answers.' Even if nobody wants to listen.

Rosa

Mum is tired but she wants to stay at the hospital with Michael and I'm bored so Mum tells Dad to take me away somewhere and so I have to go in Dad's truck which smells like rotten fish and is all hot from the sun. Dad says we will go somewhere fun and I want to go to a movie or the zoo to see the monkeys that poo on each other but Dad says, 'I'm broke.' So we can't do anything fun anyway. I just want to go home but Dad won't let me so we drive around, not really going anywhere, and then Dad gets an idea to go to the lake to see if there's any boats and I know that will be boring but I don't get a choice. There are some groups of guys rowing those long skinny orange type boats, which seems pretty stupid because they're not really going anywhere and they're not even racing but Dad gets out of the car and watches and when I say I'm bored he tells me to go play on the playground.

I pull the Velcro strap that makes a raspy noise and take off my shoes. The grass is squelchy under my feet because it rained last night for the first time in ages. It was a big thunderstorm and I wondered if the lightning would come right through the hospital and kill us all at night, and then it wouldn't matter if Michael was crazy because most of the family, except Elena, would be dead. But I bet she'd be really sad then.

The playground is ages away. It's all made of concrete and even though it's a hot day it feels cold. I crawl into a big concrete tunnel and read the writing that says 'Shayna loves Tere' and 'Jonah is gay' and 'Rita likes to suck cock' and 'Call Sarah Mathews for a good time' with a number that's been scribbled out, maybe by Sarah Mathews. It's probably the teenagers that write that stuff because no one else really cares about it but I would feel pretty yuck if someone wrote that about me, like the time Johnny Weasley kissed me on the field and everyone went 'Ooo' and said stupid things about sex and getting married and I wanted to die.

Dad is still standing by his truck, even though I've been in here for ages. He's got his hand up over his eyes to block the sun and he's still watching those stupid boats. This is what he always does. I kick the grass then practise making daisy chains. I swing on the swings until – even when I stop and lie down on the wet grass and close my eyes – it still feels like I'm swinging. No other kids come to the playground, which is good because I don't like strangers. A man walks past with his dog and I watch to see if he might be bad and kidnap me or murder me but he just keeps walking past. I give him an angry look just in case.

I chew on my fingernails. Michael might never come back to normal again and he might be like one of those crazy people in the hospital forever and that would be sad because there would be no one to play with me and swing me around and stuff and we would have to look after him all the time but it wouldn't really be him. That is why everyone is so worried.

I go back over to Dad. 'I'm bored. Can we go now?' But he's started talking to the man who yells at the rowers and tells them what to do and so he doesn't even listen to me. The sun goes behind a cloud and the wind feels cold on my arms so I go back to the truck even though it's smelly. 'I'm hungry!' I call to Dad but he still doesn't listen so I beep the horn and then when Dad finally does come over he just yells at me and calls me stupid and a 'spoiled brat' and his words feel hard in my chest so I can't stop the tears from coming out and making everything feel worse and better at the same time and Dad just laughs at me and calls me a cry baby.

Elena

I knew my chances were slim, but after years of waking up every day with bad hair there must have been some possibility that I would wake up one day with *perfect* hair. That day was today. Maybe it's the pregnancy hormones or the bath I took last night but my hair has formed into perfect ringlets. I suppose I have more important things to think about, like my dysfunctional relationship, my impending child or my crazy brother. I know I shouldn't joke about it but I just want things to be light-hearted for a change. Give me a break.

Cooking is escapism for me these days. Whenever I'm at home I'm in the kitchen. I made stew even though it's the middle of summer and ridiculously hot. I've experimented with low-sugar deserts. Some of them were disastrous but still a welcome distraction. Malcolm complains that I haven't spent any time with him despite him being at home on break but I can't sit still. I feel my body getting heavier and movement seems twice as exhausting as before. My feet are sore from standing and I have to sit down every now and then. When I do I pick up my knitting and focus on that. I turn on the radio, I sit at the computer and look up nourishing recipes. Anything to be busy. Being at the hospital makes me feel sick, but I've gone up, dutifully, every day.

God. It's only been a week. It seems so long.

We are all in Michael's room again. Mum and I are in the

chairs facing the bed where Michael is sitting, Rosa's on the floor, John is leaning against the wall. Dad is downstairs in the Whānau Room, getting dinner sorted, probably just lying on the couch watching TV. Michael looks up at us.

'Are you alright, love?' Mum says in her caring voice. Rosa fidgets with her sleeves.

'Yup,' Michael says, but his eyes are vacant. I can't bear to think of the drugs they all but forced on him. It makes me cringe.

'Just stop acting crazy,' John says. It feels awkward for a moment before Michael's laughter breaks the tension and the rest of us join in. The laughter says a lot; that we wish this was all just an act, that we're afraid it's permanent, that we need a break from all the seriousness and clinical sterility.

I've always thought John was just a little bit psycho. It's like he came into this world with a vengeance. He was a horrible little brat of a child, biting my friends when they came to visit, wrecking my toys, yelling in such a way that even Dad was stopped in his tracks. I remember a photo of him, he was about two and had just pushed his toy cart over. He looked into the camera with angry, determined eyes. I always wondered who would take a photo like that.

I was always scared of my much younger brother, with good reason, after he chased me around the garden with a metal pipe. That look in his eyes was cold and fierce; glacial or something, an avalanche, a tornado, untrustworthy, unstable. It was a frightening contrast in the otherwise innocuous face of a child. He showed such little empathy, the way he taunted Rosa. He would think nothing of running out into traffic, trying to end his own life at age six. He was creepily paranoid of Nazis too. Henry would say it's a past life thing. Maybe it is.

Now he's the sane one. He's keeping a level head while Michael, the golden boy, has lost his halo. He's the only one of us brave enough to crack jokes. I'm grateful. He doesn't care about being sensitive or socially appropriate. He sees through the bullshit and drama. A malicious Buddha.

We start to watch a movie on my laptop. It's *Beetlejuice*. We used to watch it when we were little and we all seem to be enjoying it when, halfway through, Michael clears his throat.

'I'd like you all to leave now,' he announces. So we do. We file out and loiter downstairs in the Whānau Room watching inane television until Dad brings a rotisserie chicken from the supermarket for dinner and I stuff my face with white bread rolls and soft drink to quell the gaping hunger this baby is causing, sucking up all my energy, all my life. I'm exhausted and fall asleep on the foam mattresses. I don't want to go home to Malcolm, I just want to be gone.

Every day being here it has occurred to me that I could google this. I could see if I can find out what kind of nutritional factors are linked to psychosis, maybe a mineral deficiency. Every night when I've gotten home, I've been too exhausted to do anything.

I know he's bound to be deficient in something. A diet of pies, chips and burgers is just not balanced. He's been too busy partying to think much about food, not that he usually would. But being away from Nan and Mum who usually feed him must have taken its toll, not to mention all that drinking, depleting his body of the essential nutrients it needs to function. I bet all that unsalted, low-fat, disgusting hospital food doesn't help either. I should make him some soup.

The doctors say this kind of psychosis, common with young men, is usually linked to drugs, but Mike's tests didn't show anything other than marijuana in his system. Google informs me that this could possibly have set it off, but that there's a chance that the increased correlation between cannabis use and these kinds of conditions might not be causal: that people prone to these conditions are self-medicating with the herb. I use key words like 'Nutrition' and 'Vitamins' with 'Psychosis'.

The pages appear with an array of possibilities. It could be B3. Is that niacin? Or it could be B12 but he's not the vegan (although it might explain a thing or two about Evie). Maybe it's a copper deficiency or lack of magnesium. Possibly folate, he doesn't eat a lot of fresh vegetables. I scan an article titled 'Can zinc really cure psychosis?' claiming we are in a global zinc deficiency. I'm not entirely convinced. I wish I could post about this on my blog but I feel it would cross boundaries. I couldn't do it without mentioning the situation that inspired the post in some way. I don't think Michael, or Mum, for that matter, would appreciate that.

Apparently sugar and stress are known to alter hormonal states, which can trigger psychosis. I'm not surprised. If only there was a tailor-made anti-psychosis mineral and vitamin supplement, with the aforementioned micronutrients. Even if there was, I doubt I would have any luck getting Michael to take it. He's still so paranoid and the last thing I want to do is to freak him out with yet another pill and turn him against me. I resolve to make him a mineral-rich soup – maybe free-range chicken and vegetable. Chicken soup is supposed to be healing, after all. I just hope that he'll trust me enough to eat it.

I flick over to Facebook to see if there are any messages from Henry or Tanya. I haven't seen them much lately. The little red '1' in the corner indicates a new private message. I click on it before I realise the profile picture isn't mine. A strange feeling engulfs me. It's icy and nauseating. Malcolm must have been using my computer. Who is this girl messaging him? From Kim:

Hey you. Last night was amazing. I've never cum so hard in my life. Text me if you want to hang out again later this week. X

Oh God. Malcolm was working late last night. Obviously, he was working hard. I laugh but my emotion is so mixed, so intense that tears burst out. God. He's sleeping with someone else. Who is she? A student. I click on her profile. Yep. I take a deep breath. I can't believe this. Injustice washes over me. Henry better be home.

I hear a creak and remember that Malcolm is in the bedroom reading. Fuck him. I take the car without asking Malcolm, without saying anything. I leave the browser open on the message. If he gives a damn he'll notice and he'll be sorry.

'I can't believe this.' I'm crying incessantly like I have been for the last hour since I got here, repeating the same meaningless phrases over and over. Henry is holding my hand and patting my back. Tanya brings me camomile tea. 'Thanks,' I sob.

'That cunt!' Tanya is angry. Henry nods.

'I can't believe he would be so clichéd!' he adds and I laugh through the tears. This is so weird, so surreal. How did my life get like this? An echo of Mum and Dad's divorce. I shudder.

'In a way, I'm kind of glad,' I say. 'At least he can't be mad at me for not putting out. I'm sick of him sulking all the time.' I laugh through the tears.

The emotion fluctuates, I feel manic, high … then it drops again into despair.

'Maybe if I was more interested in sex this would never have happened.'

'Shush.' Henry slaps me gently on the cheek. 'Don't you start to take responsibility for his actions.'

He wraps his arms around me and I relax.

'Just like Tanya says. He's a cunt,' Henry confirms.

'You don't even believe in monogamy.' It's an accusation.

'Not as a personal choice, honey. I just can't do it, but I don't pretend to do it either … not anymore. It kept getting me into too much trouble … and I wasn't just about to become a father.'

'Fair enough.' We've talked about this so many times and this is always my response. It's not fair to pretend to be in a monogamous relationship while you're fucking someone else. An icicle of fear shoots through me as I wonder if he's done this before. Has he been unfaithful all along? Maybe it was the fear of fatherhood that pushed him to it – such a cliché. I cringe.

'Everyone will say I should leave him.'

'You should,' Tanya shouts from the kitchen.

My phone starts ringing again and I don't answer. Again.

My head is spinning. Life without Malcolm is hard to imagine. Raising a baby on my own? God.

'You wouldn't have to do everything alone,' Henry says, reading my mind, an unnerving habit of his. 'You have me and Tanya and your family.'

I put my head in my hands. I don't want to tell them. Not even Mum. The shame is almost unbearable. How did this happen? Maybe I've been too busy with this pregnancy, with Michael in hospital, with my blog, to notice how far apart Malcolm and I have drifted. I feel nauseous.

'No.' Henry's voice is firm. 'I will not have you taking any responsibility for this.' I'm so lucky to have friends like this. I'd be lost without them. The tears keep coming, the pain comes up again and again from some infinite source. I feel release, probably my brain chemistry responding to the crying, followed by the anger of injustice.

Valerie

'*The inexorable ticking of the clock is like the throb of pain made by keen sickening fear. And so it is with the great clockwork of nature. Daisies and buttercups give way to the brown waving grasses, tinged with the warm red sorrel; the waving grasses are swept away, and the meadows lie like emeralds set in the bushy hedgerows; the tawny-tipped corn begins to bow with the weight of the full ear; the reapers are bending amongst it, and it soon stands in sheaves; then, presently, the patches of yellow stubble lie side by side with streaks of dark red earth, which the plough is turning up in preparation for the new thrashed seed. And this passage from beauty to beauty, which to the happy is like a flow of a melody, measures for many a human heart the approach of unforeseen anguish – seems hurrying on the moment when the shadow of dread will be followed up by the reality of despair.*'

Even my dear Eliot, with her scenes of clerical life, is no distraction from Michael. Nothing is. The passage I read tonight just seems to be echoing his madness. I see him in everything. Every patient is walking that fine line between sanity and emptiness, every sound in my room at night sounds like his voice calling out in words I don't understand. I can't sleep and when I do I wake from stressful dreams. Elena is pushing baby Michael in a wheelbarrow down a hill. She lets go and I scream, 'Don't let go of the wheelchair!' I wake to my own muffled shriek. All I seem to feel is guilt and anxiety. I drink coffee for every meal and I feel like I ought to be the one locked up in that place. I'm the crazy one. The woman, mother, doctor who can't even look after her own child. People at work look down when they speak to me. Everyone except the commanding head nurse who instructed me not to come in again until Michael was better. She said it in such a way that I felt scared to disobey her. So instead I sit in the waiting room or in Michael's room when he lets me. I watch him sleep and eat and seem dazed and question every word that is spoken by anyone.

Elena's been funny lately. She insists on coming in even though there's nothing else to do. When I suggested she go and spend some time with Malcolm she looked like she wanted to hit me.

'What is it, sweetheart?'

'Nothing,' she said. 'I need to use the bathroom.' And walked away.

I hope it's just the hormones. I hope she would tell me if there was something wrong. I suppose there's no point in worrying. It won't help, but I can't stop myself. I think of Evie and feel that tremendous guilt. Should I have told Michael about her health and breached confidentiality? No, of course not. I would feel much worse if I had. Unprofessional. It would be betraying her trust too. Maybe she really doesn't want him to know or maybe it's too hard to talk about. I just wish I could be there for her more. Right now, everything is eclipsed by Michael.

Caleb

I watch Jack Nicholson smile that famous smile – I don't know which movie this is but I know I've seen it before. It's probably half-finished so I grab the remote and flick to sports. Elena sighs dramatically and gets up off the couch. I've only been in the Whānau Room for five minutes and I've already pissed her off.

'I was watching that,' she snaps, as she walks out the door. She didn't even give me a chance to change it back. But there's golf on anyway. Elena's never liked sports so it's probably a good thing she left the room.

The whole time I've been here Val and Elena have avoided me. I've been trying. I've been doing the supermarket trips, buying countless rotisserie chickens and bread rolls, even though I'm broke and Val earns a lot more than me. I've never complained. I haven't even asked her for money. I've taken Rosa to the park to stop her getting on Val's nerves. I've even done the dishes in the Whānau Room every night. Val's never thanked me once. What else can I do?

I wish I could get through to Michael. I know I've let him down – let all the kids down. If I could fix it I would in a heartbeat. I need to get him out of here and back onto a fishing boat: some good old-fashioned male bonding. That will sort him out. Val babies him too much. It makes him weak. He would never have ended up here if it wasn't for her.

I hear the familiar 'Never Gonna Give You Up' tune coming

from my pocket and answer the call. 'Yeah?'

'Caleb?' I try to place the voice that reminds me of my dead uncle Hickey. 'It's Bruce from the club.' Our cheap local watering hole.

'What can I do for ya?'

'Well, actually, I've got some good news.' My heart skips a beat – just like it does when I'm about to haul a massive catch or the second after those three cherries line up before the coin starts to ching into the metal tray.

'You know our raffle?'

'Yeah.' I'm trying to figure out which one.

'Well, your son Mike – he won!' It was his Christmas present. I entered all the kids into a raffle. It must have been something big. 'A thousand dollars of overseas travel!'

My mind races as I hang up. Automatically changing the channel. A fishing programme comes up. Fishing in Brisbane. I bet for a grand both the boys and I could be on a boat like that.

'You what?'

'I just called the travel agent,' I repeat in a voice like Father Christmas.

'Michael's in hospital – with psychosis – this is hardly the time to be thinking of overseas travel.'

'Jesus, Val.' Her body goes stiff. 'He won a grand worth of travel. I haven't booked anything. I'm just making some inquiries – no need to get aggro.'

'What?'

'It was a raffle at the club – his Christmas present from me – and he won!' Her mouth's still hanging wide open like a carnival clown head. It's not that hard to understand, is it?

'So … Michael won a thousand dollars' worth of travel and you are making plans on how to spend it?'

'It was my Christmas present to him.' She makes it sound like I'm being selfish, like she's standing up for him, but really she's selfish. She just wants everything under her control. That's the way she is.

'Look, Val. I know you need to be in charge of everything, but you're not Mike's only parent. You haven't been any use in this situation. I'm surprised you even took time off work.' I know it's harsh. I can almost see her flinch as my word hit her.

Her voice is too quiet for the words that come out. 'You bastard. I'm not listening to this.' She's not looking at me, eyes out of focus on the wall behind. I soften my voice.

'Sorry, Val. I didn't mean to be an asshole. But we both know I am.' When talking to a woman always admit defeat. 'I just think this could be the perfect opportunity … you know, for Mike and John and I to bond. It could be therapeutic …' I can see her coming around. 'We could go on a fishing trip.' And I've lost her again. I feel the slap in the face before I even see it coming. It's nothing, just another reminder that I'm never right. All that's left is a tingling sensation.

Valerie

'He *what?*'

'He wants to spend it on a fishing trip.'

'*What?*' I knew Elena would take my side. It's a relief, because John obviously won't, when there's a fishing trip in Aussie in it for him.

'What is wrong with that man?'

I sigh. I don't know, but I feel guilty, time and time again, for inflicting him on my children, and yet I have an obligation not to make him the bad guy. I don't want to be one of *those* parents who turn their children against their father.

'He's your father, Elena.' Jesus taught compassion, I remind myself.

'Not *my* fault.'

She's having a very catty day. I remember those pregnancy hormones well. She's almost in tears.

'It's not *fair*, Mum. Michael's not in any fit state to make decisions. How can Dad even think about spending his travel vouchers without him being able to decide?'

'He thinks it will be good for him, male bonding.'

I shouldn't have said that. I see the pain in Elena's eyes but I don't put my arms around her because she doesn't want to admit that it's there. She looks at the ground. I'm silent. Finally she acknowledges it.

'If I had been born a boy …' she says, the rest of the sentence lost in sobs. The tears soak through my blouse. It's the same one I wore yesterday and the day before. My mind is sidetracked. I bring it back. It's true, I think. Caleb has never been able to relate to women, or girls. He's never seen us as human. I don't know if he can relate to men well either, but they're part of the same club, keeping the safe distance mediated by sport and beer, playing the man game, acting the man role. He's always been good at that. He's always treated me as his mother; someone to do the housework and make him feel good about himself, and also someone to hate, to resist, to challenge like an insolent teenager. When we lived together, it was like having an extra child to manage.

I didn't realise Elena had noticed, but I suppose it was obvious that Caleb was always doing things with the boys and never had anything in common with her – never made an effort. It's not that he doesn't love her; he just doesn't know how to interact with her. I wonder if she's thought about it much before. I suppose I was too busy to notice.

Elena rests her head against my shoulder and I pat her back like I did when she was a baby. She wipes her eyes and pulls away leaving see-through blotches on shirt.

'I know it's hardly a fishing trip,' I say, 'But we could do the typical girly thing and go shopping.'

She smiles.

'Okay, Mum. I know you need it.' She looks down at the slit of skin showing between her top and pants. 'We both do!'

Elena

It goes around and around in my head. I should leave him. I should. It's the appropriate thing to do. But I love my house. I love my life. I'm pissed as hell at him but I love him. I don't need him. I would leave if I thought it would be better for me.

Malcolm has been treading on egg shells, so repentant, so guilty, and I've been enjoying every minute of it. The part of me that felt betrayed wants him to suffer. But it's not helping. I'm not making progress with this.

'Maybe it's just the way I am,' he says. And I wonder how he can justify this situation. 'Maybe I'm like Henry.'

'Bullshit. You're nothing like Henry. I wish you were. Henry gives a damn.'

It's not even the infidelity that bothers me. It's the whole situation. My brother has psychosis, in hospital, I'm pregnant with Malcolm's child … Could he have picked a worse time? I suppose I haven't had any energy for him lately at all. I can sort of see that. Maybe he doesn't deserve my energy.

I would kick him out but then I would be home alone, so instead I ignore him. I've tried talking. It doesn't get us anywhere. Instead, I'm camped out at Henry's. God knows I need the company and the emotional support. I can't bring myself to tell Mum. I know it's not logical but I feel ashamed. I don't need anyone to judge me or to hate Malcolm. Henry is surprisingly balanced about the whole thing, which obviously means he's still taking my side, otherwise I would consider him a traitor.

'Okay, so from an NVC perspective, I'm hearing that you have a need for emotional security and that need has been threatened by this situation.' Non-Violent Communication is one of Henry's many obsessions. It makes sense in theory: remove all the bullshit, talk about what's underneath all the blame and judgement.

'Everyone has the same basic human needs: food, shelter, love, safety, security.' Henry prattles on. I've heard this speech a hundred times but I know he's just trying to help, and maybe he can.

'If we just talk about our needs and feelings then we can all at least understand where everyone else is coming from, even if we don't agree, even if we don't meet the other person's needs …'

'So what's Malcolm's need?' I ask through poisonous black emotion. 'To fuck his students? To sow his wild oats? To fuck me over?' Henry rubs my back.

'He has a need for freedom, and I guess there's a physical need involved there as well, but there are other ways of meeting that need that would make him less of a wanker, or more if you'll excuse the pun.'

I can't help but giggle. It seems to calm me down a bit.

'Freedom.'

'I think it's really about freedom. For me it is. I hate to be restricted …' Henry continues.

'Yeah, but you're honest about not wanting to be in a monogamous relationship. That's different. This whole situation is pointless and I can't resolve it. There's just no solution. I guess

I should have learnt from Mum that men are assholes.' Henry coughs.

'Except you,' I add, hugging him sideways. 'You're wonderful.'

'You're starting to get Freudian on me, Elena. Are you mirroring the relationship your Mum and Dad had?'

'Oh God, I hope not. I mean, Dad cheated on Mum but our relationship is different. We're much better than them. They hardly ever spoke when they weren't fighting. Although, that was later in the relationship. I wonder how it was before I was born. I can't imagine them ever being in love. Anyway, Dad wasn't fucking around when we were kids, not that I know of. He was just drinking and gambling and fishing all the time.'

'Is that what Malcolm's doing?'

'What?' Surprised laughter bursts from my mouth. It's deep, guttural.

'He's gambling.'

'Oh my God. You're right.' He was taking a risk – that I wouldn't find out. He was gambling on our relationship.

'And you were the stakes.'

The realisation sends a rush of energy through my body. I grab Henry and hug him ecstatically. He giggles.

'Thank you.'

'Any time.'

'Thanks, Dr Freud.'

'You're Velcom,' Henry replies in an accent that sounds more like the Count from Sesame Street. 'Vone Oedipal complex – ah ah ah ah ah ah.'

'That's enough.' I pick up one of his hideous orange paisley cushions and hit him gently on the forehead.

'Oedipal? I'm not the one fucking someone old enough to be my dad.'

'She's obviously got daddy issues. How old is she?'

'I don't know, probably the same age as most of his students. 18? I'll find her on Facebook.'

'So not all that much younger than you?'

'Six years makes a big difference!'

'Well, Malcolm would have to have been a pretty young father to have an adult daughter.'

I shoot him a look and reach for his laptop. Fortunately Malcolm's password is the same for everything. I log in to his Facebook. Funny, I never felt the need to check up on him before. I must have trusted him.

'Here she is.' I pull up the message that sent my life spinning out of control. Henry reads is.

'Tactless,' he mumbles under his breath, then clicks on the thumbnail image to bring up her profile. 'Oh my God. I know her!' He's excited now. It's contagious.

'How?' I take a closer look at her profile picture, hipster-punk, dark hair, skinny as fuck. Bitch.

'She was in my sociology paper last trimester and she lives across the street.'

'Get out.'

'Don't get any crazy ideas.'

'Would it be so crazy to confront her.'

He puts on a posh voice: 'A woman in your condition ...' I elbow him.

'Just make sure you know what you're doing, hun. Don't do anything you are likely to regret.'

I feel like I'm on cocaine, not that I've ever been on cocaine, but the way I've heard cocaine feels. I'm high as a kite, invincible. Underneath it all I'm terrified as I walk across the tar-seal and up the long driveway to what looks like a typically dilapidated student flat.

When I get to the door I almost turn away. My hand is shaking as I knock on the frosted glass. This is surreal. I'm a star in a David Lynch film. I'm just waiting for the long panning shot of symbolic lampshades and full ashtrays. Breathe.

The door opens and she's there. Suddenly I don't know what to do or say. I should have written it down. Why am I even here? Watch her facial expressions, confusion, recognition, shock. I feel light-headed.

'You're Malcolm's girlfriend.'

I nod. I need to sit down. I steady myself on the door. I want to hurl accusations at her. I want her to suffer the way that I am. I want to scream. But nothing comes out. The dizziness starts at my temples, then it engulfs me.

There's nothing.

Everything is black.

Breathe.

I'm aware of my body, of the summer heat.

I open my eyes and she's still there.

'No.' Why did I come here? I just want her to go away.

'I'm so sorry.' My vision is still blurry. She looks down at me and she's too close. I realise my head must be on her lap. I realise she's been crying and all the anger I had seeps away. It must be maternal instincts or something. Part of me still wants to be angry but I can't summon the feeling back. I feel moisture trickling between my legs and panic overwhelms me.

'My baby!' I look down but I can't see past my bump.

'Is there any blood?' I'm too terrified to move. My body is rigid.

'I can't see any.'

That has to be a good sign. I prop myself up and check. At this point I don't care at all if I make myself indecent in front of a stranger who happens to be having an affair with my partner. All I care about is the baby. Thank God. It's just sweat from the heat. I breathe, such deep relief.

I look at Kim, still sitting on the floor next to me and realise she could be me. When I first started seeing Malcolm he was still on-again off-again with his old girlfriend. He downplayed it, said the relationship was coming to an end, but she sent me abusive text messages from his phone. I wanted to believe Malcolm, so I did. I chose to think she was a bit crazy and that he was innocent.

'Malcolm …' I begin to speak. I want to explain to her what I've just been thinking but I can't find the words.

'He won't talk to me.' Her voice breaks.

She's so young, so innocent. My anger returns but it's not aimed at her anymore. How could he do this, to both of us? I still can't speak. I can't find the words.

'I feel so used.' Tears burst out and she automatically lifts her hands to brush them away.

I raise my arms – also automatically – maybe it's the mother in me, maybe it's my 'condition'. It's not rational in my mind but I do it anyway and she collapses into me. Surreal is the word. Her skin is so soft that I'm lost for a moment. I don't know this woman. I just know that she's caused me emotional distress, pain. Did she? She knew about me, obviously, but it was Malcolm who couldn't keep his dick in his pants.

Her hand brushes my hair, I feel her face, hot against my cheek. This has to be the strangest experience of my life. I'm comforting the woman who recently ruined my life, as it was. I'm holding her as she cries and I feel closer to her now than I have to anyone in a long time. We've both been betrayed; Kim by her lecturer and me by my partner. That they happen to be the same person should be grounds for us to attack each other. I thought I'd come over here and make her regret what she did, but now I'm lost in this unexpected intimacy.

'Life is a collection of moments,' I say, to no one in particular, but Kim nods. 'The only way I can tell that I'm same person from ten minutes ago is from memory, but she's almost un-recognisable.' Kim looks at me again, her sobs have subsided into the peacefulness so familiar to me after crying.

'I wonder how it's even possible to convict someone of a crime,' she says, looking down at her hands. 'If they're not in that moment anymore.'

I think of Malcolm and feel momentary nausea, but it passes. Maybe I can't hold him accountable for the person he was days ago, but I want to. 'I want to punish him,' I say, surprised that the words even come out.

'I would too, if I were you,' Kim says. 'And I would hate me.'

'I really should leave him.' I can't believe I'm talking about this with *her*. My anger returns again, but so do her tears. This time I feel like pushing her away. I want to make her suffer, but I can't. She's too much like me.

Malcolm

I stare out across the university lake. Despite the seething man-made cesspool of duck shit that it is, I still find it calming. I take a drag on my fourth cigarette and watch the tree reflections ripple. I shouldn't have bought this packet. Smoking out of stress is such a cliché. Elena would kill me again. I already feel dead. *Stop being so melodramatic*, the little critical voice in the back of my head calls out. Don't I have a right to be?

I really fucked up this time. I hate this rollercoaster. One minute I'm a scolded child, with all the shame and guilt, thinking I'll do anything I possibly can to make it up to her. I can change. I can be a better person. I'm unworthy of her greatness, et cetera. The next minute I'm thinking this is just the way I am. I need to accept that.

If Elena wants to be with me she should accept me for who I really am, not who she wants me to be. I did it. I enjoyed it. I've never felt so alive as when I was with Kim. Then the voice pops into my head – *don't be such a cock*. It wasn't real, it was just a fantasy that managed to happen for me. It's not meaningful. My relationship with Elena is meaningful – was meaningful … and it goes round again.

Sometimes I think I should leave. But that would only make it worse. If anyone gets to decide to leave it should be Elena, if that's what she wants. I've done enough damage. I don't actually want to leave her anyway. She's perfect – gorgeous, intelligent, wonderful. It would really mess me up if she left, but it would be my own fault.

When you enter a relationship you sign a contract; not one you will ever read the small print of. It's like the 'social contract' we apparently all sign by being born. We are supposed to know the rules and follow them, even if no one teaches us. Ignorance of the law is not a just defence. I couldn't plead ignorance here anyway. I could make a good case for stupidity, maybe biological imperative.

A duck waddles up and has a go at pecking one of my discarded butts. 'Sorry, buddy. I got nothing." I'm on empty.

Maybe I should have come clean rather than let Elena find out this way. If I had told her it would still have been a nightmare. I didn't say anything because I wanted to protect her – or protect myself. That worked out real well. I'm the lecturer, the ethicist. You'd think I'd know better. I suppose it's like any ethical dilemma, any thought experiment; there is no clear-cut right or wrong here. Our relationship was the fat man stuck in the cave. There was no way around its destruction. The pressure just built up to a point where I couldn't handle it anymore. Maybe that's self-sabotage. Who cares what label you give it?

I should have been more careful. If Elena didn't find out it wouldn't have hurt her – hurt us – but if our roles were reversed I would want to know and I would be just as angry as she is. Yep, I really failed on the 'do unto others' principle. What about utilitarianism? There's no way anyone's overall happiness has increased.

Hedonism in the moment can cause one hell of a hangover.

But if Elena didn't know we would all be happier, wouldn't we? I guess that's the flaw of utilitarianism, too often it's just used as an excuse to get away with things that would normally be immoral. Kim still hates utilitarianism. If she were here she could sort me out on this but I can't see her. Not anymore. I've done enough. It's bad enough that it happened, but if Elena finds out I'm still hanging out with Kim there will be no going back. Anyway, I'm still angry that Kim sent me that stupid message in the first place; I bet she wanted this to happen. She's probably jealous of Elena. But now we're playing out the classic love triangle through modern technology. I won't answer Kim's calls and texts and Elena won't answer mine or respond to the many self-deprecating emails I've sent her.

Elena's blog started all this. I've read it – over and over in the past few days. I'd never read it before. There's no clue there about anything in her life, it's all fake; all vitamins and amino acids and lacto fermentation. She's such a hypocrite, eating Burger King and donuts in secret while soapboxing about the evils of processed food. It's so much effort for something so insignificant. Maybe if she had put that effort into our relationship I wouldn't have done what I did. I briefly fantasise about going onto her blog and telling her readers that it's all bullshit, that the person they think they've been communicating with doesn't even exist. It would only make matters worse, of course.

I feel nauseous from the noxious fumes I've been self-harming with. Time to go home. I can't go home so I'm back with Mum and Dad – being doted over in the most patronising way, but I appreciate it. I begin the walk. People see me, but they have no idea what's going on inside. Maybe no one ever does. My mind is a blur of half thoughts spurred by guilt, anger, remorse, resentment. No one would want to be in here.

'You don't really want a partner, you want a mother,' Elena had accused me countless times.

'You're messier than I am.' I'd thrown back, without thinking.

'Exactly,' she sighed. 'You want me to be your mother and spend all my time cleaning.'

I hear the vacuum before I'm through the front door. Sure enough, Mum has the nozzle in one hand, an upturned chair in the other. She's vacuuming the lint off the bottom of each leg with a determined look. The sight of it makes me want to run back to the cottage with a million cultures brewing on every surface of the kitchen and knitting strewn around the lounge. It's too late. In exercising momentary freedom I've lost the freedom to maintain the life I used to have. I'm looking for the key to one of Rosa's imaginary worlds but there's no way to escape this mess. I make a beeline for my room, grabbing the phone on my way.

'Roast pork for dinner,' Mum calls down the hallway after me. It won't be free-range. Elena always hated eating here. I bet Mum will make microwaved potato bake with the little flavour sachet. Half of me loves it, the other half just wants to be home where there's no microwave or flavour sachets.

My room is the same one I left when I left high school: single bed, posters of soccer players on the wall, DIY kit mechanical gadgets and Terry Pratchett books. It's both familiar and alien. I dial home. I'm ready for Elena to rip into me again. I deserve it.

'Hello?' The voice on the other end of the line is sweet and light and happy. For a moment I think I've dialled the wrong number.

'Uh, hi.'

'Malcolm?' It's definitely Elena, but she's not pissed, even after recognising my voice.

'How are you?' The standard blah question has so much more significance with us these days.

'You know, I'm actually really good.' I don't understand why or how, but I believe her. She sounds transcendent. She doesn't ask how I am. Maybe she doesn't want to know.

'What happened?' I ask, still stunned.

'Oh, I don't know.' Her voice is floaty. 'I guess I've been processing some stuff.' There's really nothing else to say. I can tell she doesn't want anything from me. She doesn't need me. I'm speechless. I hope that this is just part of the cycle of grief. That's it. She's in denial. She will push me away then come crawling back. I loathe myself for thinking like this. I'm the one who should be crawling.

'Malcolm?' Elena asks. 'Are *you* okay?'

'Yeah. I'm just at Mum and Dad's. Let me know if you need anything.'

'I will.'

Suddenly the conversation has drawn to an end but there's still so much I need to say, so many questions I want to ask but they all centre around one thing.

'Elena. I know I messed up. I know I hurt you. I just need to know if there's a chance you'll ever forgive me.'

Elena is silent for a while.

'Yes.'

I breathe a sigh of relief. When all this settles down we can go back to normal.

'I will do my best to forgive you for what you did, Malcolm. I don't want to be burdened with that kind of grudge.' A bitterness creeps into her voice making me uneasy. 'And I will try to forgive you for what you did to Kim too.'

'Kim? What?' Now I'm confused. 'Why do you care what …' She interrupts me.

'It's irresponsible of you, Malcolm. It's horrendous. You were in a position of power and you exploited it – you exploited her – and then you just ditched her.'

My head's spinning but I register two things. Elena must have been in contact with Kim and somehow, by trying to make things better I've made them a lot worse. By avoiding Kim I've hurt Elena more. 'I thought you wouldn't want me to talk to her after …'

'You would think that because it's self-serving.' Elena's words kick me in the face. 'You only care about my feelings because they affect you and your life and the relationship and the 'happy family' that you want to have without taking any responsibility. You don't give a damn about her.'

I've been pushed so far I can't help but retaliate. 'Well, if you gave a damn about me in the first place you would have noticed that we hardly even *had* a relationship for the past six months.' I can hear her drawing in her breath. 'If you had paid any attention to me at all – a *real* person in your *real* life – rather than staring at a computer all the time pretending you're this super amazing housewife, we wouldn't be in this situation.'

'That's right Malcolm. It's all about you.' I hear the click, then the repetitive beeping of the disconnected phone line. Everything I said was true, to a point. Everything Elena said was too. That's the thing with relationships; there are always two sides. No one's ever innocent.

Gayle

It's only the second time I've visited my grandson. The first time I couldn't stand to be here, in this place. Hospitals reek of death and decay, and in mental hospitals it's the decay of the *wairua*, the spirit and the death of the mind. *Get him out.* The ancestors scream inside my head. But it's not my place to intervene. This is not my world, it's te āo Pākehā, and I've lived in this world long enough to know there's no point in trying to change it. Michael lies still, like a corpse, his eyes closed. I sit on the bed and wait.

'Nan,' he says before he opens his eyes. It's a sign.

'We need to get you out of here, boy.'

He nods. 'It's not me that's broken – it's not my mind. It's our family that's broken.' His voice is strained, high pitched.

I'm washed with guilt. 'I'm sorry.'

'It's not your fault.'

It is. It was me that moved away, it was me who started this. If I had kept the connection this never would have happened.

Michael looks me in the eye. 'It's the whole world,' he says. His voice is calm and powerful now. 'It's never just you.'

As soon as I'm home I call my sisters. We talk of old stories, of magic, of mākutu and tohunga.

'He has power,' I say. 'He has a gift.' I hear the silence of agreement and wait for the only reply.

'He needs guidance.'

Michael

There's a storm outside but it breaks through the walls. The thunder rumbles right through me. I can tell something big is coming. There's a pause – silence – before the knock. For once my room's not crowded with family and I'm glad. I've been waiting for him.

He has a walking stick and paper-white hair that flows down his head and over his chin. He hobbles in and introduces himself as Hone, leaning on his cane. I recognise him from the marae.

'Nan sent you.' He nods.

He begins to speak in Māori that flows so fast it rushes like a monsoon. The syllables join together and cascade around me, pooling in the corners of the room. All I can hear is one word which echoes in my head.

Tohunga.

The storm breaks through the walls and saturates me. The clouds roll in thunder above. I can almost see the stars and the universe beyond. I'm high above looking down at my puny body in the bed below. *Am I dying?* I'm too far away to tell.

Hone is next to me now, in the heavens. He summons the birds in whispers, tūī, kōkako, kererū. They break away and melt into constellations. I see the threads of the universe in its tight-loose weave, unravelled at the corners of my life. Hone nods. This is the work you must do. The strands are silver water in my hands and I don't know how to weave them back together. My ancestors are chanting within me, all around me, through me, we are one. My hands begin to move and I watch as we pull everything back together again.

I am Māui and I'm in the last story. The only one that terrifies me to the bone. Grief has touched everyone in the village and I am on a quest against death, against the death goddess: Hine-nui-te-pō. If I can kill her the world will be rid of death forever – can you imagine? Guaranteed immortality. My bird companions are tagging along as usual. Fantail darts from tree to tree leading the way. Kererū follows closely behind. We come out of the forest and behold the view. It's the view from Indicators, but I don't have a surfboard. I see the land shifting and recognise Hine-nui-te-pō, just the way she was drawn in the children's book; as part of the land, herself, like a mountain that descends into the sea. We make our way silently now, stealthily. We can't wake her up. The only entrance is though her tero, and she has to be asleep or it will mean the end for Māui, for me.

It's a dark cave and it's the most terrifying thing I've ever seen. It seems to go forever. There's no point in hesitating. I dive in but, like Māui in the story, my legs get stuck, and seeing flailing legs hanging out of the death goddess's vagina is enough to make fantail crack up.

'No!' I'm spiralling. Down, down, down … the secrets of the universe unfolding themselves on the way …

I guess it has to end somewhere. And every change in life is a little bit like death – every defeat, every conquest, every orgasm, every surf, every breath. We are all connected and we all share that terror of death – of our own mortality – which we know is always coming – because there is a beginning there must be an end – in the beginning was nothing – Te Kore – no one remembers the beginning – it was before awareness – maybe there was no beginning – just an endless circle – a skipping CD – an iPod stuck on repeat playing Bach or Tom Jones or Celine Dion – who the hell knows?

Maybe this is hell – round and round and no escape. Maybe death is the only escape, maybe instead of fearing it we need to harden up and look it in the face – life is the problem, death is the answer. What if it's not? What if Elena in her Buddhist phase was right – what if we just have to come back again and again – as a bug – as a bird – as a whale – that sounds a whole lot better than being human and having all these fucking questions circling around and around, a dog chasing its own tail – a shark fin in my mind – just visible above the water and no one wants to know what's beneath – I can hear the *Jaws* theme music, I can smell the sea – I'm almost there.

Mum calls me from across the room – across the sea. She dissolves. My family are all standing there – distant like a postcard, surrounded by a frame of reality while I'm out here in no man's land. The last of the air escapes – bubbles of awareness – sensations all through my body. I am. I am alive. I am me. The water ripples, the wave surges I push myself above the surface – onto the board which seems so familiar – it was my life before everything capsized – before I bailed into a different kind of world where everything made more sense and less sense at the same time – where I knew everything and yet, no one understood. Is that enlightenment?

I feel the water rushing past as the wave descends. I've missed it this time. Will there be another chance? Is this world any better than the one I've left behind? It will do for now. I look out to the horizon – it's flat on all sides. No land – total isolation – and it's surprisingly peaceful. Still. Silent. What's there to do except surrender?

The horizon begins to rise – a swell so massive it eclipses the sun and the world goes dark – a tsunami – and I know it's going to be the ride of a lifetime.

PART THREE

The aftermath

Autumn 2012

Valerie

The dishes seem to clink more loudly than ever before. My hands are rubbery and rough from being in the soapy water too long. I let out the water and dry my hands on the dish towel.

'Rosa – dry these or the TV goes off!'

I do a quick sweep of the kitchen floor. And pick up the cushions and kids' clothes in the lounge. I don't ever remember doing this much housework in my life. I've always had a cleaner on Friday afternoons and I guess we just got by with a medium level of chaos in between times, mediated by frantic bursts and desperate child nagging. I suppose housework was just another thing on the endless list of things to do. Now it seems to be *all* I do since Michael came back home. I say back, but he was hardly ever here before, so it's still not normal. He stays in his room with the curtains drawn. He watches DVDs and reads surfing magazines. He might as well be a zombie. I feel less a mother than a servant. He orders me to bring him food and I obey, I don't know what else to do. I don't know what I can say to him to make things better. There's just nothing. I feel just as helpless now as when he was in hospital.

I can't wait to be back to work but I don't want to leave Michael when he's like this. My receptionist, Walter, sent me flowers which are now wilting on the kitchen table, wilting like I am, like everything in this house is.

Rosa's barely talking to me. I thought she'd be pleased to have me around more but she can tell that my words and gestures are hollow. She can tell that I'm giving Michael everything right now, even if he doesn't care or notice, and there's nothing left for her. So I clean. I take every item out of the pantry, one by one, throw out the expired packets of noodles and the bags of nuts with moths in them. I clean everything out and put things back together and hope that I can do the same with my life. Wash away, wash away, create a clean, clear space to allow for something better.

Sometimes I pray while I clean: for mercy, for grace, for Michael's sanity and for my own. Sometimes I sing Frank Sinatra or Billie Holiday. Most of the time I just let my mind go blank. I don't know if praying ever worked. It would be nice if it did but when things are this hard – every day – I wonder whether God has any compassion at all. I think of the footprints poem. The man (of course it's a man) walking along the beach alongside Jesus who sees, looking back, that in the hardest time of his life there is only one set of footprints, and Jesus says it's because he was carrying him. Well, where is he now? I'm not going to let anyone else take any credit for my hard work! It's strange, because during all the other hard times, with the divorce, with raising all these teenagers, and so on, the thought of God being there always helped, but now it's no consolation. Maybe I don't have any energy for God anymore.

I daydream about selling this house and moving somewhere tropical, but it's mostly to escape the feeling of futility, that this whole existence is pointless.

Rosa

Michael's out of hospital now. He's staying with us but he's still not normal. He keeps asking Mum for things, the way I do when I'm sick: 'Mu-u-um, can you bring me some coffee.' Except that coffee is gross and I don't ask for that. His room is gross too because he never leaves. Mum goes in there and gets the empty plates but he never listens when she tells him to have a shower.

'Where's Evie?' I ask him.

'She's not coming back,' he says and sounds sad. His voice is slow, like he's almost asleep. Mum says it's the medicine he's taking and I wonder why it makes him all dopey when medicine is supposed to make you better.

Mum's been cleaning the house lots because she's not back at work. She yells at me when I forget to take my shoes off and when I leave crumbs on the bench. I liked it better when she wasn't here to yell as much.

It was the holidays, but this morning it's the first week back at school but Mum doesn't remember so I don't remind her, I don't want to see the bitchy girls again I just want to watch TV.

Mum asks me to bring Michael his toast but when I go to his room he's not there. Mum looks worried and checks for his car but it's gone.

'He might have been missing for hours for all we know,' she says.

She calls Nan and I hear her say, 'Oh, he's with you.' I can tell from her voice that she's relaxing now. 'Tell him he shouldn't have left without telling me.'

I bet Mum will remember about school and so I have to go again but it's alright because Elena is going to have her baby soon and then I'll be an aunty.

Michael

It's dawn when I wake up. I can hear the waves but I don't take the usual path down to the surf. I head west. We used to come out this way, adventuring, when we were kids. The path was clearer back then, now it's overgrown with gorse and flax. The prickles tear at my jeans and I know they hurt but I can hardly feel it. I can hardly feel anything.

I stumble though a thick patch of kānuka and drink in the view. The ocean, the horizon, that's all I want to see and from here I can see my destination. The overhang.

It juts out about twenty metres from the cliff, wider at first, then narrow at the end and from there it's a sheer hundred-metre drop to the rocks and crashing waves below.

Am I crazy? Everyone knows about it. I can't hide it from anyone. All my friends know. *How can I ever live this down?*

Is this real? It is now. Everything could have been a dream and I wish it was. I wish it was one of those nightmares that you wake up from and take a while to realise that it didn't actually happen. Sweet relief.

I stumble down the neck of the overhang and stop in my tracks. If I can get to the end I will be the closest I've ever come to just seeing horizon.

I step carefully over the small stones and hoist myself up onto the boulders at the end then, from all fours, I rise up.

I'm at the edge of the world, a hundred metres up from the

waves and rocks below, and if I don't turn my head all I can see is sea, sky and that dark line that connects it. To my right the sky is glowing red, to my left it's still grey.

What am I doing here? This is crazy, but maybe it has to be, to end all of my craziness. I've put my family through enough and this is the final test.

It's got to end here. One way or another.

I close my eyes and breathe deep. I have been numb. These drugs have been pulling me down. They've been suffocating me. They're poison. How could my family do this to me? The anger flares but I drop it. It's in the past now.

This is a time for a fresh start.

I open my eyes and suddenly I can feel again. The ice-cold air hits my eyes and I breath it in.

This is real. This is me. I'm flying without ever leaving the ground. I don't need to jump. I just need to know that I can.

Evie

A dead cow or sheep lying in the pasture is recognised as carrion. The same sort of carcass dressed and hung up in a butcher's stall passes as food. J H KELLOGG

I'm here because this is the responsible thing to do. My appointment has finally rolled round and I'm waiting in the Elizabeth Rothwell building, the women's outpatient clinic, waiting, waiting.

My whole body is rigid. The colposcopy came back abnormal. Just like the smear. I don't want cancer. It would seriously get in the way of my activism, and that's about all I have at the moment. Activism and friends. *Breathe.* Being sick wouldn't help. *Inhale.* Dying wouldn't help. *Exhale.* It would just make the ratio of people who care to don't care even worse. I'm doing the right thing.

I dig my heels into the well-worn carpet and study the children's art on the walls to avoid eye contact with the other outpatients. Out. That's right. Out of sorts, out of it, out of mind … out of time. On the outside. Looking in. Out to get me. I wring the piece of refill paper a little in my hands, careful not to tear it. I feel crazy. Was Michael like this? I feel a pang in my chest. I hate missing him. I try not to think of Valerie. She would want me to be here. Hell, she would hold my hand, if I had the courage to ask.

The people around me might as well be aliens. I watch them

and try to figure out their stories but it just comes out blank. People walk in and out of the waiting room, everyone looks around. It's too awkward. I put my head down as someone approaches. The shoes stop right in front of me and I look up expecting to see an official stranger – a nurse calling me for my appointment. Instead I see Val.

'How did you …?'

'They send a duplicate letter to your GP.' She sits down next to me.

'Why did you come?'

I can feel Val's arm around my shoulder but I'm looking down, trying to fight back the unexpected tears. It must be the shock of seeing her here, the surprise, that has made me cry. Yeah, that's it. Oh God, does this mean things are even worse than I've suspected?

She speaks as if in answer to my thoughts.

'I just wanted to tell you,' her voice is calm and even, 'That I've been reading all the recent research about abnormal results with young women.'

I hold my breath and grit my teeth.

'Don't worry, Evie. It's not bad.'

I relax a little.

'Actually, it's good. Well, the research shows that young women are much more likely to have spontaneous regression in their cells. Your cells are likely to go back to normal. You don't need to have this treatment today.'

'That's what Tara said. She said if I quit smoking I might not need the treatment. But why would they bother to do it?'

'That's a good question,' Val nods to herself. 'Maybe they went a bit crazy trying to make up for that Cartwright incident. Do you remember that?'

I nod, even though I only know about it from Tara.

'Maybe,' she continues, 'It will take a while for this new research to affect medical practice.'

The gynaecologist calls my name. An Indian man. I'm among the most actively non-racist people you will ever meet, but I'm uncomfortable. Mostly because he's a man, I tell myself. Why would any man, in his right mind, want to be a gynaecologist? I suppose most specialists are male. Creeps. I'd rather have the nondescript female gyno I had last time, but I don't get a choice. That's the beauty of the public health system, I suppose.

I leave Val behind in the waiting room and I'm led into a small office.

'The procedure we are going to perform today …' He begins.

'Wait,' I say. I knew this was coming, didn't I? But it feels so rushed. 'I know, it's the LEETZ, you take a heated wire loop and burn off six millimetres of my cervix.'

The doctor nods, taken aback.

'I just have some questions first.' Thank you, Tara and Val. If I didn't have this support I would surely have just been another box on the conveyer belt; churned through the system, adding to the statistics.

'What are the risks of not doing this 'treatment' today?' I ask, my voice quavering. He is the expert, after all. What would I know?

'Well,' he stammers. 'There … there would be no great risk.'

I know this already. Cervical cancer is very slow to develop, ten years, they say.

'And what are the chances that the cells will regress by themselves?'

He seems uncomfortable. 'Well, they are high-grade abnormal cells, but perhaps, fifteen to thirty per cent.'

'Alright.' I feel more confident now, especially because of what Val just told me. 'So, there's a chance that they will regress back to normal, by themselves, but you want to do this today?'

'Well, it is standard procedure.'

'Okay, one more question. With cancer, damaged cells are more likely to grow back abnormal, aren't they? I mean … any damage causes regeneration, which is more likely to result in more abnormal cells in the future.'

'Yes.'

'So in having this procedure today – when you said I don't need to and that the cells might regress on their own …' I take a deep breath. 'I might be making it more likely for abnormal cells to regenerate?'

'Yes, but the chances are fairly low.'

'Okay. But, what are the risks of me not having this treatment today?'

'Well, if you come back and have another colposcopy in four months, there is no significant risk.'

'Alright,' I smile. 'Thank you.'

He looks at me as though he has no reason to trust me.

'But you would have to come back.'

There is such a vested interest here. They look good if they treat more people. The thought makes me uncomfortable, but for my own peace of mind I will come back.

'Of course.'

Rosa

School is back now and Mrs Mills is my teacher again which is okay because she's mostly nice and it's cool 'cause Aroha is in my class and Chardon isn't but it's also not cool because the other bitches are still there and Mrs Mills put them all at the same table with Aroha again and I have to sit by Leela who dribbles all the time and Timmy who smells funny and steals my pencils.

Mrs Mills says we have to write a story about what happened in the summer.

My brother was crayzee

We had to go to the Henry Bennit centa and stay in the farno room and Mum cried lots. Now he's better but he still seems a bit dumb or tired or something. Mum says it's becuz of the medesin but I think what really hapind was that he went to a difrint werld in his hed and he is still thear some of the time. I don't know what kind of werld it is but he likes serfing a lot so maybe it is one where he gets to serf and never has to do the dishes – coz he hates dishes. I hate dishes too and I can't serf so if I ever go crayzee I want to go somewhere where there are fairies that wear little blue flowas on thear heds like in the storybooks or maybe witches and I can fly on a broom and go to the moon.

Mrs Mills looks at my story and her mouth twists down at the corners and I wonder if it's not good or it says something wrong.

'Rosa, are you alright?' she asks and it seems like she cares about me and that makes tears come out from my eyes and she hugs me.

'How can I help?' she says.

'Can Aroha sit at my table?' I ask and she says, 'Of course.' And then everything is better.

Elena

Feijoa skins

Recently, I've been bingeing on feijoas, as many New Zealanders do at this time of year. I hear they're also known as pineapple guava, but I've never heard them called that here. They grow very well in our subtropical climate and everyone seems to have trees – I'm still surprised they sell in supermarkets when they're easy to get for free. I find their juicy, sweet, tart flavour irresistible and am always surprised that some people don't like them. Some people love them so much they eat the skins which are a little sour for my tastes, but I have devised a way to get more of the goodness out of the skins before I compost them.

Fermented feijoa drink

I loosely fill a 1.5 litre sealable jar with the empty skins, then fill it almost to the top with water and add about 1/4 cup of sugar (I'm using organic fair trade sugar, but I guess honey would work too). I started off using kefir (converted milk kefir) to ferment the feijoas, but then realised that the powdery stuff on the feijoa skin is actually yeast and the kefir grains weren't doing much.

The flavour leaches out of the skins, along with vitamin C and other things, I assume, and makes a delicious feijoa tasting drink in a couple of days. When the weather was warmer it took two days on the bench to get to the fizzy drink stage but now I'm experimenting with putting them in the hot water cupboard after a few less fizzy brews. I've also tried chopping the skins up into small pieces and cooking them in honey for a while – it creates a sort of glaze which would be great over a cheese cake, or it could be poured into a jar and consumed as marmalade.

In the past few weeks, with Malcolm gone, my blog has been more important than ever, making me feel less isolated and more human, alleviating the loneliness and giving me something else to focus on.

Henry and Tanya have been over here every day. I have asked them both to move in, even if it's a huge sacrifice. They know I would do the same for them. It takes a village to raise a child and I need to start building my village. Every day things seem a little bit different. I don't care about Malcolm fucking his student anymore. It's not about that. I care that he lied to me, that he betrayed me and that he didn't have the balls to tell me about it. I hate that I found out by accident, and if I didn't find out then I might never have known. I hate feeling like a fool. But maybe that's all ego talking, maybe I need to get over my victim mentality. Grow up. I'm about to become a mother, so there's no better time than the present.

Kim and I have been hanging out too, which is probably quite strange. She's always bringing me inappropriate food and I love it. Yesterday it was donuts – the American styled ones filled with custardy stuff. I know she still feels bad about what happened and sometimes I think she should, sometimes I don't. Sometimes I'm grateful that she helped to get me out of the swamp I was stuck in. Perhaps it's a coincidence that she is one of those people for me – the ones that you meet and instantly have a connection with. These days I have trouble believing anything is a coincidence.

Michael has been out of hospital for a month now but he's still vacant, I don't know if he'll ever be right again. Nan says he spends most of his time surfing and that the spirit of the ocean and Tangaroa will bring him back his life force. I hope she's right. She's taken him to see some healers, apparently. I've given him some supplements that Gerard recommended but I don't know if he's taking them. I'm at the kitchen sink preparing my amazing feijoa skin drink when I look out the window and hold my breath for a moment too long and wonder if I will ever be able to breathe again. I feel a rumble through my spine and pain cascading out and I know I'm in labour. The tree that fell in my garden is still there, still propped up by its family and I wonder if Michael is like that, if he's gone and the memory of him is just being held intact by the rest of us. The pain increases and all thoughts of Michael are wiped from my mind. Then it's gone, the contraction, I suppose, and I'm just an ordinary woman in an ordinary kitchen slicing feijoas.

Valerie

It's 7am and I'm on my way out the door when I hear the phone. Normally, on my early morning shift when I'm running late, I would leave it, but I have this feeling of excitement, built on the knowledge that it is coming soon. Elena has been complaining all week that she's over being pregnant. She has interchanged *I just want to get this thing out of me!* with *I want to see/hold my baby* and *It's so bloody hard to walk!*

'I think I'm in labour!' She sounds terrified and terribly excited. 'I just had this intense pain and now I'm bleeding.'

'I'm on my way.' I'm dialling work on my cell before I've even hung up the phone.

The door's open and Elena is sitting in the bay window wearing a loose cotton dress.

'Nothing's happened since I called,' she says. But a few minutes later she's groaning and rotating her hips, trying to quell that deep centred pain that I remember so well from all four labours.

My mind keeps racing ahead – thinking of the hospital – but Elena wants a home birth and at least I'm a doctor. I breathe deeply. She phones her midwife who says she will be over in a few hours. I feel a slight sense of panic. What are we going to do 'til then?

'Eat something,' I say. 'This could take a long time and you will need your strength later.'

I toast a slice of her dense home-made sourdough and smother it in butter and honey. She nibbles at it despite not being hungry. In the next few hours I make soup, endless cups of peppermint tea and rub her shoulders. I struggle to set up the birthing pool. Every hour we are jolted by another contraction, which by midday are occurring half-hourly, followed by a relaxing lull. I've never been big on housework but I pick up here and there; fold some washing, clean the bathroom, just to have something to do. I try to read some home birthing books which are written in very '70s language, although the one by an Australian GP makes a lot of sense. Of course I knew that caesareans could be complicated but I hadn't given much thought to the way stress hormones affect the body. It dawns on me that Elena has told me all this before and I hadn't really listened. I smile at her across the room and she smiles back with bright shining eyes. I hadn't noticed until now how her skin has been glowing, how healthy her hair looks. I hadn't really processed that my child was becoming a mother: a little somersault in my chest. It's actually nice not to have to think of when to go to the hospital or birthing centre, or what to pack. It's nice to just allow this baby to be born when it wants to be, even though I'm still on high-alert in case anything goes wrong.

The day seems to have whizzed by as if the euphoria in the air has somehow oiled its progression. By 3pm the birthing pool is set up, filled with warm water, and contractions are every twelve minutes. The midwife still hasn't turned up, which stirs frustration in me, but she's on her way and tells Elena she can get into the pool if she wants. Elena is mid-contraction and jumps in fully clothed.

Malcolm should be here. Elena won't tell me the whole story. It's so like her to keep secrets. I can't stand it. How could he miss the birth of his child? Well, Caleb did, often enough.

'I'll call him.'

'No!' Elena is adamant. Mid-contraction. 'Just trust me, Mum. He doesn't deserve to be here.'

I sigh. Infidelity, I suppose. Either that or he ate at Burger King. I giggle quietly. I can't imagine what else would make Elena so mad. She had wanted to involve him in the birthing plan right from the beginning. I guess that's all part of the modern hippie revival childbirth paradigm, even if lots of traditional cultures left birthing to the women who knew what the hell they were doing.

Zena finally arrives and starts boiling water with the air of an emergency doctor. She's in the zone. She finds a large bowl – I'm not sure how anyone finds anything in Elena's tiny, overloaded kitchen – and carries it, filled with steaming water, over to the birthing pool in the lounge.

'This is what they call 'hot towels," she tells us, dunking a hand towel into the bowel and wringing it out, despite its obviously painful heat. Now she seems more like a silver-dreaded warrior princess. Elena doubles over from the pain of contraction, her head drooping towards the water so that the tips of her hair are submerged. Zena spreads the towel out over her lower back and I can almost feel her whole body relax into a sigh.

This is nothing like any of my births. Elena has plied me with questions about them in the last few weeks and I've felt this tightness, as if I'm clenching the memories, not wanting to give too much away, not wanting to expose my vulnerability. I told Elena bits and pieces, but I couldn't tell her everything. I don't even want to remember most of it. They were all in hospital except Rosa, who was born at a birthing unit; a much nicer, less-equipped version of a hospital. I'd never considered being in the water. It seemed like a fad.

Elena was prem. My water broke when the midwife was examining me. I had to be rushed in to the hospital and I stopped having contractions so I had to have an emergency caesar. I don't remember much, just waking up with this baby I didn't know what to do with. I felt so guilty. I was supposed to love her unconditionally and all I felt was pain – from the operation and from the shock of everything happening before I was ready. I read all the magazines and books available in the 80s and did my best to breastfeed and increase the oxytocin so that we would bond.

Michael was so big I could hardly get him out. It didn't help that the doctors wouldn't let me crouch and made me lie down in the bed instead. I resented that afterward. It wasn't a medical thing or a safety thing, it was just being in that position, being at the mercy of other people, being disempowered. I couldn't really argue. I was too busy with the contractions.

John's birth was less painful because they gave me an epidural I never asked for. Apparently, after I got into hospital, the contractions slowed so they had to induce labour with Syntocinon and decided to paralyse half of my body with an epidural while they were at it. I couldn't even feel how to push. I haven't thought about it very much but every birth was traumatic for me. It was the sacrifice I made for my babies.

Now I'm watching as my first baby goes through this herself – so much braver than I was, more willing to decide for herself, more empowered than I ever was. I'm flushed with pride and drug-like excitement.

I must admit, this feels a lot more relaxed than being in the hospital. It's home, it's safe, there are all these familiar comforting things around, there's no need to pack or make decisions about where to go, there are no strangers around. I'm starting to see why Elena wanted this, even though I wanted to convince her otherwise.

The contractions intensify, so close together now. Zena is still draping the hot towels. There's no one checking the timing or trying to see how dilated she is, which makes it feel so much calmer. But as the delivery becomes imminent I can't suppress my anxiety. Elena hasn't had any tests or scans. What if we're setting ourselves up for an awful, desperate situation? I start to pray. There's nothing else I can do.

Elena's body stiffens and begins to shake. We're getting to the crux of things, now. She isn't screaming obscenities or primal screeches, she's silent, as though she's lost in the experience, overwhelmed. She looks up at me as the contraction subsides. Her eyes are pleading and I reach for her hand.

'I'm so tired,' she says, 'I can't do this.'

'Yes you can, love. Yes, you can.' I'm not saying it but we're both thinking it. *There's no going back.*

Zena goes to the kitchen for more hot water. I move around behind her and massage her shoulders and she folds into another contraction. She breathes deeply and a soft moan escapes her mouth. Elena leans forward as Zena comes back with her bucket and I move out of the way to make room for the relief. I can see it spread across her face as the steaming towel lands on her lower back.

Elena leans back and her whole body trembles. I grab hold of her shoulders to help prop her up in the water and I can feel the vibrations of her body birthing this baby. With one deep moan her body delivers and the baby is sent out into the water which has suddenly gone from clear to deep red and panic rises in my chest: what if something has gone terribly wrong? What if there's something wrong with this baby that takes over the rest of our lives? I hold my breath and pray. I'm not equipped to deal with this. Zena reaches into the dark red pool and lifts up a beautiful, healthy boy.

Elena

I've never felt this high in my life. I look over at my baby, wrapped up next to me, sleeping so peacefully. It feels wrong that he's not touching me and I know the attachment parenting thing is to have them on you all the time, but I don't think I'm cut out for that kind of self-sacrifice. I know I would go mad. I would love to unwrap him and lie him on my belly, but he's so peaceful. Right now, he doesn't need me. If he did I'm sure he would cry like he did when he emerged from the water, with that little squished up red face, black hair and chubby thighs.

Such a strong baby, Zena said. He could hold his head up and everything. Fin. That's the name that came to me at the time. Definitive and simple, something that's necessary, essential, though it seems strange it exists at all … Actually I have no reason for naming him. I can't really justify it and I don't need to. If people ask me why, I will say, 'Because that's his name.'

I roll over and lie on my stomach again, oh God, such a relief to be free to do this – to be free to move – I'm telling you it's bliss! I feel the loose skin slide around my middle and wonder if it will ever feel like it's mine again – or will it forever be his – like a redundant marsupial pouch.

My body is tingly all over but I can't possibly sleep. Labour was the most intense experience of my life. I feel so proud. Obviously I can't completely explain it, what it feels like to reach my absolute limits and have no choice but to carry on.

To surrender completely to my body because I know that it knows what it's doing and anything I do to try to control it isn't going to help. It's only going to get in the way. What a beautiful, positive experience.

I bet no one will believe that the pain wasn't bad – that it was mostly early on – the contractions bringing on a deep ache, like period pain, emanating from the base of my spine that lasted less than a minute then disappeared. The actual 'pushing part' wasn't painful at all, and more interestingly, I didn't even push. It was like my body took over and started shaking, vibrating. It was, seriously, the strangest thing.

Zena was great; so calm and focused, so confidence inspiring. That hot towel thing was amazing. Every time I felt the damp heat land on my back the pain dissipated. It felt like it was flowing back up my body, transforming into peace. This is something midwives have been doing forever. Why is it not just a common part of a birthing experience? I can't believe that most people go through torture to bring a child into this world, sitting in a hospital bed? Really? Why not relax in a pool in your own house?

My heart goes out to the women who want to have a home birth but can't, and have their birthing dreams turned into hospital nightmares. That's a traumatic enough experience to bring on post-natal depression. Of course if there had been complications I would have called the experts on pathology and let them do whatever they could to save my baby. But if you don't have to, if you could choose instead to have a very empowering experience, why wouldn't you? I guess most people are all too willing to hand over the power when they're scared, to divorce themselves of all responsibility so that if something goes wrong it isn't their fault. Their loss, I suppose.

I lie in this ecstatic yet peaceful state, drifting in my mind until the sky outside gets lighter. It feels like an eternity and yet it could also be an instant. This is the point that I happen to be at in my life, right now. I'm in the moment. For some reason it seems like a miracle. Like I said: I've never been this high in my life.

Malcolm drifts sheepishly into the room. I'm glad he's here to share my proudest moment. I love him. Of course I do. I'm just not sure if I want to live with him after everything. I don't want to be stuck in some romance narrative trap. I don't want to go round and round in circles. I've got better things to do.

I pass Fin to him and watch his face as every possible emotion passes over it and through me. Maybe we will get back together some day, whatever that means. For now, we both need some time and space. I need to learn how to be more independent. He needs to learn how not to be an asshole. I need to process all the changes in my life and family these past few months. I need to remember that there are no happily-ever-afters, just happy moments, just this amazing, shifting, evolving journey we call life. In the centre right now is Fin and me in our little bubble, and then my friends and family, spiralling outward.

Malcolm passes Fin back and pauses for a moment. 'If you need anything …' The only words he utters. I nod. He leaves. Peace.

I look down at Fin's squished up newborn face and suddenly I'm terrified. All this responsibility: he's completely dependent on me. Breathe.

There's a knock at the door.

'Michael?' I would recognise that rat-tat-tat-tat anywhere.

'Hey.' His face is full of love and light. He's practically bursting with it. 'Hey, baby,' he coos, taking Fin from my outstretched arms as if he's holding the Holy Grail and everything feels as if it is falling together again.

Valerie

It's so unlike my life that it feels like a dream. Every morning I've woken up with this warm tropical breeze luring me out to the beach, the scent of coconut oil. It's the first time I've been on holiday. Ever. I don't think family vacations count because they are more work than anything else. This island paradise is the perfect escape. I don't know how I will ever bring myself to leave.

It's funny. I occasionally find myself feeling guilty because I'm not busy: I'm not working or worrying about my kids. I still do the mental checklist: Rosa is with Elena, talked to them both last night, they're fine. John and Michael are on their fishing trip with Caleb. I promised Elena that I will take her on a trip sometime to compensate. She promised me she would get over the unfairness of it if I took a holiday by myself. But despite being coerced into coming here, I don't regret it at all.

After four days of tropical fruit, swimming and sunbathing, I'm starting to feel comfortable in my bathing suit.

'Sunbathing?' Elena asked in mock horror on the phone last night. 'Think of the melanoma!'

'At my age, and after years of avoiding the sun, I think my skin deserves a little bit of abuse.'

'Good for your vitamin D levels.' I can't believe Elena and I actually agree about something.

Maybe I'm relaxing a bit, maybe I don't need to be in control all the time. When I think about going back to work, back to the real world, the stress comes back.

'How do you think Rosa would feel about moving to Rarotonga?' I ask Elena through the phone line.

'What have you done with my mother?' Elena laughs.

'It's just a thought. Just a daydream, I suppose. But surely they must need doctors here.'

'I don't know if I could cope without you two,' Elena admits, and I feel appreciated. It's not like her to concede dependency.

'Well, who knows?' I shrug. 'But either way, we are definitely all coming back here at some point.'

'I'll hold you to that. I need a tropical escape!'

I dip my toes into a rock pool on my meandering way across the beach. I've read three novels already, none of them just to get to sleep. I left George Eliot at home. I have made friends with the resort bar staff.

'Friends?' Elena can't believe it.

I drink piña coladas in the evening, taking in the safe, warm, humid breeze, looking out at the horizon that disappears into the void of the sky. It feels like it could swallow me up. I've never seen this in New Zealand.

I hope Michael's enjoying his fishing trip. He's back to normal – more or less. The experience seems to have changed him in the way that travel or children or losing a loved one might. He's more reserved, more adult, but sometimes it seems like he's somewhere else. His psychosis was a nightmare for me, and now if feels like an old dream, vague and hazy, like it might not really have happened at all except that it seems to have changed all of us. It has brought us closer in the knowledge of fragility. The young male invincibility that he used to possess was just an illusion. Maybe that's what's missing from him now. I suppose it's easier for us not to take each other for granted now.

My feet sink into the sand as I walk along the shore line. The wind picks up, rippling my sundress in all its magenta hibiscus glory, and sending my mind in a different direction.

I don't know if this was all part of God's plan or not. I don't know if I need to think that anymore. Elena said that I use religion as a crutch and it's true; I have used it to get me through some of the hardest times in my life. I suppose I'm still a bit disillusioned. Sometimes it's just not a strong enough crutch for everything life throws at you. When Michael was in that hospital I couldn't believe that God would put me through that – put us all through that. For what? To test my faith? What's the point? I was angry. I know people have been through much worse, but that just made me more angry. Now I'm relieved. I'm surprised I'm not praying constantly in gratitude. I haven't prayed since the heightened experience of Fin's birth. Right now I have no need of God, or maybe our relationship is just so fractured I don't even want to think about it. I suppose Elena is right. We construct God in our own image. My version of God was convenient for me until I felt he was failing me.

The baby waves wash over my feet. I stop and look out at the ocean, so vividly aqua-blue that it takes my breath away when I bother to look properly.

I hear that familiar whisper in the back of my mind: calm, gentle and loving.

Just trust me. I look behind me, back along the beach and see two distinct sets of footsteps and tingles run through my body. This is real. The Holy Spirit feels beautiful. I allow Jesus' love to wash over me and through me. I look out at the horizon and embrace the feeling. I walk directly into the water, sundress and all, let go my inhibitions and just dive in. This is my baptism: both ridiculous and ridiculously happy. If only Elena could see me now.

Rosa

Fin reaches his chubby little arm up and grabs my thumb with his sausage fingers. That's what Elena calls them and we both call him a little sausage, which sounds funny and cute. Being an aunty is cool because you still have a mum and you still have a big sister but you also have a baby sometimes and you can look after him and hold him and then he cries and you feel bad but at least you don't get tired like Elena who has to look after him crying all night.

Elena puts him in her sling which has a pretty purple flower pattern on it. She picks up the jug of lemonade off the table that we just made while Fin was having a nap and we go out to the garden. It's a hot day but all the leaves are turning brown and orange and falling off the trees so I know it will be winter and cold soon.

I help Elena spread the blanket on the ground and we sit down. The lemonade is too sour, but I think Elena likes it. It's probably healthier.

'Do you hate Malcolm?'

'No.' Elena breathes all the air out of her and her shoulders go down like she's sad. Maybe I said the wrong thing. I do that lots.

'Why doesn't he stay here anymore?' I ask her. 'Did you have a fight?'

'No. Yes. We just need to spend some time away from each other.' Elena looks at me like she wants to say something important.

'You know, when people spend too much time together it's not very healthy.'

Elena always wants to be healthy.

'Yeah,' I say. 'Like when I spend too much time with Mum and she's stressed and she yells at me.'

Elena smiles. 'Just like that.'

I look out at the grass and wonder if there are fairies. If they were anywhere they would be in this garden with the little mushroom statues and all the flowers. It's probably a crazy thing to think. I think about being crazy all the time. When I look at the wall or the footpath for too long, or the grass, with the leaves like this and I start to see zigzag patterns or little dots that move. I don't tell Mum this but I wonder if there's a secret code and if I work it out, like a puzzle, I can get to one of those secret worlds. I probably am crazy some of the time. Just not like Michael. He's still strange. He's very quiet and I can tell that he thinks a lot about everything, but doesn't say most of what he thinks. Sometimes he's more like he used to be and he picks me up and carries me round on his shoulders and pretends to drop me.

'Michael loves Fin,' Elena says, and I wonder if she can read my thoughts and knows I was just thinking about him.

'I know. I love Fin too,' I say and tickle his toes while Elena feeds him. He wriggles them but doesn't look up.

'I watched a scary movie last night,' I say, because I keep thinking about it. 'At Aroha's house, and there was this crazy man who kills people.'

'A psychopath,' Elena says. She's not mad that I watched a scary movie. Mum would be.

'Michael wasn't like that,' I say. I'm pretty sure.

'No, he wasn't.' She shrugs, but I don't know why. 'There are lots of types of crazy.'

I wonder what type I am.

'Psychopaths don't feel emotion. Only power. That's why they can hurt people so easily.' Elena knows everything.

I wonder if that's what Chardon is. Or is she just a bitch? I take my off my shoes and put my feet on the grass. It feels nice.

'What other kinds of crazy are there?' I ask.

'As many kinds as there are people!' Elena pats my arm and laughs.

Maybe one day Michael will be normal again and by then the rest of us will be crazy and we will all have to be in hospital with yuck food and weird doctors and nothing to do. I don't want to ever be in there like that, so even if I am crazy I will pretend that I'm not so that no one will know.

Evie

A human being is a part of the whole, called by us the 'Universe', a part limited in time and space. He experiences himself, his thoughts and feelings, as something separate from the rest – a kind of optical delusion of his consciousness. This delusion is a kind of prison for us, restricting us to our personal desires and to affection for a few persons nearest to us. Our task must be to free ourselves from this prison by widening our circle of compassion to embrace all living creatures and the whole of nature in its beauty. Nobody is able to achieve this completely, but the striving for such achievement is in itself a part of the liberation and a foundation for inner security.

ALBERT EINSTEIN

I hear the beating of wings and look up through the tree canopy to see two kererū disappear into a nīkau palm. My feet find the grooves in the path between gnarled tree roots, my boots sink slightly into the damp earth of the forest floor. I'm in heaven and I know it. I've been doing voluntary conservation work for a few months now.

Sometimes I think about Michael, about that whole situation, and how I could have dealt with it better. I don't think I was really in my right mind at the time. All that stuff with my abnormal cervix was getting in the way. I wasn't thinking clearly. It was like a wall had come down between us, like our realities had diverged so severely that there was no middle ground. No 'us'. Nothing.

He couldn't be there for me because I didn't let him. I didn't want him to know and I didn't believe he could actually help. I couldn't be there for him either because I didn't know him anymore. I couldn't recognise him through the veil of his psychosis and he couldn't see me either, couldn't trust me, couldn't trust anyone.

When something horrible happens to someone you love you want, more than anything, to be there. But the reality is you can't. You never can be there enough. Even Val and the whole family camped out in the hospital couldn't help as much as they wanted to. It helps not to be alone, but no one can really be there inside your head. Michael had to do it by himself, really.

Some days I think that, in some possible future, Michael and I could conceivably get back together. Other days, the thought is ludicrous. We couldn't be more different. I think, more than anything, I loved his family and the way they cared about each other. Of course, they don't always get along, but they still have that closeness that I've never had with my parents or siblings. I miss Val and Rosa the most, but even Elena plays on my mind as I do this solitary work. I imagine the conversations I could be having with her, the arguments. I imagine myself arriving at Sunday dinner and surprising them all. Of course I'll never do it, but the thought tugs at my heart in a way that's both joyful and painful. I was included. Now I'm not, but maybe I could be.

Maybe I'll find another dysfunctional family to adopt me. I don't think I have the energy.

I suppose you want to know about the results. Well, I'm happy to tell anyone about my cervix now. I'm sick of it being a secret, if it's so common to have abnormal cells and the surgery to remove them, we need to start talking about it. We need to know what's going on so that the medical profession don't get carried away with making their statistics look good. Anyway. I stopped smoking. I did the juice fast with Tara. I ate lots of seaweed and drank kombucha and ate lots of other fermented foods. Elena would have been proud. I went back for another colposcopy, which was much like the first: uncomfortable and invasive, but worthwhile in the end. It's good to know that my cells have regressed, that my cervix is normal again and not at risk of developing cancer. It just makes me wonder how many other people have been in my situation and had the treatment and lost six millimetres of the inside of their cervix without needing to, when they could have made a couple of lifestyle changes and their cells might have regressed all on their own.

I check the possum traps, one by one. No corpses so far. It's the grossest part of the job, but killing possums still seems right in the broader scheme of things. They are like humans, destroying the native habitat. They shouldn't be here and neither should we. Sometimes though, when I'm up on the mountain on a misty morning it feels like there's more to it, there's more meaning … like, maybe we actually are evolving, maybe human beings are just nature, after all … maybe we need a little destruction in order to grow.

Michael

Six months ago I was normal. I was enjoying the summer, hanging out with my friends, being carefree, just cruising. It was probably one of the best summers I've ever had. No. It was *definitely* the best. We would go surfing and then have a bit of a smoke, have some beers and barbecue some steak and seafood if we caught any. We would go on road trips to different beaches, go to concerts and crash on the couches of people we hardly knew. My car broke down in Gizzy and I had to call Mum and beg her to drive down and pick us up. I remember that. But I'm not sure about the things that happened after.

I was crazy – that's what they tell me. But I wasn't crazy; everything else was. The world flipped inside out and I was the only one who could see it. Now I'm not sure – about anything – but it's calm.

'I was crazy.' I tell everyone that because they wouldn't believe me otherwise. I tell everyone and I smile, I laugh. It's a joke. Everyone knows. There's no point in trying to hide it. That would just make the shame more real. Something like this stays with you forever: the humiliation of not being right, of losing my mind, the shame of being locked up, of being weak, of being wrong, of not being normal. No one will ever believe me again. That's their loss.

You're probably wondering what happened with the boys while I was out of it. Dave's taken off down south – to find a new outlet for his P addiction probably. He's not a mate anymore. Maybe he never was. Nan doesn't understand, but I can't tell her everything. Nico and the other boyz are all good. They don't really believe me about Dave. They think they would have known if he had been cranking the amphetamines, but you never do know. I'm by myself a lot more now. I have a lot of thinking to do, a lot of time to spend with the ocean. I do hang with the boyz a bit though. We go for a skate sometimes or have a few beers. They take the piss out of my 'episode'. I need that. I need people to make it into a joke, not like my family who can barely talk about it, who just look at me with worried eyes as if I'm about to do something insane again.

The fog started to lift as soon as I stopped taking the meds, as soon as I came back to Whaingaroa. I watch the fantails dance through the trees, hear the beating wings of the kererū overhead and they remind me of my journey. They remind me never to forget where I came from, what I lost and what I got back.

No one else was there when the tohunga came, so no one knows if he was real or some kind of delusion. When I talked to Mum and Elena they looked worried, but whether he was there in the flesh or not, I know I saw him. His presence was there, his wairua. Nan understands. When I told her she just nodded her head, not smiling, not frowning, just knowing.

'Did you ask him to come?'

'I called my sister Mariana,' was all she told me. That's enough. There doesn't need to be a mystery, everything is resolved enough as it is.

'When you're old enough,' Nan said, 'you can go up the

mountain and begin your next journey.' I don't know how, but I knew exactly what she meant. This is my calling, one day I will be the old man – wrinkled and wise, and I will be the one who visits the crazies in the hospital to help them reconnect with culture and weave their fragmented minds back together. But for now I'm just an average guy with an average life, or at least I'm trying to be. There's my last year at uni to think about and whatever comes after that, but more importantly: there's the surf to keep me sane.

About the author

Isa Pearl Ritchie is a Wellington-based writer. She grew up as a Pākehā child in a bicultural family and Māori was her first written language. She has completed a PhD on food sovereignty in Aotearoa. She is passionate about food, wellbeing and social justice. *Fishing for Māui* is her second novel.

www.isaritchie.com